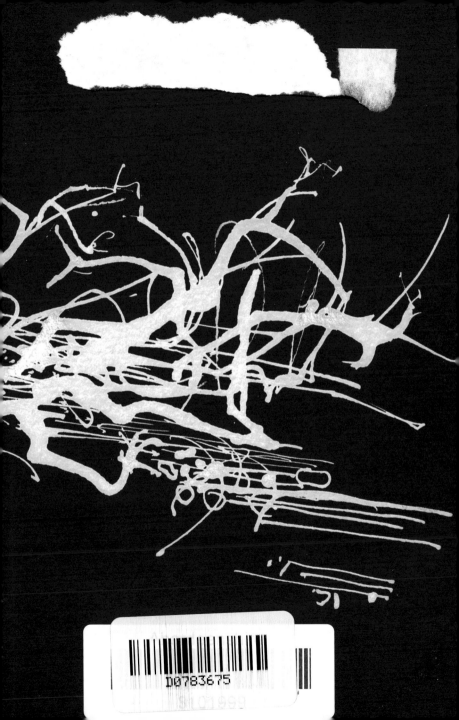

THE
ANGEL
CANTATA

A NOVEL

THE
ANGEL
CANTATA

A NOVEL

JENNIFER POTTER

IMAGES
FFIONA LEWIS

FULL CIRCLE EDITIONS

By the same author

Fiction
The Taking of Agnès
The Long Lost Journey
After Breathless

Non-Fiction
Secret Gardens
Lost Gardens
'Sacred Grove' in *When The Wild Comes*
    Leaping Up
Strange Blooms, The Curious Lives and
    Adventures of John Tradescants
The Rose, A True History

For Chris, Emma, Louis and Robert

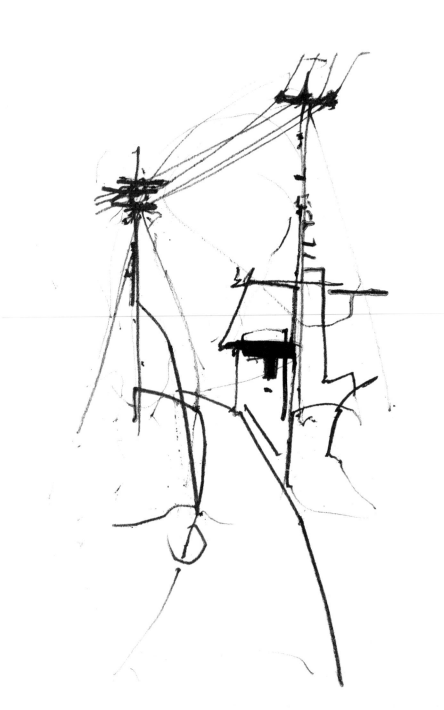

I went outside and found the landscape
which had eaten my heart.

'Viral landscape' from *Of Mutability* by Jo Shapcott

1

Her voice hooked him first, rough and muddy in the lower registers then soaring like a skylark in the thermals. He caught it sliding out of the evening mist as he walked the mudflats at low tide, disheartened by yet another day without progress. Filmmakers call it the magic hour, the time of transformation as light bleeds slowly out of the day. He equated it rather with the long slow sliding of his favourite Schubert *Notturno*. Either way the hour suited his mood of quiet melancholy. Maybe the gamble wouldn't pay off. Maybe he wasn't as good as he thought.

Then the voice slithered out of the sea fog and he found his spirits quickening, imagining at first that its sexy, vibrant tones came from inside his head. Hearing voices went with the territory, even ones as earthbound as this. But when he realised that the source was external – the pub on the beach, most likely – he knew that he had to investigate further, suddenly hopeful that the voice might provide a way out of his predicament.

Afterwards he would say it was a memory of something that hadn't yet happened.

Ridiculous, I know, but that's how it felt, honestly. Ask Stas, he knows about such things. I remembered your voice despite never having heard it before in my life.

Surprised by his own urgency, he clambered up the shingle ledge towards the pub, stopping only to slip on his shoes. That voice: it came to him from another time, another place, and wired itself directly into his brain. He had to get closer to feel its power more keenly. But as he crossed from the beach to the apron of cracked

11

concrete that served as a parking lot, the band gave up without warning, mid-song. No fanfare, no rolling drums, just the girl singer lurching to a halt amid a smattering of applause. Although he would hear her again that night, and wonder that a mere waif in a polka-dot miniskirt could produce such contradictory sounds – Ariel revoiced as Caliban, or Puck recast as Bottom – it would be some time before he understood what she was really trying to say to him.

When his music was eventually written, he christened it the *Angel Cantata* in her honour and for ever afterwards his name was bracketed with other visionaries of the English landscape: William Langland, William Blake, Samuel Palmer, Benjamin Britten, men (and they are all men) whose accomplishments transcend the narrow boundaries of their art. Although the truth was a little different, he did not object, knowing full well that you need a good story to sell yourself in the market place, and that angels in the landscape make as good a story as any. Had the schoolboy Blake really seen angels up a tree in Peckham Rye, or was that a metaphysical alibi for missing his tea?

Only one person ever came close to discovering the true gestation of his piece, a young music journalist who reminded him of Nancy Flight, she of the polka-dot miniskirt and unearthly voice. Commissioned to write a profile of him for the *Guardian's* Saturday Review pages in celebration of his seventieth birthday, the journalist had asked him where it came from, the much-lauded *Angel Cantata* which had launched his distinguished career (re-launched, he thought to himself, but if she hadn't deduced his wilderness years from his press cuttings he wouldn't allude to them now). Word was that he had written the piece in and around the Pevensey Levels, a place she had often visited as a child to see her grandfather who lived in one of the oyster bungalows on the Beachlands estate.

'Those prefabs on the way out to Normans Bay? Good God yes, I remember those.'

The memory set him off, and he talked to her about Nancy, and Maddy his wife – his first wife, that is, he had remarried twice since - and his own grandfather who had retired to the Suffolk coast, and a strange Russian whose place in the story the journalist couldn't quite fathom, and the landscape of course, the low-lying fields criss-crossed by drainage channels that would one day cause an almighty flood, and angels everywhere. He spoke so quickly that he left the journalist far behind, distracted by childhood memories of her own, unable to follow the twists and turns of his imagination, or to elicit the missing bits of information that might have made sense of his complicated tale.

Afterwards he fretted that he had talked too much, given away too many secrets. Ideas came to him in different ways – from paintings, skies, woodlands, city streets, eavesdropped conversations, his feelings for other people, women especially; sometimes a line of melody simply stuck in his head in that strangest of moments between sleeping and waking. He had once conceived the idea for a whole sonata from a sardine can, or rather from the satisfaction of inserting the key and knowing that the metal will perform precisely as intended. At other times, of course, the metal tongue snaps off at the first turn, rendering the key completely useless, or you open the cardboard box and find the key is missing altogether. His sonata said all these things and more, earning praise for its technical mastery of form. But his *Angel Cantata* was different. This work gave him a theme to which he would return again and again: England in all her tawdry glory, the tired land strewn with rusting relics of the past that somehow looked forwards to a better future. England was broke but he would fix her, he believed, looking backwards into the future like Walter Benjamin's wayward angel. No wonder the journalist couldn't keep up.

But the woman's visit had disturbed his hard-won equanimity. After they had talked for nearly three hours (or rather, he had talked and she had made a show of listening), and he had watched her tottering in high heels down the gravelled drive to the taxi waiting at the gates, his mind returned to that day more than twenty years previously when he had first set eyes on Nancy Flight, and sat with her in the bar of the beachside public house after she had finished her final set. Then as now he had done most of the talking while Nancy sat perfectly straight in her chair, listening with apparent indifference like an only child in the company of grown-ups. When he offered to buy her a drink, he wondered if he shouldn't first check her age, but her request for a straight vodka, no ice, silenced his qualms. Her speaking voice was more Ariel than Caliban, soft and husky with an upward inflection that left her intentions hanging in the air. He found it enchanting, as he found everything about her enchanting: her boyish frame and spiky hair, a sort of bleached strawberry blonde, her choice of clothes (bright red tank top and skimpy polka-dot skirt, no bigger than a tea towel), even her gnawed fingernails.

The only time she became animated was when he remarked on the butterfly tattooed onto the fleshy part of her left shoulder, its pale blue wings shading off to smoke and a darker edge of grey. His fingers itched to touch the memory of it now.

'That's a Chalkhill Blue,' she said, 'a male. The females are more sort of chocolatey brown. You get loads of them round here, because of the chalk. Blues follow the vetch and the vetch follows the chalk. Horseshoe vetch,' she added, 'you know?'

He didn't.

'So you live locally?' he asked.

She looked at him warily, as if she knew exactly where this conversation was leading, but she nonetheless volunteered that no, she wasn't local, had merely stayed here many times as a kid with her Aunt Edie, her great aunt really, and that she was staying in Edie's house now, up beyond the Martello tower, with Derek and George from the band.

'Derek fixes things and also plays Spanish guitar. George is the drummer, when he remembers to get out of bed.'

'And the butterflies,' he asked, 'who taught you about those? Was it Edie?'

'Edie's dying,' she announced, 'and don't fucking tell me you're sorry. Shit like that happens, to all of us.'

'I can still feel sorry, can't I?'

She shrugged and clammed up. He was almost relieved when the girl was claimed by the bald-headed man from the band, their fixer Derek, evidently, who laid a proprietorial hand over Nancy's Chalkhill Blue. He and Derek exchanged a few noncommittal remarks about the band's performance, then Derek and Nancy left the pub together. The girl didn't seem to object to being treated as the man's chattel but perhaps she was glad to get away.

None of this encounter appeared in the *Guardian* profile, not even the Chalkhill Blue, which was germane to the story. In fact very little of the *Angel Cantata*'s gestation made it into the public domain, apart from Blake's angel and the ones he himself had seen. But he liked the large black-and-white photograph they had taken of him in his study against a backdrop of books. It made him look suitably bohemian, caught in the act of pondering a problem somewhere to the right of the photographer's trousers. He hadn't lost any of his angular good looks or his hair, which had turned quite white by now. Thank God the journalist had drawn a veil over what his angels were doing – or maybe he hadn't explained that part very well. She really should have listened more attentively, and then she might have grasped where his ideas came from, and what his *Angel Cantata* was all about.

2

He woke to the sounds of the sea folding and re-folding in his head. Aside from a dash of peach on the eastern horizon, the view from his big white bed was of steely greyness – grey sky, grey sea, dun-grey beach of flinty shingle enlivened by a crop of scarlet poppies planted on the foreshore before the real beach began.

As a rule he hated waking up when Maddy was away in America, missing the shape and feel of her physical form that never ceased to amaze him with its strange familiarity, the sound of her breathing (she slept much better than he did) and the joy of watching her sleeping face freed from the faint flush of irritation that inevitably crept over her waking self. Maddy asleep was a vision that illuminated his entire life. Maddy awake was reassuringly less than perfect.

For the first time since coming here he experienced a sense of promise, which manifested itself as a sense of heightened awareness and a slight tingling in his nerve ends. As he carried his tea outside to the small concrete patio between the house and the beach, he found himself humming the opening bars from something the girl had sung the night before (he didn't know what, but it certainly wasn't about angels).

His mood on arrival had been very different. In the short taxi ride from the station, a box of precious scores on his knee, he felt he had made a terrible mistake. The station was close by Pevensey Castle, where William the Conqueror had established his first encampment. Now history had moved on, leaving in its wake a muddle of caravan parks, prefabs, overhead power lines, pot-holed roads and enough speed humps to quell an invasion on their own.

It was Maddy's fault, really. If she hadn't gone back for another semester at Princeton he could have stayed home on Wandsworth Common, but with Maddy gone he was forever bumping into her shadow.

'OK, guvnor?' called the driver over his shoulder as the front tyres hit another rut.

'Fine, thanks.'

He shut his eyes, hoping that when the taxi finally stopped, the other houses would have disappeared. *Quiet retreat on Sussex coast*, that's what the advertisement had said in the back pages of the *Times Literary Supplement, suit single artist or similar. Has own garden and piano.* When he had telephoned to enquire, he had made a point of checking that the house was on its own.

'Oh, it's perfectly detached,' the woman had gaily replied. 'No worries on that score.' Her laugh was strident as a donkey's but mercifully short. He held the phone away from his ear. 'I promise, you can get up to all sorts of jinks.'

When the taxi at last lurched to a halt, he counted to ten then opened his eyes. The houses were still strung out in a line as he knew they would be.

'You did say number 584, didn't you mate?'

'That's right.'

'Well here we are, then. Want a hand with your things?'

'No thanks. I'll be fine. Just feeling a bit queasy.'

'It's all them holes in the road, I expect. Council's rubbish round here, same as any place. You from far, mate?'

'No, not really. London, that's all.'

'I expect it's no different there. All them lot's rubbish. Don't know why we bother with them. Mind you, could be worse. At least we're not killing each other like they do in some parts. Here, you sure you're all right? You look proper poorly, if you don't mind my saying. I could take you on to the hospital, if you're willing to chance your life in their hands. Go in healthy, come out feet first, as often as not.'

'No, really, I'm quite all right. I expect the sea air will do me good.'

'Suit yourself. But take my card: you never know when you might need it.'

Once he had unloaded all his things from the cab, and the driver had disappeared with a friendly wave, he had to negotiate the swing gate and the long narrow front garden to the wooden steps leading up into the house. Hauling his things across the lawn took several trips. The lawn grass was shaved flat, but the bed to the left of the path had lain fallow for weeks. Thigh-high grass choked the few flowers that hadn't already given up the ghost: pink thrift at the front, a stunted rose or two further back. By the time he had carried everything up the steep steps to the raised wooden veranda by the front door, he was feeling unpleasantly hot.

To reassure himself, he glanced back into the landscape. Mean slivers of front garden ended in a medley of sheds and makeshift garages, each one botched together without thought for its neighbour. The marshes began on the other side of the road. An empty diesel train rattled across a dyke from right to left. Beyond the tracks lay the marshland proper, low and flat under wide-open skies. Feeling his spirits lift just a fraction, he hunted in his pockets for the key.

The door caught on a protruding strip of draught excluder.

He stepped inside the small kitchen. Cheap units, scuffed lino, an impression of browns and dirty cream, polystyrene tiles on the low ceiling. No, this really wouldn't do.

Worst of all was the smell: trapped air and the faintest seepage of gas, not a dirty smell exactly but neither was it clean. He was back in his grandmother's kitchen at Bawdsey on the Suffolk coast, any second now she would bustle through the door and plant a wet, warbling kiss on his cheek, followed by the old man fumbling for the watch chain strung across his chest.

You're late again, boy, what's been keeping you this time?

Nothing Grandpa, me and Dickie ...

Dickie and I, boy, what's happened to your grammar?

He couldn't compose a jingle in a place like this, let alone the piece that was supposed to revitalise his career. He would call the woman who had rented him the house, tell her he had made a big mistake. Nothing personal, it just wasn't right.

Yet something made him hesitate. Through the kitchen doorway he could see into the dazzlingly white main room, which opened directly onto a sunroom that was shaded on three sides by vertical blinds. Sunlight filtered through the angled strips, creating a frieze of diagonal stripes on the shiny wooden floor.

The key to the French doors lay on a small footstool by one of the cane chairs.

Once he had drawn back the blinds and opened the sliding glass doors, he stared in quiet awe at the sea.

The light filled his head.

He hadn't expected the sea to be quite so close. Although she had lied about the proximity of the other houses, the woman had omitted to mention that the house was right on the shingle.

How strange. Maybe she was so used to it being there that she didn't find it worthy of comment. Of course the sea is right there – where else would it be? This is a beach house, silly.

Scarlet poppies distracted his eye, and a clump of viper's bugloss against the breeze-block wall that demarcated his patch of foreshore from next door's. He sat at the piano, pushed against one wall of the main room, and opened the lid. From the notes he tried, he judged it surprisingly in tune. He could maybe find a way of working here after all. Give it a week, maybe two, and see what happens.

Yet as the days slid past, he found progress hard to achieve. His problem was not so much the place (which he was quickly growing to like), or Maddy's absence, or even the annoyingly present neighbours on either side (he could hear them moving about at night, and a child's fretful crying), but rather his own lack of inspiration.

Despite his previous successes – a quintet performed at the Wigmore Hall in his late teens, a tune especially composed for the late Queen Mother, an opera fragment commissioned by a festival in Heidelberg, a much-praised series of talks for Radio Three on the *Landscapes of Composition* – there were rumours that he had lost his way, that his early promise had produced nothing of real maturity. Nobody said it to his face, of course, but he couldn't help noticing that his phone no longer rang quite so often and the invitations to judge this or that competition, to appear at this or that musical festival, even to dinner, for God's sake, were becoming less frequent.

So when the call came out of the blue to write a post-9/11 piece for a small New York music festival he had jumped at the opportunity, despite the uncomfortable suspicion that he had nothing he particularly wanted to say. Actually what they really wanted was a post-post 9/11 piece, if he had properly understood the conversation, which made the commission easier to contemplate.

'The world has moved on, you know. Pain, suffering, financial meltdown, greedy bankers, all that shit. Now we're looking forwards. Hope, healing, you know. Say, are you with us on this?'

The caller was a heavily Americanised Dutchman. Per Woudstra, he said his name was, *Call me Pete*. He had a way of talking in nouns that left you in some doubt about how they all strung together. Ashes. Death. Destruction. New World Order. Do a Mahler for me. How about it?

Mahler?

Resurrection, you know, great theme. World's a fuck-up but what the hell. That's where you come in. Joy, hope, happiness, you know. Oh yeah, and give us a decent tune, will you? None of that atonal shit.... I am talking to the right man, aren't I? Michael Anders, *the* Michael Anders?

'That's right,' said Michael, '*the* Michael Anders.'

'You got me worried for a second. Thought I might have to start all over again with some other guy.'

Woudstra claimed to know Michael well from a festival they had both attended in Cologne the previous year. He had certainly visited the festival in question, where he had met many foreigners including, he thought, the odd Dutchman but no one called Woudstra as far as he could recall. He could only assume they had met at the bar one particularly raucous night when Michael, no drinker, had lost the key to his room and managed to talk his way into the lodgings of a lady harpist who took him in like a stray cat and petted him all night long on the day bed. To Michael's embarrassment, it became the talk of the festival. After that, he became more circumspect with his keys and gave harpists a wide berth, a caution he extended to his work.

Now he wondered if Woudstra really had approached the right man. He had once been mistaken for another English composer called Michael Anvers (was he there too, in Cologne?). Well Anvers could easily sound like Anders to a Dutchman, especially a drunken Dutchman, who knows? And Anvers had a reputation for bringing pomp to every circumstance. Yes, the more he thought about it, the more convinced he became that it was Anvers they really wanted. Writing compositions to order was hard enough but writing them under false pretences was harder still and Michael felt tempted to call Woudstra and regretfully decline the commission. He badly needed the exposure, however, so he kept his peace, hoping valiantly that the work would come together in time. It always had in the past, so why not now?

The idea he had mapped so far was of planes flying through espionage chatter, each plane containing the germ of its own destruction. Originally he had thought of linking the big bang of the planes' impact to the big bang that kicked off the universe but as soon as he went down this route he lost the spy chatter that was integral to his intentions. It was all too cerebral and not emotionally felt, unlike the radar chatter which had come to him out of the blue, he wasn't sure why.

What he wanted was another idea to collide with the first because that's where his best pieces came from. Something that would talk to him of place – New York, of course, where the commission had originated, but also of England. New York for him meant speed and danger and dazzling vertigo, big black baseball players and streets choked wall-to-wall with yellow cabs, steaming manholes, the hot stench of the subway rattling underfoot in a fuzz of concrete columns and crowded platforms – all the things he had expected to hate about the city and actually found exhilarating.

I bet they really wanted Anvers after all, he thought. Anvers would turn out a competent piece of work, something tricksy and flash that would catch the mood of the moment without stretching anyone too far, man in the landscape sort of idea. Hey – maybe that's it. Go back to New York not as a place but to how it makes you feel, hot and bluesy. Bring in the blues, an *Englishman's* response to the blues.

He played a few notes on the piano and felt a sudden lightening in his head.

What was the first blues he ever heard, in the rundown shack at Shingle Street, between the Suffolk beach and the road that ran nowhere? His grandfather had forbidden him to go there, but that came later. The shack belonged to his friend Dickie's Uncle Jack, Mad Captain Jack they called him, although he wasn't mad and he wasn't a captain either, just looked as they imagined a captain should be.

Mad Jack was drunk when he played them his all-time favourite, Muddy Waters' *Long Distance Call*.

'Now whaddya think of this one, laddie?' the old man had asked as he laid the record reverentially on the turntable, clicking back the arm and dropping the needle on to the vinyl because the self-starting mechanism was shot to pieces, like everything else in Jack's shack. And because he was drunk, he overshot the beginning and had to try again, yanking the arm back across the record to the start, but his hand was shaking so much from drink that he misjudged the distance. The needle made a ripping sound as it hit the record, etching an alien groove into Muddy Waters' signature beat. Even then, as his young ears struggled to catch the sliding rhythms, he knew from his thumping heart that this music would stay with him for life and forever after; and whenever he heard Jack's favourite track, he waited for the scratch that never came, same as Christmas in July.

The telephone rang just as his head started jumping, static and blues, a sweep of radar noise like the folding of the sea. Its squeaky high-pitched tone startled him. He thought it was a fire alarm and when he realised it was the telephone, he couldn't for the life of him remember where it was. Under the plain leather couch? Out in the sun room? Over by the bed?

Several seconds passed before his brain came down to earth.

You don't have to answer, he thought. Just because someone chooses to call doesn't mean you are duty bound to respond. If they really need you, they'll call again some other time. But what if it's Maddy? She doesn't usually call at this time but she might want something …. Shit.

He looked wildly around the room. The sound was coming from a bookcase in the far corner. Scanning the shelves he found the phone stuffed into one of the lower shelves, above a ragged pile of paperbacks placed on their side. As he reached for the receiver, the ringing stopped, leaving its promise suspended mid-air. There was a number you could dial to check who had called. One four something something. Maddy was forever checking when she was home. She said her mother always rang off without leaving a message. It didn't work with foreign calls or anyone ex-directory, but you could at least hazard a guess who might have called. One four what the hell was it?

He was just putting the phone back on the shelf when it rang again.

'Hello,' he said, sounding eager.

'So you *are* there,' a woman's voice said gustily, 'I thought you would be. Most artists I know like to get their work done in the mornings.'

He struggled to put a face to the voice, which sounded familiar but no image came.

'Is everything all *right*?' enquired the voice with an exaggerated lilt he found as baffling as her identity. 'I'm just calling to see that you have everything you *need*.'

'I'm sorry?'

'I've been meaning to call these past few days but oh, you know how it is. One thing runs into another and all my good intentions drop like flies.'

She was sounding less and less familiar. Perhaps she thought he was someone else. Anvers' ghost was turning into a *doppelganger*. Then her braying laugh gave her away.

'It's *Alice*,' she said, 'Alice Pearson. Your *land*lady. As I said, I'm calling to see that you have everything you *want*. I mean, if there's anything you need – anything at all, really …' her pauses were getting longer, 'I can drive down in the quickest of jiffies, no trouble at all, really. That's what I'm here for. I like to give my visitors *every* satisfaction …'

Good God, he thought, what on earth did she mean?

'Yes of course, everything's fine. It took me a day or two to settle but then it always does. I mean, well, there are a few things that aren't quite as I … expected …'

'Tell me,' she gasped, 'I need to know so that I can put them right. No one has *ever* complained. I take that as a matter of pride.'

'I'm not complaining. It's just that, well, I can't play much here, you see, for fear of disturbing the neighbours. The other houses are much closer than I thought.'

'Oh dear,' she said crossly, 'you can hardly expect me to spirit the neighbours away just to let you *play*, can you? That's hardly fair.'

'You misunderstand me, Mrs Pearson. I mention it only because you asked.'

'Call me Alice, *please* do. And it's Miss not Mrs. Well, miz, really but what's a title, between friends? And you *are* my friend, aren't you? I'm not doing this as a business, you know. I like to help out where I can.'

'That's very good of you. But honestly … Alice … I have everything I need and now that I'm settled, I'm starting to make progress.'

'*Ex*cellent. I shall expect an invitation when your work is first performed. Do you know when that will be?'

'Not till the autumn, in New York.'

'Ah, that might be tricky. Unless I can persuade my friend Geraldine to come with me, she's always zipping over there, in fact she's there right now, I expect she'll remember to send me a postcard on departure. But never mind that, I must let you get on. I know you *artists* dislike being disturbed. If there's anything you need, anything at all, you have only to call and I'll sort it all out for you. That's what I'm here for.'

'Thank you, that's very kind. I promise I'll call if I need you.'

'You have my number to hand, I take it?'

'I think so.'

She gave it to him again, just in case, enunciating the numbers slowly and clearly on the assumption that he was writing them down.

'Well, bye for now,' she said. 'It's been *so* nice talking to you.'

'Yes, it has indeed been a pleasure, good bye,' he said, relieved at the final click.

Absent-mindedly he stuffed the telephone back into the bookcase. The wires led to a socket under the sofa. He pulled out the end and left it dangling on the radiator. Maddy would not be able to reach him but he was invariably the one to call her. He would explain when they next spoke – she would surely understand.

3

Few of the Post-it notes stuck to the fridge door made much sense, even to Alice. Telephone numbers detached from their owners. A shopping list (cat food, fly spray, bin bags, bread, piccalilli, beeswax polish, royal jelly) that segued into an inventory of flowers (larkspur, bugle, Himalayan poppy, *Allium christophii*, caryopteris, Californian lilac, hound's tongue, speedwell, plumbago, Canterbury bells, *Hyacinthoides non-scripta*, Miss Wilmott's Ghost, columbine). A fridge magnet from a local plumber in Camden Town (she would never use *him* again). Half the instructions for removing red wine stains from antique fabric. A whole stack of recipes. Good heavens, that looks interesting: mussels and pork, who would have thought it? Incomprehensible map references (she never knew which came first, eastings or northings). Instructions on how to reach an unspecified destination without once hitting a roundabout (Milton Keynes, surely?) The faded beginnings of a letter in her own hand, *I just wanted you to know that I found your recent exhibition without equal in the contemporary art scene* (who on *earth* was that to?)

Ah, there it was, she recognised the New York code, at least she hoped it was New York, 001 was certainly America. Give it a whirl and see what happens. If it isn't Geraldine's number it might belong to someone more interesting.

Lark was rubbing against her legs. *Not now sweetheart,* she said firmly, *you'll just have to wait your turn. Can't you see I'm busy?*

The Burmese cat arched its back and turned away with feigned indifference.

She thought carefully before dialling the number. *The world turns clockwise so in America they must be behind us, not in front. If I call now, let's see, what time is it … Geraldine should be just about ready to head out to the shops. She likes an early start. Says it works up a good appetite for lunch, and she should know.*

Confident that she had mastered the time difference, she dialled the number quickly.

'Glenmarsh Hotel,' came the immediate response. The man's deep southern voice gave her a thrill.

'Geraldine Beddoes, please, she's one of your guests.'

'Say ma'am, you don' happen to have her room number handy, by any chance?'

'No, I'm afraid I don't. I'm calling from England, from London, actually.'

'Is that right? Well, you jus' hold on a moment, ma'am, ah'll be as quick as I can be.'

The cat had forsaken her legs for the fridge door. She heard the receptionist consulting his colleagues. There seemed to be some kind of problem, or maybe they weren't very efficient at locating their guests. It was unlike Geraldine to forsake her usual haunts. The Chelsea was much more her style.

The man came back on the line. 'Now listen up, ma'am, ah'm truly sorry but last night Miz Beddoes gave orders not to be disturbed. Must be sleepin' late. No one's seen her at breakfast.'

'That's impossible,' said Alice, 'I'm her best friend. Geraldine never sleeps late.'

He chuckled. 'Well, ma'am. I'd like to help you if ah possibly can, but when a guest asks spe-*cif*-ically not to be disturbed … you see mah problem?'

'Yes I do, but this is urgent. I have a suggestion to make.'

'Fire away, lady.'

'You could call her room and ask if she wants to speak to me. My name is Alice, Alice Pearson.'

'You say Parson?'

'No, Pearson.'

''Scuse me ma'am?'

'Oh, just say it's Alice.'

'Alice with a 'P',' he said lightly, chuckling some more. 'Well, ah can't see any harm in that, if you really are her best friend, like you say.'

The line went dead.

Alice wondered if Geraldine was sick. Sooner or later the stress was bound to catch up with her. Geraldine said that the only people who suffered from jet lag were the pantomime donkeys whose hind legs couldn't keep up with their front. As long as you walked tall, your body could cope with any number of *décalages*.

'*Alice*,' came her friend's sleepy voice, 'what's the matter? Do you know what time it is?'

'One fifteen,' said Alice smartly.

'Well it's eight fifteen here and I asked not to be disturbed. Can't it wait till I get back to London? I'm leaving Thursday night – back some God-awful time Friday morning, like I said.'

'No it can't wait till then,' said Alice, stifling her qualms. 'Listen, I need your advice.'

'Come on, Alice, when did you ever listen to anything I have to say?'

Alice said: 'It's about my new guest, down at the Pevensey house. I don't think I told you about him, did I? He's a composer, quite famous, I think.'

She paused for Geraldine's response. When none came (she distinctly heard Geraldine yawn) she said, 'I really ought to protect his privacy so I'll not tell you his name. You will have heard of him, for sure. Everyone has – he's bigger than that Finnish flautist who stayed last year, remember him? Well, Mi – this composer is working on a new piece right now, in my house. It'll be premiered with a big fanfare in New York later in the year. We were talking about it on the phone only this morning. The thing is, I think he'd be happier if he had someone to look after him. You know, someone who might slip in to cook his meals, give the place a quick dustover. What do you think?'

'Don't ask me to play the charlady, if that's what you're after.'

'Don't be silly. I thought I might offer.'

'But Alice, that's a crazy idea. If he's rented the house, you'll have nowhere to stay down there. You live in London, remember, north London, right on the other side of town. Think of all the travelling – it would drive you nuts.'

'Not if I'm being … *useful*,' she said hopefully.

'No, really Alice, I think that's the stupidest notion I've ever heard. If you really want to help the poor man, call him up and ask if he needs a cleaner. I'm sure you'd be able to fix one, if that's what he wants.'

'That's just it. I don't think any of the local girls would do. You have to be so sensitive where creativity is involved. He's an artist, don't forget.'

'Most of the artists I know wouldn't recognise a dust storm if it flew up their noses.'

'Yes, but they're painters like you. Musicians are a different breed altogether – much cleaner for a start, more … fastidious. Then there's the matter of his meals. I could rustle him up one of my Spanish omelettes perhaps, or try out some of the recipes I'm putting together for my book.'

'He'd be better off nipping down to that take-away veggie Balti place you're always on about.'

'Geraldine, what's the matter with you? I was hoping you might sympathise with my dilemma.'

'I do, honey, it's just that, well, I'm kind of busy.'

'All that shopping, I suppose.'

'Actually no, I haven't been inside a shop since I left London.'

'So what are you doing?'

'Oh, things …' said Geraldine vaguely. 'Galleries, mainly, and walking in between … We've seen a few shows, nothing earth-shatteringly good but there was one that made us laugh, sort of off-off-Broadway but not quite. Off-colour, too,' she laughed.

'Did you say "we"?' asked Alice quietly.

'Yes. Bill came too. Or rather he was here already, so we thought we'd make a few days of it.' Alice heard a muffled voice at her friend's side, then Geraldine's exaggeratedly cheerful 'Bill sends his best regards and asks to be remembered to Lark.'

'You could have told me you weren't alone,' she said. 'I would never have confided my problem in front of a third party.'

'Bill's not third party, where's your sense of proportion?'

'So it was Bill who chose the hotel, I suppose? I wondered why you had abandoned the Chelsea.'

'I chose it myself,' said Geraldine. 'A friend told me about it – the bathrooms are down the hall, it's all quite primitive, and they give you breakfast in the basement if you're really desperate. But it's cheap and we've got a lovely room, one of their Queens, definitely worth splashing out if you're slumming it. Hey, stop it,' she said, her voice turning all throaty.

'Stop what?'

'That wasn't for you, honey. You know what Bill's like.'

'Yes I do,' said Alice, marshalling her dignity as best she could. 'He was my friend first, remember.'

'Now don't start me on the guilt trip. Yes, he was your friend first, still is, as far as I know, but this is something else. I'm not poaching your friendship, believe me. Isn't that true, Bill?'

Alice noticed how her friend's voice changed when she spoke to the man in her bed. Bill was saying something in her ear. He sounded horribly close, although thankfully not close enough for Alice to catch his drift. She heard what she thought was another gasp then Geraldine said, 'This must be costing a bomb. How's the book going?'

'Fine,' said Alice, as lightly as she could. 'I start writing tomorrow.'

For several minutes afterwards Alice sat at her kitchen table. Dark purple tulips held themselves stiffly in a painted vase, one of a batch of seconds she had picked up from the gift shop at Charleston. The others she had given away as Christmas presents to her cousins in Canada and Australia, saving the prettiest for Geraldine.

You could always count on the Bloomsbury set to get their colours right, she thought carefully, running her hand over the rippled surface of the vase: yellow, watery green, dusky pink and a light sky blue, all hand-painted and fixed with a cream glaze. In a couple of days the tulips would turn blowsy and droop, which was how she liked them best. Shame you can't say the same about people, she thought. Take Geraldine, for instance, now there's someone who is really letting herself go.

She sat up straight, both hands in front of her on the table. Open in front of her was the book she had been reading in preparation for her own, a text she knew almost by heart, Elizabeth David's *A Book of Mediterranean Food*, the John Lehmann edition illustrated by John Minton. She spotted a nasty stain on the page she had been reading and instinctively blamed Lark who liked sitting on her things. The cat was not as clean as he used to be. That blasted hotel receptionist, she thought. If he had followed Geraldine's instructions she would never have known what her so-called friends were up to behind her back. People should do as they are asked. That's what you pay them for, isn't it?

4

It was no use. His landlady's call had broken the spell of Michael's inspiration and all he could show for his morning's work were a few chords and a stubborn musical phrase he might have borrowed from someone else. She had taken up residence in his head like some ghastly cuckoo and displaced any original ideas of his own. Hoping that the sea air might help to dislodge her, he put on his jacket, locked the doors and went out by the French windows to the sea.

From Alice's bungalow you could walk eastwards to Bexhill or westwards to Eastbourne, either following the beach or taking the coast road sunk below the shingle ridge on which the houses were built. The lower part of the beach was passable only at low tide, when the retreating sea exposed stretches of hard sand moulded into ripples; otherwise it was a slow trudge across the shingle. As the tide was high he slipped down the concrete steps between the houses and soon found himself walking along the road in the direction of the pub.

At the prospect of seeing her again, he quickened his step, his view to the sea blocked by the ribbon of beach houses strung out along the shingle ridge. The development on the landward side was patchier: first a zigzag of cheap two-storey houses set back from the road, then a narrow grassed enclosure lined with rusting cars that were virtually antiques, Volvos, Morris Minor estates, a couple of old Citroëns, a solitary Cadillac, and on past the Beachlands estate, its neat lines of suntrap bungalows plucked from a modernist catalogue and deposited on the edge of the marshes.

But as soon as he turned into the cul-de-sac where the pub was situated he knew from the general lack of trade that he was out of luck. Inside the bar, a few solitary drinkers (all men) slouched over their pints, and a smattering of families occupied the tables scattered about the bar and dining areas. He recognised the barman, at least: a young and not particularly attentive Australian who had poured him a pint the previous night instead of the requested half. 'No worries,' the barman had said, without offering to remedy his mistake.

When the barman brought his lime and soda, he asked if the band might be playing later.

'Today's Thursday', said the Australian.

'How about tomorrow?'

'Tomorrow's Friday.'

'I know.'

'Band only plays here Wednesdays and Saturdays,' said the barman, nodding at a blackboard behind the bar chalked with names and dates. *Nancy Flight and the Whodunnits* were playing again in two days' time.

'Do you know if they might be playing somewhere else before then,' said Michael, 'somewhere local? I'm looking for Nancy.'

'No idea mate, sorry, I'm new around here. But you could ask him,' said the Australian, indicating a man at the far end of the bar whom Michael didn't at first recognise. Dressed in black from neck to toe, he wore a tight, neutral-coloured skullcap pulled low over his shiny bald head. Of course: it was Nancy's fixer, the man she had introduced as Derek.

'It's not that important,' he said but the barman had already called the man over, saying he had a customer who was looking for Nancy.

'Cheers,' said the barman, leaving the two men alone.

About a foot shorter than Michael and stockily built, Derek had plainly recognised him. Although they had spoken the night before, Michael hadn't introduced himself so now he held out his hand.

'Michael Anders.'

'Derek de Villiers.'

'French?'

'South African. Tell me, you're not the Michael Anders who wrote *Lighthouse Blues* are you?'

'That's one of mine, yes. Where on earth did you hear it?'

'Helsinki. They played it as the finale.'

'I know, I was there. They played it twice, if I remember.'

'Three times, I thought.'

'More if you count the encores. I hope you liked it.'

Derek shrugged. 'I nearly used it once, for a gig at Hartland Point.'

'But you didn't?'

'Nah,' said Derek. 'Too many double basses for the helicopter. I went for jazz in the end, it worked better all round. The players had to arrive after the audience, and a helicopter was the only way in.'

Not sure whether he was supposed to feel offended, Michael overcame his awkwardness by asking about Nancy. Derek smiled at some secret memory, or maybe he just wanted to look mysterious.

'Have you known her long?' asked Michael.

'First time I used Nancy was at the Warehouse project, you hear about that? A three-day performance, 24/7, in a disused China warehouse in Shad Thames. That's China as in oriental.

The developers wanted to put the place on the map so I filled it with ghosts, singing ghosts and a couple of tap dancers, you know, plus a chamber orchestra up on the roof. Nancy was the best ghost I had. Shame about the rain.'

'So that's when you started managing her, right?'

Derek eyed him keenly. 'I look after her interests, if that's what you mean. The developers screwed me over the warehouse gig, but that's history. I'm a showman, not a weatherman. It's made me what I am. Careful. What's your interest in Nancy?'

Ordinarily reluctant to discuss work in progress, Michael explained as airily as he could that he was working on a commission for New York, a festival at Brooklyn's Prospect Park, nothing major, but the piece was turning into something English and different. He was stuck, in fact, and when he listened to Nancy the night before he thought she offered a way out of his predicament. Nancy's voice had a quality he couldn't put into words but if he could put it into his music, well, problem solved.

'She's quite untrained,' said Derek.

'But she can read music?'

'Sure, with a little coaxing.'

'So where did you find her?'

'Art school,' said Derek, without elaborating further.

The man's opacity was getting on Michael's nerves. 'Look,' he said, 'I only want to talk to her. Possibly get her to sing for me, I don't know.'

'I see,' said Derek, fractionally raising one eyebrow.

He looked away.

'Okay,' said Derek at last, after an awkward silence, 'if you want her that badly, I have an idea. We could share her if you like, share her professionally I mean. I'm grooming her for a gig

I'm planning later in the year. Can't explain more, sorry. You know how it is if word gets out. All I ask is the credit for having put the two of you together. Plus the usual percentages but we'll talk about that later when we know what we have. Does that sound like a deal?'

This time it was Derek who held out his hand and Michael who hesitated. Handshakes implied trust and trusting Derek struck him as a step too far.

Nancy's slinky voice at dusk slid into the equation. He took the other's hand, and immediately Derek turned his back and was talking on his mobile phone to Nancy, telling her to get on down to the pub on the beach as they had business to discuss with the guy she had met the night before, that's right, the older guy who reminded her of Gregory Peck.

'Well that's fixed,' said Derek, turning back to Michael. 'Nancy's coming over. But not a word about Gregory Peck. Nancy thinks he's smart and she wouldn't want you to know it.'

When Nancy finally arrived, Derek formally introduced the two of them, giving Nancy a short but reasonably accurate résumé of Michael's career, unprompted, then left the bar, much to Michael's relief, who had found making small talk with him a trial. Nancy looked even younger than she had the night before. Her tight jeans had gone into holes around the knees, and her ruby-red top was all but transparent. In the light of day, Michael could see quite plainly the darker roots to her strawberry blonde hair. Aside from lipstick (the same ruby red as her top), she was wearing no makeup. He liked that, even if her skin was flawed. And he liked the fact that she didn't seem in the least bit curious about why she had been summonsed. Derek had okayed their

45

conversation, and that was fine by her.

Michael began by asking what kind of music she liked to sing. Jazz-café, indie pop, blues, reggae, white rap, cabaret, salsa, bebop, Bartok, skiffle, plain old-fashioned rock, Cuban dance numbers, garage, fusion; she shrugged, as if it was all the same to her. And no, she didn't have any particular musical heroes, at least none that meant anything to Michael, although she liked Little Richard singing *Long Tall Sally*, and there were several Laurie Anderson numbers she had taken into her repertoire. But he had to know that Laurie Anderson was by no means a musical hero of hers – she took herself far too seriously and some of her lyrics were just plain dumb. Did he know the one about Hansel and Gretel, and Hansel's one true love, the wicked witch? No? He should check it out some day. Gretel was a cocktail waitress, and Hansel got himself a part in a Fassbinder film, that was all crap, but she liked the bit about the angel of history being blown backwards into the future.. It made her feel apocalyptic.

'Can you sing it for me?' said Michael.

She obliged without demur. Even at half voice, every man at the bar turned his head. Michael felt the same tightening in his chest he had experienced on the beach. 'That's Walter Benjamin,' he said.

'No way. Laurie Anderson, that's who.'

'Fine, but she borrowed the angel from Walter Benjamin. You know who I mean?'

'Sure.'

'Really? He's long dead now.'

'Even dead people sing the blues.'

'He was a writer, not a singer.

'So what's the problem? I sing lots of people – Beethoven,

Brecht, Billie Holiday. They're dead too.'

He could see that he was beginning to annoy her. She was looking at her watch and the butterfly tattoo on her shoulder was twitching visibly. He didn't want to lose her, not yet, so he related a little of what he had told Derek, how he was writing a piece for New York and felt there was a place for her voice somewhere in there, although he wasn't sure if he wanted her as a performer or simply as a muse, a line of melody, well, not exactly melody, he didn't write tunes but he wanted to capture her spirit in sound.

'Sounds okay,' she said, looking – he was sure – mildly interested.

What he wanted, he said, was to go for a walk with her, away from the pub, which was beginning to fill up with afternoon drinkers, so that he could get to know her better.

'Can't it wait?' she asked. 'I'm off to see Edie and there's other stuff I should do.'

'It's important,' he said.

'Important to you, maybe, but so is Edie to me.'

'That's your dying aunt, right?'

'Who said she's dying? Edie's my great aunt, anyway.'

'I thought you told me that yourself.'

'Did I? Edie's old but she's hardly dying. If we went out now it could only be for half an hour or so, and if you want anything more from me, you'll have to check with Derek first.'

'So he manages your time as well as everything else?'

'Fuck that,' she said with a scowl.

Michael's gaffe was soon forgotten as they walked back along the coast road towards Alice's beach house, Nancy wheeling her bicycle on the pavement and Michael ambling along beside her. He would rather have walked into the marshes but Nancy said there was no path this side of the railway line, and the many drainage channels meant you couldn't just cut across country or you'd end up in a ditch like her great uncle Arthur. Anyway, she had to get home and then either Derek would give her a lift to Eastbourne or she'd catch the train from Normans Bay.

The modern terraces beyond Beachlands gave way to marshland. He heard cows coughing and sheep bleating and once the shrill *peewit peewit* of a lapwing, identified for him by Nancy, who told him that she had learned her flora and fauna from Arthur, to whom the naming of names had clearly been as important as it was now to her.

He let her stride on beside him, bumping him occasionally with her bike as she enumerated a litany of birds, plants, butterflies, bugs and beetles that made the Levels special to her. Her knowledge of birds astonished him as she slipped between the common snipe and the common redshank, sedge warblers and reed warblers, wintering golden plover and breeding yellow wagtails. He wondered at his own fascination for this punk cygnet with dirty fingernails and a butterfly tattoo that rattled its wings intermittently. Auburn beauties like Maddy were more usually his style. When she reached the various dragonflies, damselflies, snails and spiders of the marshes, he gave up on the names and listened only to the modulations of her voice, which evoked for him the God of Genesis (a God he had long since left behind), who brought forth every living creature after his kind, cattle and beasts of the earth and every thing that creepeth upon the earth. He saw them marching across the Levels towards an imaginary Ark where they joined the fish of the sea and the fowl of the air in a maelstrom of life and imminent annihilation, altogether thrilling.

They passed Alice's bungalow then the campsite and the Martello tower and had just reached the junction for the level crossing and the station in the marshes when Nancy stopped and waved energetically to a man emerging from one of the caravans parked like sardines in the site to their left. The man didn't see her at first, so she thrust her bicycle into Michael's hands and ran towards him. Catching sight of Nancy, the fellow opened his arms in welcome. He looked a strange fish: long-faced and crinkly haired, with a scrape to his face that implied a recent fight.

Annoyed at the intrusion, Michael wheeled Nancy's bicycle towards the embracing couple, who ignored him completely. When they had finished, Nancy extricated herself from the stranger's grasp and flashed him a smile.

'This is Stas. We don't quite know how he got here. I found him in a field. He's supposed to be visiting the Observatory at Herstmonceux but they're not expecting him for another month. He's Russian, you see,' she added, as if that explained everything.

The men shook hands, a little warily on Michael's part. Scabs of dried blood stuck to the Russian's right eyebrow and the bruise around his eye socket was turning a bilious yellow.

'*Menya zovut* ... My name is Stanislav Gregorovich Vasilyev. Call me Stas, please.'

'Stash?'

'Stas, that is correct.'

'Michael ... Michael Anders.'

At close quarters the man looked harmless enough, but Michael wondered if Nancy knew what she was doing. His clothes didn't fit properly, and his leather jacket came from a different era. Even his smile looked stuck on.

'Here's your bicycle,' he said, trying to push it into Nancy's hands and managing only to run over her feet. 'Shall we go on?'

She smiled up at the Russian. 'You go. I think I'll stay here with Stas.'

'Won't that make you very late for Edie?'

'Edie's not expecting me till tomorrow.'

The Russian followed their conversation with an air of concentration, keeping his eyes on Nancy.

Unable to insist, Michael was nonetheless aggrieved by Nancy's desertion. He felt a stirring in his memory. The Russian held one arm loosely around Nancy's waist then slid his hand over the top of her jeans, letting it rest on the crease of her buttocks. At one of the far caravans they stopped, embraced briefly then went inside. The door had evidently been left unlocked.

In her haste to be with the Russian, Nancy had asked him to look after her bicycle until she came round to collect it. At least this meant she had his address, although he suspected she wasn't listening too carefully when he gave her the number of Alice's house.

He set off gingerly, wobbling as he meandered about the road. The low seat forced his knees into the handlebars, but his confidence soon returned and he cycled slowly home, his head filling with sounds that came from nowhere: a flute and a rumbling tuba and the distant echoes of a male voice choir intercut with the tramping feet of pilgrims, followed by the pentatonic strains of a solo violin. By the time he reached Alice's house the noises in his head had started to coalesce into something approaching an idea.

It was dusk when he had finally worked himself out and he felt almost sick with hunger. Rifling through the fridge he found some cold potato and shrivelled French beans he had cooked the night before. Still famished, he opened a tin of tuna chunks in olive oil, eating straight from the tin.

As it was early for his nightly call to Maddy, he wasn't perturbed when he got her answering machine but there was so much he wanted to tell her, about how the piece was going and about his meeting with the girl-singer Nancy and the scar-faced Russian in borrowed clothes.

This is Madeleine Fairweather speaking – she emphasised the 'Fair' in her name; that was just like Maddy, always looking on the bright side of life. But he couldn't help noticing that she was beginning to sound a little American. Either his ears were especially acute or she had re-recorded her message as he hadn't picked that up before. Oh dear yes, this was definitely a re-recording because the next bit was new. Instead of saying, as she usually did, *I can't get to the phone right now so please, leave a message and I'll call you back as soon as I can,* she was explaining how she wouldn't be able to return any calls for several days so if it was urgent, the caller should try her cell phone. *Cell* phone? What on earth was going on? Maddy's dear, sweet Americanised voice gave a string of numbers, slowly and clearly as he would have expected, but he didn't have a pen to hand, or a notepad. Panicked, he hit the redial button. Up came the message again. Oh Christ, he still didn't have a pen. After he had run over to his desk and back, she was halfway through the number. He would have to try again.

Michael stared at the string of numbers Maddy had given him. When he was feeling quite calm he dialled the number but the call failed before he had even finished dialling. He tried again, and again. The same thing happened each time. Of course, he should have dialled America first. This time he added 001 to the number he had written down and although it made the right connection, Maddy must have switched off her phone because he connected straight away to a computerised voice which told him that if he wished to re-record his message, he could press '1' at any time.

'It's me,' he said, trying not to sound alarmed. Maddy hated it when he fussed. 'I was just calling to see how you are. Where are you? You didn't tell me you were going away. I'm still here, in the Pevensey house. You've got the number but I'll give it to you again just in case you don't have it with you. Everything's fine, I'm working hard and I've met some people who should be able to help. I'll tell you about them when we talk next. Call me when you can. I love you … but you know that already…'

Did telling Maddy that he loved her merit a re-record? As a psychoanalyst, she was wary of hearts worn too lightly on one's sleeve. He let his message drift into silence that ended in a sharp click as his time ran out.

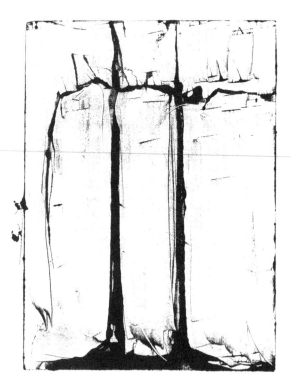

5

The smell of urine soon took the smile off her face. She could never breathe in here, not properly, so the first thing she did was to open as many windows as she could, in whatever room she found Edie, usually against the wishes of the care staff who preferred to keep the temperature subtropical.

In the hall she stepped over Solomon the bulldog. Over the years he had inflated to massive proportions from the scraps that rained down from the dinner table. Although Nancy didn't care for Solomon, and felt disgusted by the solid ripples of fat gartering his belly, she saw he had a point. The residents cuddled him like a baby and loved him to bits. Only Edie dissented from the general view. Edie said the dog poisoned the air with his farts, but at least his existence proved you were not the ugliest creature in the universe.

She found Edie in the day room, chatting with a couple of the old men. Someone had already opened the windows but Nancy shifted the sash a few more inches then gave her aunt a big hug. Edie was wearing a stained pink cardigan she didn't recognise. Clothes were handed out at random more often than not, although she had sewn nametapes onto all Edie's belongings as required, even her knickers, *Edith Fisher* written in red italic script.

'You took your time,' said her aunt cheerfully, 'no flowers?' Fat fingers clutched the mock leather handbag on her lap.

'Next time I'll get you some anemones from the fruit shop.'

'Ooh, my favourites.'

Nancy pulled up a chair. 'Aren't you going to introduce me?' she said.

'And have you run off with my beaux? Not bloody likely.'
Edie grinned then said in a loud whisper – louder than her normal voice – 'Them lot's crackers but it's better'n Scrabble, any day.'

'Shhh.'

'No shushing me, girl. I never could spell right, so what's the point in learning now? This is my niece,' she said to her companions. 'My great niece. She's a good girl, so don't go thinkin' you can play one of your filthy tricks or I'll set the fartin' dog on you.'

Edie looked her over with crafty eyes. 'I wondered when you'd be comin' to see me. I'm in the dog house, as I 'spect you know.'

'What was it this time?'

'Nothing much. And don't believe a fuckin' word they tell you. That lot couldn't blow straight into a paper bag if you held it wide open. Arthur was tellin' me just the other day…'

'Edie …'

'Arthur *Willis*, there's more'n one Arthur in the world, girl, and trust my luck to pick the wrong one, Arthur *Fisher* I mean, my late lamented, oh what the hell do I mean?' She sucked at her cheeks in a flicker of distress.

Nancy stroked her arm. 'It's okay, Edie, really. I'm here now. I would've come earlier but I had a late night' – a vision of Stas slipped into her head, Stas over by the window of his rented caravan, struggling with the buttons on his shirt – 'and then, well, there was all sorts of shit to sort out this morning.'

'Don't go usin' language like that with me, young lady.'

'I'm sorry. I was forgetting myself. I'm having a hard time, that's all.'

'At least they don't shut you away with the loonies. That's what this place is, a loony bin. And don't think we don't all know, because we know *everything*.'

The two men beside her nodded their heads vigorously. Edie was a hothead, no doubt about that.

'I'll get you home as soon as I can,' said Nancy.

'Is that a promise?'

'Cross my heart and hope to die.'

'Dyin's too good for either of us, girl. But you may have to get me home feet first, you realise that, don't you?' said Edie with a fierce cackle that flipped the switch on her companions. Even Nancy found herself smiling.

Jenny put her head round the door. 'Everything okay in here, Mrs Fisher?'

'Mrs Fisher, Mrs Fisher,' said Edie to Nancy. 'When you're not here, Nancy girl, plain Edie is good enough for me.'

'Oh Edie.' She held her aunt in her arms. Edie's soapy smell wasn't strong enough to disguise a faint whiff of faeces.

The room was filling up as two of the care staff started to set the long dining table. It was not yet eleven and already the place was preparing for lunch. Meals had a function here, like Solomon the dog.

Cradled in Nancy's arms, Edie fell still. She could feel the loose skin of Edie's forearms where the fat had dropped off during her recent illness. The pink cardigan was scratchy to the touch and Edie hated pink. Said it was for babies. Why was nobody looking after her properly? Nancy hugged her more tightly.

'Now let me look at you, girl,' said Edie, pulling away. 'My,' she said, 'you don't half look peaky. What've you been doin' with yourself?'

'This and that. You don't really want to know.'

''Spect I don't, my girl, 'spect I don't.' Edie looked her niece up and down, shaking her head. 'You need feedin' up, that's your problem. Get some nice dinners inside you. Girl like you should have a nice bit of fat on her. Men always like something to get their hands on.'

'I'm fine as I am.'

'That's what you think.'

They smiled at each other complicitly. Edie was always trying to fatten her up like some ghastly broiler chicken while Nancy was really quite happy in her body. If anything, she ate rather too much than too little and if she didn't put on the fat that Edie wanted, her metabolism was more likely to blame. One of Edie's admirers was dozing in his chair. The other was looking at Edie with rheumy eyes. She reached for her aunt's porky hand.

'So when are you goin' to get yourself a boyfriend?' asked Edie. 'A real boyfriend, not like the last one – bald as a coot and not in the least bit interested in you, I could see that plain as day. Looking after number one, that's all he cared about. What you need most of all is a husband, some feller who'll look after you and keep you in your place.'

'I'm not sure that's really my style.'

'It's *every* girl's style,' said Edie emphatically. 'Oh, the fuckers'll let you down soon enough, like my Arthur, getting himself drowned in a ditch, I ask you. But I'll not be happy till I see you settled.'

'You know Edie, I may have a boyfriend.'

'May? May? What do you mean, *may* have a boyfriend. Don't you know what's what, at your age?'

'Of course I do, but ...'

'But what, girl? I've never heard anything so daft in all my life. In my day, we knew if we had a boyfriend or not, I can tell you.'

'Times have changed.'

'So I bloody see. Tell me about him, then, this boyfriend of yours. Better still, bring him in to see me. I'll soon find out if he's worth anything, same as I did with the last one. I hope you sent him packing, like I told you to.'

'You may not like this new one either. He's Russian, and we've only just met.'

Edie's eyes opened wide. Then she snorted so loudly her sleeping beau woke with a wild start. 'Going with a Russki?' said Edie, clasping the handbag in her lap. 'I can tell you plainly what Arthur – my Arthur – would've had to say about that. Well, in present company I should probably keep shtum but Arthur would very definitely not have been at all happy about one of his own going with a Russki. He spent the whole of his service time listenin' to them, that's how we met, me and your uncle Arthur, when he ended up at RAF Pevensey. *Listenin'* to the Russkies is one thing. *Fraternisin'* with them is quite another. We had a word for girls like you, and you wouldn't care for it, I can tell you.'

'I thought the Russians were on our side during the war,' said Nancy.

'Not after the war they bloody weren't. Never trust a Russki, that's what Arthur always said.'

Edie had wrapped her handkerchief around the handle of her bag and was twisting it round and round like a tourniquet. Nancy wanted to reach out and hold her again but Edie pushed her away. 'You better tell me all about him,' she said firmly, a determined look in her eyes which Nancy knew only too well.

'What's he like, this Russian fellow of yours?'

Nancy told Edie all about her new 'boyfriend' as the day room clattered around them with the sounds of lunch approaching, anticipated by a growing number of elderly residents who hovered between the serving hatch and the table, or clustered about the window, having mentioned him only to keep Edie happy and now wishing she had kept silent. What was she thinking of? Edie wouldn't take to Stas in a million years and he wasn't really her boyfriend, just someone she liked in a way that hadn't happened to her for a long time. She told her aunt all she knew, and a bit more for good measure as Edie seemed to think she had something to hide.

By the time Edie was called away to the dinner table – 'Fish bloody pie, must be Friday' – the two had called a truce in their warring over Nancy's boyfriends, Nancy saying she would bring Stas for Edie's inspection and Edie saying she would reserve judgement, if Arthur would let her.

She caught the train back to Normans Bay, where she was the only passenger to alight, stopping at the level crossing to say hello to the attendant, Frank Rollings his name was, she'd known him since he was a boy. Big Frankie they had called him even then, because it was obvious he would turn into a giant. Frank Rollings said it looked like rain. They were warning of serious storms by the weekend. She said she remained an optimist at heart. Whatever they told you on the telly was usually wrong. He laughed and said wasn't that just like a woman, to disbelieve the experts.

Instead of turning left to visit Stas in his caravan site, she climbed the shingle ridge to the dyke that stopped the seas pouring into the Levels. She used to play here as a child, in the months her mother used to leave her and her brother Clive with Edie and Arthur. Her father was often away, working the rigs in Scotland and sometimes in America, until one day he never came back.

Edie was a cousin of Nancy's maternal grandmother – a kind of great aunt once removed – who ran a south-coast boarding house frequented mostly by travelling salesmen. It never became fancy enough for the holiday trade but because of the family connection, Nancy's mother used to spend a summer fortnight here with her two children in return for help around the house. One summer she went off for a weekend, leaving the children with Edie, and didn't return for a month. Edie was resigned to taking the children permanently under her wing, convinced she could give them a better life than their mother, who laboured all hours in the sweat shops of Kentish Town until she had saved enough to start her own workshop where she worked others as hard as she had worked herself, turning out copies of catwalk fashions for the markets and tat shops around London. In the end an uneasy compromise was reached and the two children spent most of their summers here with Edie and other holidays too, leaving their mother free to work. Nancy respected her mother's ambition but they weren't especially close, and her affection for Edie stood between them like a reproach.

The fields and ditches where she played as a child had all but disappeared. Summer grazing it was then, used to fatten the bullocks and the barren cows. Well, there may have been the odd caravan or two, maybe even a smallish site, but nothing like this. Now the stretch between the shingle ridge and the railway line was packed with regimented caravans parcelled out for summer weeks that were always too short, unless the rain narrowed the holidaymakers' options to card games and Scrabble and traipsing the ruins of Pevensey Castle, huddled against the walls to keep dry.

Edie had told her tales of a great flood, centuries back, before the marshes were properly drained. After weeks and weeks of rain, the winds blew and the mists descended and a great sea came crashing through the shingle ridge, choking and drowning men and women as they slumbered in their beds, and their livestock and suckling babes with them, while those who took to the trees for safety fell into the swirling seas and drowned. Stas in his tinny caravan wouldn't stand a chance.

The house was quiet when Nancy finally got home. For all its air of dilapidation, Edie's house had a soul that lit up whenever there was life inside, but now the blackened bay windows stared back at her, dull and empty.

She lingered for a few moments in the front garden, where the flint wall sharpened into a point, like a ship's prow. Pink valerian grew out of the crevices, and a felting of orange lichen crept along the sides. Arthur's tidy lawn had grown into a hayfield, fast losing ground to the advancing line of brambles and scrub.

'Anybody home?' she called as she pushed open the front door.

George may have been out, or sleeping, and Derek had still not returned from London. He was organising an extended coming-of-age gig for some celebrity's child, hip-hop meets avant-garde, Derek said, all hush-hush, and there was a singer he needed to see and possibly engage, that skinny model who had hung around with them the last time they had played in London, heroin chic and a voice that cut like glass. Derek liked her, obviously, which might explain his now frequent disappearances. Derek liked anything crossover, and strange. They were playing the pub again the following night, so she hoped he could find a way to drag his way back before then.

For Derek, she thought, *everything is wondrously simple. You put one foot in front of the other and carry on in a straight line. No zigzags, there. Dear Derek. Go fuck that skinny child and turn her into a star. She'll like that. So will you. It'll be like doing it with sticks, but don't try to bend her or the poor little thing will snap. Oh shit, why do I feel like this? It's not as if she's done me any harm. My choice, as Derek would say, yes, but who wants choices when life should just happen, of its own accord?*

She remembered Edie's warning to her as she left the home, how she needed to catch her man before time ran away with her.

'What you need is an egg timer, young lady, and we both know what sort of eggs you'll be wanting to drop.'

6

Despite his progress of the previous day, Michael felt like Sisyphus pushing his rock up a precipice and watching it crash back down again. Having been here before many times, he knew that he had to give his music the space to advance of itself so he took Nancy's bike from the storeroom under the front steps and headed towards the village. He might just as easily have walked, but if Nancy dropped by to collect her bike when he was out, he couldn't return it anyway, so he might as well cycle as walk. Staying home on the off chance she might call was pointless.

At the village, he cycled through the visitors' car park and on to the beach. The sea was at its lowest ebb and once he had pushed the bike over and down the shingle ridge, he found the firm sand much easier. A group of kids hung around the entrance to a huge outfall, daring each other to venture into its gaping black jaws that disgorged a dribble of marsh water into the sea. You wouldn't see it at high tide. He wondered if anyone had ever been sucked unsuspectingly inside.

At the far end of the bay, he reached the abandoned villa he had noticed on his first day. Once an art deco palace in pink stucco, it lay like a broken liner in dry dock, its private foreshore coiled with barbed wire. This time, however, he saw that somebody had opened the windows facing the sea. Sounds of hammering came from deep inside the house. Tap-tap-tap-TAP. Tap-TAP. Tap-tap-tap-tap-tap-TAP. Tap-TAP. Tap-tap-tap-TAP. You didn't need instruments to make music. The rough and readiness of everyday sounds could work just as well. Though he had often incorporated raw sounds into his recordings, he had never yet constructed an entire piece from the flotsam of his life. It could be skiffle all over again, reinvented for the twenty-first century. Take away Lonnie Donegan's cheap Spanish guitar and what did you have? Washboard riffs, tea chests, broom handles, jugs, anything that came to hand. He remembered roller-skating with Dickie in the cavernous barn on the lane leading down to the sea at Bawdsey, and Dickie's all-time favourite, *Freight Train*, infinitely sweet, played over and over again on Fairground Jim's Dansette record player while they skated and danced across the pitted concrete, a barn full of jumping kids, their knees bloodied from countless tumbles. Good heavens, Fairground Jim: he hadn't thought of him in years but that's who the Russian reminded him of, not in looks but rather in a certain kind of physical cockiness – the way he'd run his hand over Nancy's backside. What was that Scottish woman called, Dickie's favourite singer? Nancy Whiskey, that's it, voice like a clarion, but sweet, too. Nancy Flight, Nancy Whiskey, same thing, that's why her voice had thrown him a fishhook while he stood on the edge of the twilight strand. She could help him put the piece together. Raw sound was Nancy's province. Rawness and roughness. Oh yes – he would like working with Nancy, he would like that very much indeed.

His head full of Nancy, he cycled fast into the Levels proper. The road slipped in and out of arching hedgerows that hid a variety of ditches, stagnant and rubbish-strewn. A profusion of dog roses grew in the shadows, opening pink and fading to a papery white around a fluff of yellow stamens. Bright yellow flag irises lit up the darkness. Hawthorns and more hawthorns. Then out into the light. Straight drainage channels cut like lines of perspective, some choked with pondweed, others clear, one or two coated with a thick russet crust. Pollarded willows straight out of Cuyp or van Ruisdael – so very English, he couldn't help thinking, despite the Dutch comparison, the England he loved yet feared lost for ever. Biscuit-coloured cows patiently chewing their cud. Bald-looking sheep. Horses standing patiently by a gate. Signs of abandonment too – dilapidated barns and farm buildings sliding into ruin; rusting cars and old sofas dumped in a field. In one small hamlet, neat and orderly, he cycled through a bank of CCTV cameras, and notices warning of loose dogs, forbidding entry to doorstep callers – a watchful place, waiting for something to happen.

Some pieces happen in reverse: you start at the end and then work your way backwards to the beginning. This one was different again: he would block out the separate elements and wait to find the connecting thread. This time the music wouldn't fail.

When the voices started coming out of the marshes, he knew he was ready and turned his bike to home. One was Nancy's, no doubt about that, muddy and earthed, the other rising clear and pure as a skylark – how Maddy would sing if she would only let herself go. She never did but he would teach her the way, now that he knew what he wanted. She could do it. The world was full of infinite possibilities. He felt his spirits soar.

At first he couldn't place the sound – a sort of buzz, followed by a hollow tinkle, all quite distant. It happened again in reverse – tinkle, buzz, right on the edge of his consciousness. They weren't noises he associated with the beach house. He blinked and shook his head as if to shake the sounds out of his ears. Another buzz, and a tinkle, then the unmistakeable scrape of the door catching on the draught excluder and a woman's voice calling 'Hel-loooo, anybody home?'

She was standing in front of the sink, an apparition in floaty silks tie-dyed in various shades of purple and blue. Long dark hair, Alice band, a pleasant enough face from what he could see (the light was behind her), chubby and smiling, more accommodating than he had imagined from her voice and somehow larger, because now that his wits had caught up with him there was only one person this could be and it was someone he would have gone miles out of his way to avoid.

'So *there* you are,' she said, holding out a welcoming hand. 'Alice Pearson. I hoped you would be home. You must be Michael Anders. If you're not, I don't know what you're doing here.' She laughed as she gave his hand a sharp squeeze. 'Don't be startled,' she said. 'You look as if you've seen a ghost.'

'I wasn't expecting you. Or did we arrange …?'

'We didn't arrange anything. But you sounded rather put *out*, the last time we spoke so I thought I should motor on down, you know, to see how you are. I got quite worried about you so I've brought you some provisions. I thought you might need, well, looking after.'

Without waiting for encouragement, she opened the freezer door and started packing the empty shelves with foil containers she fished out of a voluminous straw basket.

'Just a few odds and ends to keep the wolf from your door. I didn't know if you're a meat eater or not but if you aren't, there are plenty of veggies for you to choose. Of course I could have telephoned to check but I knew you'd only say "no". Politeness is *such* a curse, don't you think, and heavens, I'd have done just the same myself.'

The cartons kept on coming. He wondered how many wolves she had counted at his door.

'There,' she said at last. 'They will need defrosting so you'll have to remember to take them out one by one, when you've had time to plan your menus.'

She stood up straight and looked at him closely. 'Just as I thought. You're as thin as a scarecrow. What you need, my dear Michael, is what you are about to receive. Go and put on your best shirt because I'm taking you out for dinner, that's right. We'll go to the Anchor where the fish is quite excellent. And if you don't like fish, I'm sure they'll be able to rustle up something that'll suit. Come on,' she chivvied, 'there's a table booked but if we're very late, they might give it away to someone else and where would that leave us? Jolly hungry, I'd say.'

'I'm not sure … I was still working …'

She clapped her hands. 'This is on me,' she said. 'I absolutely insist. Still working indeed, it's way past seven and it's Friday, the start of the weekend. There's a time and place for everything and right now it's time for eating. You won't deny me the pleasure, surely?'

He didn't know how to refuse.

'Well hurry along then. The sooner you change the sooner we can get down to the Anchor where we shall eat, drink, and en*joy* ourselves for a change.'

He did as he was told, and after he had changed into a clean shirt he found her standing next to his desk, holding Maddy's portrait in its silver frame. 'Who's this?' she asked, rather sharply he thought.

'That's Maddy my wife. She's lovely, isn't she?'

'I don't mean to pry, but I rented the house to you on the

express understanding that you were single. That's what the advert says, "suit single artist or similar". The place is very small, as you know, and while it's perfectly fine for a single person I can't allow doubles.'

'You needn't worry about that. Maddy's away in America, teaching at Princeton. She's been there for several months already and it looks as if she'll stay on until the fall. Unless she's changed her plans again. The last time I called, she had gone away without telling me, and I don't know where she is.'

'Oh dear,' said Alice, looking concerned and then brightening a little. 'I expect she knows what she's doing. Wives are fairly good at looking after themselves, don't you think?'

For all her failings, Alice was much better company than he might have imagined. Once he had acquiesced at her taking charge he began to relax, flattered by the way she laughed at anything he said that was remotely amusing. They talked about places and musical venues, discovering a common bond in a performance of Britten's *Peter Grimes* they had both attended at the Aldeburgh Festival, quite possibly on the same night (Alice, who was rather vague about dates, was almost positive she had gone on a Friday, staying overnight with a flautist she knew). She sat entranced as he explained how Britten painted his picture of the sea, using the high melodic line of violins to suggest the sky, their bright tones dulled by a couple of flutes ('that's my flautist,' she exclaimed, 'an interpretive genius') to produce the cold grey morning he had indicated in the score.

'And if you listen very closely,' he said, 'you can hear the slow wheeling of the herring gull in the appoggiatura F-E that keeps returning'. He hummed the refrain. She nodded, it was all so clear, she said, once you heard it from the horse's mouth. 'It takes a composer to understand another. I mean, you're both working with the same material, notes, tunes. What hope is there for us poor mortals, our feet planted so very firmly in the mud?'

They talked about mudflats after that, and salt marshes, which Michael loved and Alice tolerated, preferring the cleaner edges of the sea. She had tried to buy a cottage in the Aldeburgh environs, but anything close to the sea was already far above her price range so she had turned her attention to the south coast which didn't have quite the same cachet, admittedly, but offered more opportunities to someone like herself of modest means. Suddenly demure, she dropped her eyes to the white tablecloth spattered here and there with the courses she had ordered for herself, *Coquilles St Jacques* to start with, followed by a heavenly *Sole Meunière* with a double helping of buttery new potatoes and broccoli au gratin. Michael had ordered the sole, too, but lightly grilled and served with a simple salad.

'No wonder you keep your figure so trim,' she said. 'I have to be very strict with myself, most of the time, but that allows me to splash out once in a while.'

She ordered another bottle of wine.

Michael tried to protest, saying he needed to keep a clear head for work in the morning.

'You'll help me out, surely? I'm driving, remember.' She was smiling at him coyly. Well if she needed his help, it would be churlish to refuse. He let the waitress fill his glass to the brim and noticed how the girl avoided his eye. He wondered if she had taken against them. Alice was rather loud.

'Here's to a happy stay,' said Alice, clinking his glass. 'I must say, this wine is jolly good.'

As their plates were cleared for the advent of the sweet trolley, they drifted back to the subject of the sea. He told her how the marshes around Pevensey reminded him of a summer he had spent as a boy with his grandparents on his father's side at the Suffolk village of Bawdsey – reasonably close to Aldeburgh as the crow flies but a long drive round by car, on account of all the inlets and salt marshes in between. Of course the coastlines were a little different: Pevensey looked south and Suffolk east, and at Bawdsey there were sandbanks out to sea. But they both had Martello towers, and the inland marshes felt and smelt exactly the same.

She wrinkled her nose. Yes, it did smell a bit briny, like trapped dishwater with a whiff of rancid snail.

'But where were your parents?' she asked. 'Heavens, you weren't orphaned, were you?'

'In a way, yes. My mother had what I can only imagine was a breakdown, they didn't tell me at the time, only that she had gone away "for a rest", and my father had no time for me. He was a doctor, you see, with a large country practice in Lancashire, and his patients needed him more than I did, or there were more of them, which amounts to the same thing. I was sent to my grandparents at Bawdsey. Then I went away to school – it's all a bit hazy. There was a music teacher who took me under his wing, became my mentor if you like. He died just a few years back. He was the one who persuaded me to apply for a scholarship to music school. Without his encouragement, I might never have persevered. Grandfather wanted me to become a lay preacher like him – either that or try for the civil service. I think he saw me as a superior kind of clerk. He could never understand why I threw it all away for music, a career he viewed as scarcely better than the stage.'

'And your mother?' Alice's hand brushed against his so lightly it might have been an accident.

He felt an ancient pain. 'She died soon afterwards. They let her out of asylum, thinking my father would look after her, but he still had his patients to attend to and she still had her sadnesses. She went wandering the fields in her nightgown and died of exposure. I'm sorry, it's not something I talk about much. What about you?'

'Oh, my childhood was plain sailing. We lived in Nottingham, can you imagine. I often wonder if a little tragedy might have given me a different outlook on life. But you are what you are – no point torturing yourself unnecessarily for things that didn't happen.'

'That's just what Maddy says.'

'Your wife in America? Oh, don't let's speak of her now. You can tell me all about that wife of yours some other day, please.' With a flourish of her napkin, Alice turned towards the trolley. 'Golly,' she said, beaming at the girl, 'you really are trying to tempt me, aren't you? I was going to stick to coffee and one of your delicious mints, but now that I see the full spread, I can't resist the raspberry fool, with maybe a touch of trifle on the side. Michael dear, what will you have?'

'Nothing, really. I've eaten enough to last me for several days.'

'How about a nice bit of cheese? I've never known a man who can resist their Gorgonzola, it's positively heaven.'

They lingered over coffee. Alice ordered a brandy – 'I'm paying, what the hell' – but this time he managed to refuse a glass for himself. He had drunk quite enough wine already. The bill came while Alice was away in the Ladies. He wondered if he should do the gentlemanly thing and settle it himself. Sneaking a glance at the final tally, he decided against making any sort of gesture: this was her treat, after all. When Alice came back, trailing her diaphanous scarves, he saw that she had combed her hair and repainted her lips. Without looking at the bill, she pulled out a plastic card and waved the saucer away.

Nancy was sitting at a table for two close to the entrance. He saw her as they got up to leave. She was with the scar-faced Russian from the caravan site. The pair had much to say to each other, evidently. The Russian was manoeuvring small objects around the table, salt, pepper, a small plate and a single red rose in its vase, which he banged down next to Nancy's plate. Neither seemed hungry and Nancy watched her companion's every move.

As he tried to side-step out of Nancy's line of vision, she raised her head and looked straight at him.

'Hi there,' she said, lifting one hand in a gesture of welcome. Her smile made him feel warm. The Russian, too, seemed pleased to see him, unless he was a natural mimic.

'Hello Nancy,' he said. 'What are you doing here?'

'Same as you, I expect.'

'Well, yes, the food's pretty good.'

Alice was beckoning to him from the door. Nancy looked at Michael then over towards Alice. He saw her eyebrows flicker.

'Must go, sorry,' he said, and followed Alice outside.

'I can see I shall have to keep an eye on you,' she said darkly. 'You know who that was, don't you?

'That's Nancy, I met her here the other day.'

'Nancy she may be, but she's also the local tart.'

Alice drove fiercely along the potholed road, swerving from side to side to avoid the worst of the ruts. Instead of dropping him off, as he had hoped, she invited herself inside. 'Just a little nightcap, come on,' she said as they climbed the steps, then she disappeared into the bathroom where she stayed an inordinate length of time. He heard the water cistern gurgling in the kitchen, wondering how on earth he could extricate himself without causing offence. This was her house, after all, even if he was technically the occupant. He hadn't the heart – or the will - to throw her out of her own place.

When he heard the turn of the lock, saw her coming towards him with her arms outstretched, he knew there was no such thing as a free lunch, or tea, or especially dinner, and Maddy was too far away to send out semaphore signals about the boundary he was about to cross ....

7

Muffled bangs and thuds from the living room next door warned him that Alice was up already and about her business. Every morning she exercised for ten fast and furious minutes, she had told him, followed most days by ten more minutes of yogic meditation.

'At home I exercise completely in the pink, that *always* makes me feel good, even if I haven't quite got the figure for it.'

'In the pink? Oh, I see.' He had protested, of course, but perhaps not as vehemently as she might have liked.

Now that the worst had happened, he resigned himself to staying where he was until he heard her enter the bathroom. Then he would slip on some shorts and head off for a run. Although he was dying to use the bathroom himself, he didn't think he could do it silently enough to avoid a confrontation, and the last thing he wanted was to give any sign of life until she was fully clothed and on her way out.

Alice in bed had revealed herself as terrifyingly, voraciously raunchy. All that huffing and puffing, she clearly hadn't had a man in months, and while he felt flattered by her exaggerated moaning, he didn't believe his technique deserved quite such a display of sexual gratification. But he liked it when she sucked him, liked it so much indeed that he forgot his usual caution and came in her face way before she was ready for him. He knew he would have to come again, for both their sakes. The one surprise was that after he had finally performed to her satisfaction, and she lay languidly among a disorder of pillows and bedsheets – *mmmn that was good,* she had said pleasingly, *so, so good* – he had fallen instantly asleep and slept until morning, his conscience unpricked by any feelings of guilt. Maddy might not like what he had done, and he wasn't feeling particularly pleased with himself either, but sleeping with Alice did not in any way constitute a betrayal of his wife's trust. He had simply found himself outmanoeuvred. Looking back over the evening, the only thing he could have done to avert its final conclusion was to have refused her offer of a meal, declined her pre-packed dinners and avoided any dealings with the woman beyond the usual civilities between landlord and tenant. Hindsight was all very well but he believed in treating people with a modicum of decency.

The house fell into a deep silence. Checking his watch, he dozed in and out of sleep. After ten minutes exactly, he heard the bathroom door click shut and quickly seized his chance. As quietly as he could, he found his shorts in the drawer then tiptoed across the living room to the glass doors which were thankfully open to the beach so he wouldn't need to rummage for the key.

Already several adults and children were spilling out from the house next door on to their patch of foreshore. He bade them a quick hello then headed eastwards up the beach towards the Martello tower where he hoped to pee discreetly round the side. Only when the houses ran out did he stop to look back. A lone peacock-coloured figure was standing on the ridge near his house: Alice most likely. He wondered how long he could decently carry on running.

Alice was looking subdued when he finally ran back home, sitting outside at the white plastic table she had lain with breakfast things for two: croissants, brioche, grapes, melon, a white coffee pot (where on earth did she keep that hidden?).

'Aren't you a dark horse,' she said. 'You never told me you *ran*.'

'I don't run regularly. But my work gives me very little exercise.'

'I'm sure. Sitting around all day will do your heart no good at all. Why don't you take a shower and I'll freshen up this coffee. I could do with another blast or two myself.'

Prudently he omitted to say that he would much prefer tea.

But after he had showered and changed into clean clothes, he couldn't help noticing how much better he felt. A morning run wasn't such a bad idea. Now all he had to do was to get rid of Alice and settle down to work. Alice had other ideas, however. The De La Warr pavilion down the coast at Bexhill was always worth a visit, she said, just to see the stairwell, even if their exhibitions were sometimes a little thin on *content*. Or she could show him Pevensey Castle, which simply *reeked* of history.

The telephone rang while Alice was in the kitchen, clearing away breakfast.

'I'll get it,' she called.

He jumped to his feet. 'No, please.' It could be Maddy, calling from America at the end of a long night.

The foreign chap on the end of the line didn't seem to know what he wanted. 'I expect you've got the wrong number,' said Michael helpfully. 'Sorry.'

Alice went, eventually, but only after he had agreed to a further visit in a fortnight's time.

'You really must snatch a day off every once in a while, you know. Working day in, day out without a break withers the spirits, believe me, and I've known *hundreds* of creative people in my time. *All work and no play makes Jack a dull boy.*' She pulled an ugly face. 'You never saw *The Shining?* Jack Nicholson losing his cool in a snowstorm? Oh never mind, it's jolly frightening. Each time I see the axe come through the door I jump right out of my skin.'

Now that she was leaving, he hoped he hadn't treated her too badly but what had happened was clearly of Alice's choosing. He couldn't be held responsible. As they said goodbye on the raised stairway looking out into the marshes he wondered if he should kiss her or give her hand a good squeeze. Alice stood on her toes, clearly expecting a kiss. He went the wrong way and banged her nose. 'Sorry,' he mumbled, disturbed by a faint smell of face powder and dried roses. She smiled graciously and set off lightly down the steps.

He watched her walk along the garden path, pulling out weeds as she went. Across the marshes, a turquoise-and-yellow diesel train gathered speed as it disappeared towards Bexhill. By the gates she turned and waved. He waved back. She blew him a kiss then squeezed through the side door into the garage that had barely enough space to accommodate her small car.

Sensing the need to empty his mind before settling to his work, Michael made himself some black China tea, letting his thoughts focus on the kettle's boiling water sounds which he visualised as an ionic spiral, ending with a click as the rising steam cut the current. The kettle steamed like a smoking gun. When he was quite calm, he carried his tea over to his worktable, still covered with the jottings he was making at the moment of Alice's arrival.

First he tidied. Then he sat. The everyday noises from next door gradually fell away, and the sea's distant drag.

Instead of picking up yesterday's thread, his mind went back to the beginning, looking for a shape that would encompass the work and all he wanted to say. An image slipped into mind, one he couldn't place at first: a massive concrete parabola held aloft by metal girders. He saw it first in black and white. Only gradually did colour bleed into the image, rust-red doors, muddy concrete walls, coal black tyres discarded like rubber doughnuts on a patchwork of concrete roadway laid in strips, weeds already colonising the cracks.

The clue to its identity came as he drew closer, a huge metal bolt secured by a giant padlock that looked locked but wasn't. The bolt clanged as he pulled it aside then heaved with all his young boy's weight against the metal doors that shifted on their oiled castors just enough to let him inside. Sounds of skiffle on a cheap Dansette. His friend Dickie with Fairground Jim, their heads bent over cardboard boxes full of records, the other kids on their cheap roller-skates, wobbling and whooping as they skated around the barn's makeshift arena, its circumference marked with straw bales to soften their inevitable tumbles. Round and round they went, avoiding the pits in the concrete as best they could, colliding giddily with each other and cracking their heads as they fell.

His concentration is such that he steps inside the memory, both experiencing the moment and observing himself within it.

Now you're skating with the others on your rented skates. Feel the joy well up from deep inside – joy at the music that fills your body; at the unexpected freedom of gliding over the concrete, however unsteadily; at the animal pleasure of knocking into the other lads and showing off to the girls, bearing down on them then shooting past at the last moment, when they've already started to shriek. You're good at this. Everyone can see that you have rhythm and native agility and your skating skills are getting better all the time.

You're so busy enjoying yourself that you don't see the girl in the strapless top and skin-tight shorts when she enters the barn, neither does Dickie who has taken charge of the record selection, leaving Jim to lounge around on the straw, Jim who takes your money and rents out the skates to the ones – like you – who don't have skates of their own. She must have slipped into the opening while you were practising one of your newly invented spin turns.

First thing you notice is Jim staring towards the open doors, chest puffed out like a bantam cock. Leaning against the metal doors, she shows her body in profile, lots of rounded curves silhouetted against the white light outside. Short shorts. Firm wide thighs. Tight top that leaves her shoulders bare. Whatever she wants, even you can tell that roller-skating isn't on her mind.

The needle scraping across black vinyl pulls you up sharp. Without the music to hold them up, kids all around you knock into each other crazily, arms flailing like windmills. Some fall over. Above the racket of girls squealing their heads off Jim shouts at you all to clear off.

But we've paid our money, mister, you can't get rid of us like this – it's not fair.

That's your voice raised in protest. Although younger than many of the others, you feel responsible because you have the strongest sense of right and wrong – something you have undoubtedly inherited from your grandfather, however hard you seek to deny his influence. Jim flicks you off like a flea but the girl in the short shorts takes an interest in your juvenile protest, detecting in your mettle a kindred spirit.

Sashaying across the makeshift rink she comes over to where you are standing your ground, boyish fists clenched at the unfairness of adult ways. She's got funny urchin hair, red-blonde darkening into brown at the roots. The way she looks you up and down makes you feel hot all over but you are not, absolutely not, going to give way on the business of who owes what to whom. You and the others have paid for Jim's music and his lousy skates and a decent skating time you shall have.

How much did ya pay him, sonny?

The girl's drawly voice sounds copied in the dark from matinée movies. One and sixpence, that sounds about right, hire of skates included. *Okay,* she says in her borrowed voice, *you've already had some skatin' time, so how about I give you a shillin' for your trouble? Will you take that as adequate com-pen-sation?* Without waiting for a reply she holds out a shiny bright coin. *Here, boy, take it. This's a deal between you and me, okay?*

She's holding out the shilling. You're staring at it hard, tempted by its shiny brightness and what it will buy you, your complicity notwithstanding. There's something tugging you back to that moment – Nancy's song and the backwards angel, that's it, that's why you experienced such a frisson when you first heard her voice on the twilight beach and later in the bar, singing those words that originated with Walter Benjamin, about the storm blowing in from Paradise and the angel looking backwards into the future.

Hang on a minute. You're getting ahead of yourself. All that comes later. Stick with the barn and your youthful joy. Remember it's the shape you're after now, a simple parabola and monumental space, obsolete space like a disused aircraft hangar, rotting, rusting after the planes have taken off for the last time, hear their blades whirring up into sky, grey sky, blue sky, red sky at night, space turned over to other uses because that's the way the world is: nothing goes to waste in this other world, not even the broken bits.

The sounds in his head grew sharper, clangier. He had what he wanted and could now move on.

By four in the afternoon he had worked himself out. His tea stood scummy and cold on the table in front of him. At some point he must have stopped long enough to open the sliding doors to the beach and to remove his shirt and jeans which lay discarded at his feet – he found himself sitting in his underpants – but he couldn't remember that. His head felt like the inside of a punchball.

For an hour he slept in the white-painted bedroom, lying between white sheets that smelt of roses.

As soon as he woke, he called Maddy on the cell phone number he had copied down and kept next to the phone. She answered straight away, sounding surprised when she realised who was calling her.

'I miss you,' he said, which he knew at once was the wrong thing to say. He needed better words than that those to fill the silence that cracked open between them. 'How are you?' he asked in a rush, 'it seems ages since we last spoke. You're so far away I had almost forgotten what you sound like. I've been working, yes, it's going well at last, you'll like it, I think, the piece. I mean, it's really taking shape, I had an idea today that puts it all into, well, context, I suppose. It's still a bit of a muddle, because the context is Suffolk and childhood, and my piece is about the here and now, about Pevensey and the marshes, then there's New York to consider, they might not like any of it …'

'Hey Michael, hold on a minute. I was gonna call you later. You see, something's happened …'

He cut her off before she could start her explanation, babbled some more about his work and the memories welling up, even told her about Alice's unexpected visit – although not how it ended – and the meal they had shared the night before. He marvelled that a woman could eat so much without swelling up like a whale. The words were spewing uncensored out of his mouth. As long as he kept on talking, he wouldn't have to face whatever it was she wanted to explain, nor would he have to listen to the new voice at the other end of the phone. It frightened him. What he loved about Maddy was her Englishness, her class, her Cambridge vowels, her intelligence, her precision. This woman was an impostor but if he talked for long enough, he could coax the real Maddy back.

When he told her for the second time about the book his landlady was writing – *The Joy of Food* – and how she had threatened to include the meal they had eaten together under memorable menus, the woman whose voice he no longer recognised broke in and said: 'Listen Michael, I think we should talk.'

'But we *are* talking.'

'No we're not. You're speaking. I'm not even listening any more.'

He breathed deeply. 'Okay. Tell me what's wrong. I called the other night, that's how I got this number. Your message seemed to suggest you were going away.'

'That's right.'

'Where are you now? Are you at home?'

'Not exactly.'

'Then are you at somebody else's home, is that what you're trying to tell me?'

'I think you're missing the point. No, there's nothing like that going on, I promise you. The semester has ended and it's a few weeks before I start summer school and I feel the need to get right away for as long as I've got. Go on a journey, oh I know it sounds corny but I feel that if I go on a journey I might find myself again. Am I making any sense?'

'Yes. No. Not at all. Maddy, you've got to be clearer than this. I have to know what's going on, what you want.'

'That's what I'm trying to tell you. What I want is this.'

'What?'

'What I'm doing.'

'But you haven't told me what that is.'

'Don't push me Michael. That's part of the problem.'

'Why don't you come home, if you've got some time, then fly back for the start of summer school? We can find the money, I know I'm not making much at the moment, but with your Princeton salary, you can surely spare a few hundred pounds. I'll add what I can. Or I could fly out to see you. I know it would cost a bit and I hate flying.'

'This isn't about money, Michael.'

'Then what is it about?'

He could hear her thinking, searching for the words that would explain herself to him and maybe to herself. Maddy slipping off to find herself was unthinkable – he knew no one in the entire world with a surer grip of who she was. Maddy was his rock, his shining light, Peter and the Virgin Mary rolled into one. *Please, Maddy, I beg you, don't go all West Coast on me.*

I'm lost without you.

He started to tell her about Walter Benjamin and the angel who mends things that are broken, that's what you do when things fall apart: you mustn't just throw them away, you fix them, however long it takes, but he could tell that Maddy wasn't interested in viewing their predicament from his point of view.

'I believe we have reached a turning point,' said Maddy slowly in the mid-Atlantic voice he had begun to hate because it took away the Maddy he loved, 'and now it's time to start thinking about who we are. About what really matters, to each of us.'

'You're what matters to me. Not my work, not … success … not all the things I do to fill my day. Without you I'm nothing.'

The crack between them opened into a crevasse.

'That's not fair, Michael. You can't expect me to carry that sort of weight. I shall carry on talking and then I'm gonna put down the phone and you're not going call me for a few days because I need the space to find myself again. I know this sounds cruel but I'm lost, Michael, and I'll not be of any use to anyone – to you, to me, to anyone at all – if I don't go hunting, so try to keep calm, hold on to the things that matter and I'll call again in a few days. Concentrate on your work, on doing the very best you can and all this will sort itself out, if you'll only trust me to do the right thing, by both of us. So listen Michael, be strong and brave, and when it all gets too much you know I'm out here, working things out. Trust me. I'll get back to you as soon as I can, as soon as it's right …'

He didn't hear the final click as the line went dead. He was trying to do what she said – hold on to the things that mattered and to trust her, whatever she was doing, although he wondered if he would ever be able to trust anyone again.

8

Lark, looking sleeker than ever, and cross, was sitting in the hall when Alice returned to London.

'I'm home,' said Alice, dropping her keys into the china bowl.

The cat eyed her archly then marched off down the hall.

Oh be like that, thought Alice, *but I have to get away once in a while and it's not my fault if I get delayed. I can't plan for everything.*

She considered phoning Geraldine, who would be back from New York, but it was Saturday and limpet Bill might be stuck to her still, assuming he was fast on his way to becoming a permanent fixture. *Why should I always be the one to call? What are friends for, if they can't share in your triumphs and commiserate over your defeats? If Geraldine thinks Bill is a good catch she needs an eye test, or a shrink. She'll have to wait before I breathe one word about my latest development. In fact, I've a good mind to wait until the premiere, that would be fun. I could ask if she'd like a ticket to Michael's latest work – a comp, of course. Oh, didn't I tell you that our friendship has grown into something quite special? Can't say more, some other time perhaps …*

Just thinking about it gave her the heart to deal with Lark's litter tray, which she emptied and scrubbed then re-filled with organic wood chippings, a task usually reserved for Sundays. After that she opened the post, bills and junk mail mostly, and flyers posted indiscriminately through the letter box offering 2-4-1 pizzas (anything that mangled the English language went straight into the bin), aluminium windows, airport taxis, handymen-gardeners and sundry babysitting services.

She was so busy throwing things away that she almost missed

Geraldine's card, a black-and-white shot of Brooklyn Bridge looking back towards Manhattan and a clear view of the Twin Towers. Her friend's bad taste took her breath away. She had walked the bridge herself with that Chinese actor she had met at the science cabaret on Cornelia Street, soaring along the pedestrian walkway high above the traffic, so high she imagined she was flying. It was the only time she had felt the Twin Towers earned their place on the Manhattan skyline but trust Geraldine to send it to her now, when they were only a memory.

Hope you're having fun, Geraldine had written in her dashed-off scrawl, *Bill sends his love, as ever.*

Brooklyn Bridge joined the other rejects in the bin.

Alice tried not to think about it as she changed into her work clothes. It was silly, really – too silly even to mention to her friends – but she had long recognised that she did her best work when looking tolerably smart, a hangover from the days she had worked her way up the chain of command at the academic publishers who had given her the break into publishing that everybody desired. Even when she took proofs home to correct, she would sit at her desk wearing a skirt and polished shoes, none of that loafing around in jeans and flip-flops. Her natural progression to editor's chair was halted overnight when the publishers sold out to new owners – Americans, to boot – and she had found herself first sidelined and then discarded as the company marched deliberately downmarket. The pittance she received in lieu of notice, the absolute legal minimum despite her many years of dedicated service, made her wonder if there were any decency left in the world, or gratitude. The experience taught her nonetheless that it is possible to live on one's wits, which she had done ever since, preferring to devote herself to books she wanted to write rather than attempting to double-guess ones that unknown others might wish to read. It was an exchange that worked in her favour, morally if not financially.

From her still generous wardrobe she selected a denim skirt, three-quarter length, and a russet top that suited her colouring. The skirt was getting tight around the waist. She would have to lose a pound or two, she thought, inspecting herself critically in the mirror. From the front she looked fine, statuesque even with her dark hennaed hair bouncing around her shoulders. Sideways on was a different matter. Her stomach sagged forward unless she held it in tight and her shoulders slouched disgracefully. *Poached salmon for you tonight, my girl, served with a light green salad and four of the teeniest new potatoes, unbuttered, and absolutely no alcohol.*

Michael sleeping had an angel's grace – lofty, composed and so good-looking, his brain quietly recuperating like a rechargeable battery plugged into the mains. That wife of his clearly wasn't looking after him properly. Fancy going off to Princeton and then disappearing into the ether without so much as a smoke signal. Michael needed a proper woman who would put his interests first, sacrificing her own ambitions on the altar of his achievements. Unlike his so-called wife, she would serve him to the best of her considerable abilities, and she wouldn't count the cost.

The prospect filled her with quiet elation as she settled to work in the book-lined alcove under the stairs. Lark jumped up behind her on the chair, purring noisily. She was forgiven, and felt glad. *If food be the music of love,* she thought glibly, picking up her pen, *play on.*

Usually, when she started a new book, she would conduct her research as thoroughly as possible and then start writing at the beginning, working her way slowly and methodically to the end, her sights set on the latter stages when she had climbed over the book's hump and was careering down to its joyful finale.

This time, however, she felt the urge to start in the middle, at a chapter she had planned around the theme of aphrodisiacs. As well as the pile of papers relating to her completed research, she kept in constant view the dictionary definition, which told her that 'aphrodisiac' is a noun meaning a food, drink or drug that stimulates sexual desire, and that it also has a figurative meaning indicating an abstract quality regarded as having such an effect, as in *power is an aphrodisiac*. The origin of the word was eighteenth century (what in heaven's name did they use before then?), from the Greek *aphrodisiakos*, itself derived from Aphrodite, the Greek goddess of beauty, fertility and sexual desire, whose name means literally 'foam-born', from *aphros* meaning 'foam'. Alice smiled at her memories of the night before.

Pitching her tone midway between the scholarly and the informal, she began to write.

Only two substances may properly be said to exert a direct physiological effect on human sexual desire, cantharides, the broken dried remains of the blister beetle – more commonly known as Spanish fly – and yohimbine, a crystalline alkaloid derived from the bark of the yohimbé tree, Pausinystalia yohimbe. *Both excite passion by irritating the urinary tract and producing a rush of blood to the sex organs. Spanish fly has traditionally been fed to male livestock to encourage mating. It is not recommended for humans, however. As well as burning the mouth and throat, it can lead to infections, scarring of the urethra, and death. The use of yohimbine as an aphrodisiac is even more problematic. Any measurable boost to the libido can be achieved only by toxic doses, a very real* Liebestod, *and one that plays straight into Wagner's hands.*

After reading the paragraph aloud, making one or two minor changes and writing a Post-it note reminding her to ask Michael about Wagner, she continued with verve, ranging easily and lightly over subjects as diverse as food labelling and regulation, sensible diet, the doctrine of signatures (one of her best passages, she thought with a smile; did Casanova *really* start each day with a breakfast of fifty oysters slithering deliciously down his throat?), the role of Aphrodite, foods considered to enflame sexual desire (anise, banana, basil, carrot, garlic, ginger, gladiolus corms, honey, mustard, nutmeg, orchid bulbs, pistachios, river snails, rocket, sage, salvia, sea fennel, skink flesh, sparrows, truffles, turnip, the heavenly vanilla pod and chocolate), and the mercifully shorter list of foods to avoid if one wished to circumvent an embarrassing wilt (cornflakes, dill, okra, wild lettuce, marjoram, rue, and water lily). By the time she reached the fig, the most sexual fruit of all, she was positively enflamed. *Slice it open,* she wrote with a flourish, *and breathe deeply of its redly moist female genitalia, best scooped out with the fingers or sucked, for obvious reasons.*

Without pausing for breath she danced twice round the room then searched her bookcase for a well-thumbed copy of the *Kama Sutra,* which she valued not for its smut (trust the West to trivialise the true meaning of sex) but rather as a manual setting out everything a man or woman might require to enjoy the fruits of earthly bliss. The scholarly authors of the Sanskrit text had naturally given food a leading role in the art of seduction and she was looking for recipes to adapt for western audiences. Two looked especially promising: a Kama Sutra Shake involving clarified butter, honey, liquorice powder, milk and blended fennel juice; and a much simpler decoction of oat straw boiled in water. Both she determined to try out on Michael in a blind tasting that would allow her to test their efficacy.

When she had finished for the day, Alice ran herself a bath and luxuriated for a full twenty minutes to the sounds of jazz on Radio 3. Classical music would have suited her mood better, but the selection was suitably languid. After she had dried herself and changed into something more comfortable, she rifled her CD collection, kept in a kitchen cupboard as listening to music while she cooked was one of her greatest pleasures. Her heart gave a little leap. There it was: Schubert's *Notturno* for piano, violin and cello in E♭ major, she knew she had it somewhere. It was even the correct recording, at least she thought it was the one he had mentioned. Hephzibah Menuhin on piano, Yehudi on violin, Maurice Gendron on cello.

Oh, if only he were here now, he could *explain* it all for her, tell her – show her – what it meant. When he had talked of it before, she was doing her best to listen but there was so much else going on, all that static created when two people are getting to know each other and thoughts come bustling in. He was telling her about his mother, she recalled, although why a mother should two-step with Schubert she hadn't the foggiest. As he spoke to her about his mother walking out into the frozen fields she was thinking summer evenings, dancing on the lawn, May Balls, fireflies on the river, Snape Maltings, Aldeburgh, opera al fresco.

There's so much I want to share with you, you lovely, lovely man, if you will only let me.

Reverentially, she inserted the CD into its slot. The drawer slid shut with a satisfying click. She pointed the remote control towards the machine and clicked on '6'. After a slight whirring Hephzibah's glorious arpeggiated chords rose out of silence like gently lapping waves, conjuring out of the ether visions of Venice, gondolas, moonlight slivers on inky black canals and head notes of ghostly white lily smells to mask the base notes of undiluted bilge water. Their gondolier was smiling down at them as she and Michael buried themselves on brocaded cushions. Ecstasy reborn, timeless and contemplative, then the cello's joyful plucking. Poor Schubert, dying of syphilis yet able to compose melodies of such sublimity.

Michael lifts his arms and she waltzes him serenely onto the cobblestones of the Piazza San Marco to a fluttering of pigeons' wings. He dances awkwardly but she'll show him the way. Michael will lead her to a greater understanding of what the melodies mean and she will teach him how to dance with all his body - a fair exchange, surely? Feet and hands are just the beginning. It's how your body flows that matters, how the separate parts connect to one another in joyous harmony.

She feels his English awkwardness slip away.

Still waltzing in her imagination she let herself into the garden. For nearly a week now she had barely ventured outside and her neglect was all too evident. Leaves clogged the pump of her small water feature, the raised stone flags needed a jolly good sweep, shrubs flopped into each other because she always planted them too close together, and her neighbour's Russian vine had started its annual sprint along the shared trellis, swamping the one clematis that had decided to reward her attention. There was always too much to do – writing, friends, the landlady business, looking after Lark – and she found gardening a bit of a chore.

After she had discreetly chopped at the Russian vine she threw the clippings in her bin, having turned down the council's offer of a green-waste composter, which was fine in principle but quite hideous in practice. The only free space in her garden lay directly in front of her window and she wasn't going to spend her days looking out at a plastic Dalek without arms, thank you very much. No, she would get round to constructing a proper compost heap one of these days, one that worked aesthetically as well as functionally. In the meantime, she would continue to bin her peelings, clippings and organic waste, experiencing a faint stab of conscience every time she threw away substances more properly intended to improve her soil. Life was like that – a quicksand of shifting compromises you had to negotiate as best you could.

Her neighbours two doors down were having a barbecue, evidently; sounds of laughter drifted over the fence in a cloud of weekend entertaining. Alice knew them only vaguely and suppressed the thought that tonight might have presented a good opportunity to get to know them better. Determined not to feel left out she thought how nice it would be to have people round herself – Geraldine and Bill and some of her other friends. Her weeks in London would feel increasingly lonesome. With her book in mind, she toyed with the idea of a themed evening, a hundred and one things to do with offal, that kind of thing.

Bill had always raved about her devilled kidneys. Or how about a little impromptu avant-garde dinner, something light and frothy from the *Futurist Cookbook*?

A menu that appeals to all five senses: touch, taste, smell, sight, hearing. Bill would adore the joke, and he must be starving by now. Geraldine couldn't grill a slice of toast without setting the kitchen on fire.

Her energy levels restored, she went inside for her cookbooks and poured herself a glass of chilled white wine, which she carried to her dining area under the mimosa tree, remembering her earlier resolve to avoid alcohol only as she put the glass to her lips.

Oh sod it, she thought, what's the harm in one little glass? If they had thought to ask me to their party, it would be five or six glasses at least and platefuls of party food, so I think I can allow myself this one little treat.

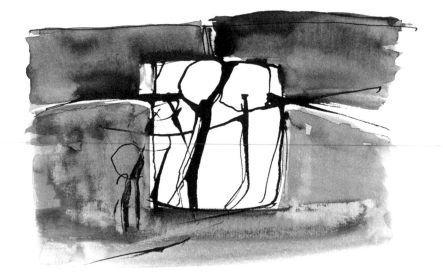

9

The door at the top of Michael's rickety steps was wide open. That didn't feel right. She paused and listened. No sound of anyone moving within. If Derek hadn't insisted, she would have turned and run. But she wanted her bicycle back, even if the guy gave her the creeps.

As silently as she could, she removed her shoes and tiptoed through the kitchen to the small interior hall, from where she could look straight ahead into the bedroom (empty) and sideways through the main room to the sliding doors that opened to the sea.

He had drawn an armchair up to the glass and there he sat, absolutely motionless, facing the sea. The chair hid most of him. All she could see was half a head of grey-brown hair protruding above the backrest. He looked as if he was waiting for something.

'It's me,' she said quietly, 'Nancy Flight.'

'I know,' he replied without looking round. 'I was expecting you.'

'How's that?'

'You promised you would come. Don't you remember?'

'Actually I've come for my bike. And I have a message from Derek.'

'Derek?'

'He wants to know how you're getting on. You don't have to tell him, but I promised I would ask.'

'I can tell *you*, because you're part of it.'

'Tell me when it's done, isn't that best?'

'Come here,' he said, looking at her for the first time. She stepped behind his chair and laid both hands on his shoulders. She didn't need Derek to tell her what to do.

'All these voices,' he said, speaking to the sea as Nancy worked the muscles between his shoulder blades. 'They're driving me crazy. You're in there, and Maddy, and you're getting horribly mixed up.'

'Who's Maddy?'

'She's my wife. You keep running in to each other. Maddy's voice – that's the soprano voice – has turned into an alto, which is your part, really, and I don't need another, so either I change the parts around or I go with what I've got. What would you do?'

'Follow your instinct.'

'That's the trouble. I don't know if the voices are real or simply imagined.'

'Of course they're not real. I mean, there's no one actually inside there, talking to you, is there?'

'Yes there is, as a matter of fact. There's Maddy, for a start – several Maddies and I don't know which is the right one. She says things she can't possible mean, horrid things, cruel and uncaring, as if she wants me to hate her. You talk to me, too.'

'Me?'

'Your voice at any rate, the part I think of as the real alto. I was pleased with you at first, the way you came into my head fully formed with an earthy quality that was just right. Now Maddy is going the same way and I can't tell you apart. It's never happened to me before. It feels as if she's changing into someone else and I don't have control any more. Perhaps I never did. I write these things and I don't know why. Perhaps they're writing me. Perhaps I'm a figment of someone else's imagination and not me at all – in Maddy's head perhaps, or yours.'

'Not in mine, you're not,' she said firmly.

'I have the angel to think about, too. It's like a bad dream. I walk into the marshes, and there it is, this flaming apparition flapping its wings. Does that mean anything? Do you know if there are stories, sightings, I don't know, anything that might link a great shining angel to the marshes of Pevensey Bay?'

'Edie might know. I could ask her.'

'Will you? Please, I'd like that very much. The angel is what this piece is all about, I'm sure of that. Colour and speed, that's what Brodsky said they have, angels, I mean, and that's why you find them everywhere. Except when you go looking for them, of course, and then they vanish.'

He reached for her hand on his shoulder and squeezed it hard. 'Why should my wife suddenly turn on me? She's good and kind and beautiful, all the things you could possibly want in a wife, and now she's turning into a harpy.'

'Stop it,' said Nancy, pulling at her hand, 'you're hurting me.'

'You've got to help me,' he implored, swaying to his feet. 'I need to know what's going on. I've just spoken to her.'

'In your head?'

'On the telephone. She was quite horrid.'

'Maybe she's trying to dump you,' said Nancy, who'd had enough. 'That's what women do. They go hard and mean to provoke you into making the first move, because that way they feel a hell of a lot better at walking out on you, believe me.'

'No, no, no, no, no, no, no, Maddy's not like that at all. You don't know her.'

'Of course I don't know her, she's your fucking wife, not mine.'

'Then why do you torment me like this?'

The guy was out of his skull. She was only trying to help, calm him down, be *nice* to him, for fuck's sake, as Derek had asked. Why did everything she touch get so muddled? Without knowing why, she moved closer and fearlessly let him put his arms around her. Daniel stepping into the lions' den, that's how it felt. He made a series of guttural noises like an animal and pulled her to his chest, as if she were the one who needed comfort, not him. They stood without speaking for nearly a minute, his arms holding her fast but not suffocatingly so, and although she could tell that he wanted her – they were, after all, pressed close together – she felt perfectly in control. And when she had had enough, she unwrapped his arms and said she really had to go. She was singing that night at the pub, an evening of songs devoted to the weather, Derek's idea but she was game, and it gave George plenty of scope. He was welcome to come if he wished. She planned to sing the Laurie Anderson number he liked so much – the one with the storm blowing in from Paradise - and he might get to meet Stas, the Russian guy who was staying at the caravan site. Stas was a physicist, would you believe? The smartest guy she had ever known. Stas knew all about space and time and loads of stuff like that.

He was feeling her hair, running his hand against the grain. If he dropped his hand any lower she would knee him in the groin. As he let go of her, he looked hard into her eyes. It felt as if he was sucking at her soul.

She found her bicycle under the house, in the unlocked storeroom behind the wooden steps, and cycled exultantly home, her head ringing with the sounds of Muddy Waters, *Blow Wind Blow*. When she had sung it earlier in rehearsal George on drums had caught at the coat-tails of her elation, nodding and grinning like Julie Andrews on speed. Derek on electric guitar was more circumspect, but even he was slipping into her slipstream, she could tell from the way he watched her, following wherever she might lead. She loved the magic she worked on people when she sang, and the power she used to make them feel good. As she cycled past the campsite at Normans Bay a gaggle of young boys threw stones at her wheels and she nearly fell off.

When she got to the pub a few hours later, her good spirits momentarily deserted her. Michael and Stas were sitting at a table in the front row locked in conversation, Michael with the wrapt expression of someone who has just found God. She could tell from the objects Stas waved in the air – a full glass of beer, a beer mat, a laminated promotion for wines – that he was holding forth about space and time and points of view. When he'd done it to her, she was a wilting rose and he was a side plate. Jesus Christ. There was Derek, snooping around in the background, apparently to check the equipment but more likely to hear what was said. He could sidle across an empty room and you wouldn't notice him until he knifed you in the back.

Instead of joining them she went to the Ladies, ignoring the other women's protests as she sidestepped the queue and locked herself in a cubicle. She was ten minutes late already. Afterwards she washed her hands and looked herself over in the mirror. Her lipstick had smudged and a spot had erupted on her chin. Fuck it. They must take her as she comes.

★ ★ ★

Michael saw Nancy subliminally when she came into the bar

– in her tartan knickers and lime-green top she was hard to ignore – but he was too engrossed in his conversation with Stas to pay her much heed. He had found the Russian already occupying a front table when he reached the pub about half an hour before Nancy and the others were scheduled to perform. After buying himself a pint, he wandered over to Stas's table and asked if he could join him. They shook hands formally. Stas's black eye was turning green and the zigzag scar through his right eyebrow gave his face a lopsided air. Michael reminded him that they had now met three times: once at the caravan site, once over dinner, and now here, waiting for Nancy. The Russian's face broke into a grin.

'I like English girl,' he said, 'I like very much indeed.'

'Me too,' said Michael, but it was not Nancy he wished to discuss. 'She says you know about time, is that right?'

Stas nodded vigorously. 'I am physicist at Pulkovo Observatory. Fine place, very beautiful, near Petersburg. Quantum cosmology, causality, closed timelike curves, wormholes, shortcuts through time, you know?'

'Not really. But Pulkovo, yes, and St Petersburg. I studied for a time at the Conservatory.'

'Rimsky-Korsakov,' said Stas. 'Yes, I know. Fine place, too.'

Michael asked what had brought him to Pevensey Bay. Stas's answer was difficult to follow, and not simply for his singular grammar. As far as Michael could ascertain, Stas was part of a delegation of Russian scientists making an exchange visit to Herstmonceux Observatory, whose great dome Michael had seen on his walks into the Levels. Stas, who worked mostly from home ('My physics all here,' he said, tapping his head, 'I am not needing office to think') had arrived at the airport with his ticket on the appointed day but his colleagues were nowhere to be seen. When he had telephoned the Observatory, a bemused switchboard operator had told him that all their internal connections had jammed and they had taken the system down in order to work out what the hell was going on.

As Stas held part of the float for the trip, he continued his journey alone, making his way successfully from Heathrow airport to London Victoria where he caught a train to Pevensey Bay. But then his difficulties began in earnest. Finding no taxi rank, he had accepted a lift to the Observatory from a helpful young man in a dented old Ford Mondeo who had driven him along country lanes towards the Observatory dome, its constant presence in the landscape reassuring him that everything was well. Then the car had broken down and the man – who still seemed friendly enough – had asked him to get out and walk the rest of the way along a grassy lane that disappeared into a tunnel of bushy trees. The sides of the path were cluttered with broken-down machines, he remembered, and his bag had snagged on the undergrowth. The next thing he knew he was lying flat on his back in a field between great chunks of concrete, his bag and his money gone and his head hurting like hell. At least his passport was still inside the pocket to his leather jacket, which Stas opened to show Michael how he kept it safe. The padded lining was badly torn and smelt of dead squirrel.

'They take money but who want to be Russian, now?'

'Did you phone the police?' asked Michael, concerned.

'More trouble than worth. Anyway, phone in bag, so phone gone too. Cops only make shit. Maybe they send me back, if they know money gone. Then Nancy arrive like good fairy. I like Nancy very much. I want to tell Elena of Nancy but wives not like that sort of talk.'

He pronounced her name 'Nanci-er', as if she were more than Nancy. Michael liked that. 'Elena is your wife?' he asked.

'Sure. Elena is good woman. Much bigger than Nancy.' Grinning, he used his hands to indicate a woman of large girth.

'Nancy call friend – that man Derek, you know? – and Derek is driving me and Nancy to Observatory. Only ...'

Here, Stas looked genuinely perplexed. At the Observatory, a security guard on the gate had asked them to wait in the car while she called through to the house. Nobody had told her of any Russians staying, certainly not a Russian requiring urgent medical attention. After a short wait, a chauffeur-driven car had delivered a smartly dressed woman who talked first with Nancy and then with him. Yes they were expecting Russians from Pulkovo, she confirmed, but not for another month.

'She say to Nancy I am impostor, perhaps. That is .. mmm ... lie. I have passport to prove who I am. Name on list, too, so she know I am not pretending to be me.'

'What did you do?'

'No choice. Woman not have me for one month more. No money. Home too far away. ... Nancy find me place to stay – very cheap. I pretend this is holiday. Here Nancy, there Elena – same thing, you know? I ... mmm ... think, same as home sweet home.'

'And what do you think about?'

'Oh – many things, I think all time. Space travel. Moon travel. Big bangs. Now Pulkovo have not much money I think space and time most often. You not know what is happening tomorrow because maybe you forget it. Look,' he said, marshalling Michael's glass, a beer mat and a wine menu. 'You are beer,' he said, catching Michael's eye. 'This table we see in three ... mmm ... dimensions, Euclidean space, you know. You born here,' he placed the beer mat in front of Michael, 'you die here.' Down went the wine menu at the opposite side of the table. 'On table, they are different places. You draw line from one to other, we call that ... mmm ... time. You locked in present moment, only because you down here.' He slammed Michael's beer glass down on the table, splashing its contents and causing several drinkers to turn in their direction. 'From up here,' he said, slopping more beer as he raised the glass into the air, 'you see everything in same moment'.

Michael felt a shiver of engagement. 'Do you think that you might have travelled here in time?' he asked. 'That you've got ahead of yourself, somehow? I mean, if everything is equivalent and everything co-exists, as long as you shift your viewpoint, isn't that plausible?'

Stas was shaking his head. 'In theory perhaps, but in life, not likely. In general relativity – Einstein, you know? - spacetime have geometry ... mmm ... have topology. If I have pen and paper, I draw you how time looks in general relativity, sometimes like tube, sometimes like egg in frying pan. Time able to loop round and intersect itself, so you can meet older or younger self. But in special relativity, Einstein says that nothing go faster than light. Theory and practice not same thing at all. You know grandfather paradox? Person ask his grandson to make journey back in time to kill him as baby. If baby die, then baby not able to grow up and have grandchildren, so grandson cannot kill baby. If grandson alive and shoot, how come grandfather not die? Okay, maybe all grandsons are bad shooters, and all guns they ... mmm ... jam. But look at mathematics. I promise you.

You able to *imagine* time machine, but build one, no. Not even Einstein can do that.'

'In that case, why spend your time thinking about things that can never happen? Things that are practicably impossible?'

'I am physicist. This is what I ... mmm ... do. I explore look for shortcuts and other ways round Einstein's laws. Time relates to causality, like sequence to consequence, you know? In my world, we suppose an effect can precede a cause. Why write music if you not able to eat it?'

'Because it sustains me.'

'Physics same thing.'

'And where does memory fit in all this – that's surely a form of time travel?'

'Ah,' said Stas, looking suddenly mischievous. 'Memory change everything, even things that are not happening.'

10

Sunday at Edie's care home was always special. Early in the morning, the local poodle parlour came to give Solomon his weekly wash. 'It's a miracle they can squeeze him into the bloomin' tub,' said Edie. 'They should try a wheelie bin, best place for that dog.' Next came the chaplain, who held a short service for communicants in the main day room, forcing those who did not wish to attend to hang about the hall or keep to their rooms until God's business was done. Edie favoured the small garden, but since her stroke could go there only in a wheelchair, so Sunday visitors were especially welcome. The trains didn't stop at Normans Bay on Sundays, however, so Nancy and Stas had to walk on to Cooden Beach, and Edie was sat in the hall with her handbag looking glum as a post when they arrived, long after the chaplain had left.

'You took your bloomin' time,' said Edie to Nancy, ignoring Stas completely, even when he presented her with Nancy's flowers, the promised blue anemones, which Edie sniffed then handed to Nancy, saying she should ask Jenny for a vase and to be quick about it. 'Them flowers look half dead already,' she said. 'Don't want 'em to die on us completely.'

'This is my new boyfriend,' said Nancy 'I told you about him last time. Stas has come all the way from Russia.'

'Just to see me, has he?' asked Edie with a crafty look that Nancy knew only too well. 'He shouldn't have bothered. What did you call him? Stash? What sort of a name is that?'

'His real name is Stanislav.'

'Is it indeed?' said Edie, looking him up and down. 'Bin in a fight then, has he? Off you go, Nancy, get them flowers fixed.'

When Nancy returned to the hall, the other two did not appear to have exchanged a single word.

'Are you warm enough?' asked Nancy, as Stas pushed the wheelchair down the gentle ramp leading into the garden. Although the day had started out bright, a string of dark clouds was crossing the sun, and a keen wind blew in from the sea.

'Stop clacking over me like an old hen,' said Edie. 'I've got my rug with me if I need it. This place'd have you wrapped up like a parcel soon as they could throw you. Don't you start on me too.'

They made a turn of the garden, Stas valiantly manoeuvring the wheelchair along the cracked concrete path. The garden itself was well cared for by a young man who came once a week, spending most of his time on the roses. Behind Edie's back, Nancy tried to encourage Stas to talk but he shook his head and made a soothing gesture with one hand, as you would to stroke a cat. Edie, who missed nothing, said the path had got a damn sight worse since she was last in the garden, or didn't they have wheelchairs in Russia? Stas inclined his head and said nothing.

On their second turn, Stas stopped the wheelchair in front of the roses which were coming into flower, vigorous bushes with shiny dark green leaves and a mass of clear pink flowers.

'Ooooh,' said Edie, 'those are lovely. "Queen Elizabeth", Arthur's favourites. "You're my Queenie," he used to say, whenever he brought me in a bunch from the garden. Hope you're looking after them, Nancy girl. Them roses are a treat.'

Heedless of who might be looking, Stas stepped into the rose bed and snapped off a stem. He looked quite mad, grinning at them from head-high roses. Nancy laughed out loud. Even Edie gave a little snort. Then he climbed out of the rose bush and knelt before Edie's wheelchair, one hand behind his back and in the other an opening pink rose, which he held out to Edie.

Edie started to smile, then clearly thought better of it.

'If you think you can buy me with a rose, young man, you've got another think coming. Roses are for sweethearts, not for old bags like me.'

'Ah,' said Stas, as solemn as a secret policeman, 'roses are for sweethearts and for old ... mmm ... what you call it.' With this he produced from behind his back another pink rose, which he presented to Nancy like a conjuror pulling rabbits out of a hat. She laughed and kissed him on the lips.

'Hmmph,' said Edie, allowing herself the tiniest of smiles, 'so I'm an old bag am I? Don't know where he gets his manners from, but there's a Russki for you.'

Stas resumed his place behind Edie's wheelchair and they made another couple of turns around the garden in a warmer spirit, until Edie said they should go inside and see whether all the priming and primping had made the slightest difference to Solomon the dog. Even bulldogs might fly if they tried hard enough.

The day room smelt of Sunday roast and boiled sprouts. Edie let Stas help her into an armchair and when they had settled her, she said: 'I can say one thing about you, young man – you're not much of a looker, are you? Neither was my Arthur, come to think of it. Know who you remind me of? Eeyore, that's who. Must be the long nose, and the gloominess of you.'

'That's not very kind, Aunt Edie,' said Nancy.

'Nothing wrong with Eeyore, my girl. He may have been a donkey, but he didn't act like one. You loved Eeyore, when you was little. 'Spect that's why you like 'im now. Oh he's all right,' she said to Nancy, looking Stas up and down, 'if that's the best you can do. Better than Piglet, any day. You wouldn't want to be hitched up to a midget.'

If they had only left then, everything would have been all right. Stas might have felt a little uncertain of Edie's good opinion, but Nancy knew Edie almost as well as herself, and Edie liked him a lot, she could tell. Edie's opinions were as clear as her eyes, and just as keen. That was the problem.

She was telling Edie about the mystery surrounding Stas's arrival, and how she had found him wandering the lane from the Wartling road to Pylons Farm.

'When was that?' asked Edie.

'Ages ago,' said Nancy. 'I can't remember exactly when.'

'I remember,' said Stas. 'Ten days ago, that is when we are meeting.'

'Blimey,' said Edie, looking at him admiringly, 'you're a fast worker. Just like my Arthur. The minute he clapped eyes on me he said I was the one. 'Spect he said that to all the girls and I was the first to believe him, more fool me. You better watch out, Nancy, or this fellow of yours will be gone before he's arrived. Near Pylons Farm you say? What was he doing there? More to the point, what were you doing there?'

'I was out walking, and yes, before you ask, I was on my own, until I found Stas, who looked as though he'd had an accident.'

Stas tried to explain about the field in which he had found himself, a field full of concrete blocks as big as hen houses. It was all a bit confused, and the knock on his head hadn't helped.

'You can say that again,' said Edie. 'If Arthur was still with us, he'd know exactly where you was. The masts came down long before your time, girl, but round about Pylons is where Arthur listened in to you Russkies. RAF Pevensey. You could see the masts for miles around. I used to go to dances at the Pier Ballroom over in Eastbourne with lads from the Wartling station. That's where we met. He was a lovely dancer was Arthur, the best of the bunch. The *paso doble* was his forte. You'd think he had springs for kneecaps. He could sweep a girl across the floor, steering you round the traffic and never once treading on your toes. All the girls wanted to dance with him, and I was first in line.'

Edie's eyes went quite misty, remembering. She hummed a snatch of Spanish gypsy music, waving her hands to the beat. In a gesture Nancy would long regret, Stas leant towards Edie as if he wanted to waltz her out of her chair. Somehow their hands got entangled and Edie found herself fingering the ring on Stas's right hand. She let go of her handbag for a moment while she inspected her own hands. Edie wore her rings on the left: a gold band and a sapphire engagement embedded in the fat of her finger.

Nancy exhaled with relief.

'Thought for a minute you was married there,' said Edie to Stas, patting his hand as she smiled up at him.

Stas was looking at Nancy with his Eyore eyes. Edie's statement didn't need an answer. Edie hadn't asked him a question, so his silence couldn't be construed as a lie. She was shaking her head, warning him to stay silent. She might want the truth for herself but concealing it from Edie was an act of kindness, couldn't he see that?

'I am ... mmm ... married,' said Stas, fingering his wedding band. 'I have wife already, back in Russia.'

Edie sucked in her cheeks. 'So you can't marry Nancy?'

'No. I can love Nancy but I not free to marry her.'

'So what the bloody hell use is that?' said Edie. 'Oh Nancy,' she said, opening her bag and rustling around inside. 'And I thought you'd finally gone and done it. Surprised us all, I mean.'

'I did too,' said Nancy quietly, almost to herself.

She couldn't be angry with him. Stas was who he was, which was why she liked him and why she suspected Edie did too. Husbands were really not her style, as Edie knew only too well. But the sparkle had gone out of their visit, and after a few attempts at banter, Nancy took Stas away, promising to bring him back before too long.

They wandered slowly down towards the seafront, admiring the striations of sunlight that swept across the bay. Stas bought her an ice cream and kissed her before she had finished, saying that she tasted of strawberries and cream.

On the promenade, beside the squashed Aladdin's hat of the Bandstand's dome, they stopped to listen to four young singers rehearsing old Abba numbers, which they belted out with joyful élan to an audience of empty chairs. A girl with long dark hair and a big bottom pranced about the sunken stage, projecting upwards to the small crowd that had gathered on the upper level. Behind her back, an Abba-like blonde and two boys wearing shades and matching yellow-and-black shirts executed a choreographed two-step and sang mostly in tune.

'You like?' asked Stas.

'What do you think?'

They carried on down the promenade, past swags of Union Jack bunting and strips of fluorescent carpet bedding. On the rusting pier they held hands as they peered between cracks in the planking at the sparkly sea. A seagull kept them in its sights, like a good omen.

Nancy suggested they should walk to the end of the pier but Stas wanted to take her back to his caravan, he said, and lie with her till the sun went down. Okay, she said, and they caught the local train that rattled back across the marshes, alighting at Cooden Beach then walking back along the road that dog-legged into Hooe Level then crossed the railway line and continued on to Normans Bay.

Back at the caravan site the smell of barbecued food was overwhelming. Stas inadvertently walked into a family game of cricket and caught an easy ball that was flying off to the boundary. Nancy apologised on his behalf, hoping that his English did not stretch to the catholic vocabulary of these little savages and bundling him inside the caravan where the sickly-sweet smell of camping gaz made her gag.

But after Stas had pulled out the thin, lumpy mattress, already fitted with sheets and threadbare bedding, he called her into his polaroid world where time stayed forever fixed in the moment, removing from her any sense of before, or after, just of time itself that wrapped the pair of them in the gestures of an endless present and delivered them each to the other. She liked that, and from Stas's gentleness with her, she knew that he did too.

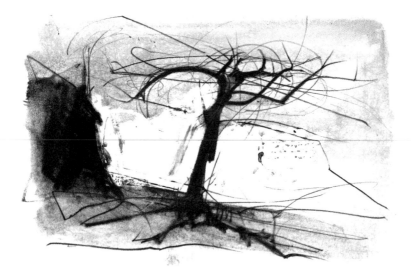

11

Spy chatter, part electronic, part human voice – a woman's voice, early 1950s diction, neither Maddy's nor Nancy's, aping the clipped tones of radio announcers heard in childhood. Apparently random numbers used to transmit coded messages on short-wave radio. CIA, most likely, or any handful of intelligence services, MI6, KGB, Stasi. Easy to pick up but virtually impossible to crack without the number pad issued to the lone agent in the field. Used once and then discarded. Perfect.

Number clusters enunciated in the woman's crystal monotone. Three – zero – nine – three - one – three – zero – nine – three – one – three – zero – nine – three - one - a double drumbeat underscores the 'one', adding tension as well as emphasis. Radar crackle rakes the skies in a circular sweep, breaking like waves upon the shore. As the sequence grows, the 'zero' becomes increasingly insistent.

Beneath the numbers, an electronic blip surfaces like a heartbeat. You the listener are wired up to the machine and the bleep is getting louder, pushing through the crackle. Despite its regularity, the rising sound suggests a fast approaching crisis. More numbers beneath the surface static, spoken by the same woman, who now sounds obviously foreign. The numbers are modulated like speech. You don't need a code book to break these. The heartbeat reaches a peak of intensity: bip, bip, bip, bip, bip, bip, bip, bip, bip, bip, bip, bip, bip, bip.

Just when you feel you can bear the tension no longer you become aware of the distant drone of aeroplanes growing ever stronger, commercial planes at first (the Boeing 757s and 767s of the September 11 attacks) but soon morphing into the throatier sounds of German Messerschmitts and Soviet MiG-17s from the 1940s and 1950s.

These grow louder, louder, louder and then – bliss - they begin to recede in precisely the same arc, to be replaced by waves of other invading armies, first the Romans, then the Nordic Saxons, then the Normans, lapping at the shores until the clash of conquest signals a temporary ascendancy of one side over the other. Napoleon is in there too, his presence indicated by squat Martello towers introduced as bulbous bursts of oboes and bassoons, although Napoleon (like Hitler) never comes.

Michael has still to map out exactly how he will characterise the separate invasions, wishing neither to run them together into a single soup, nor to risk the banal by transcribing each one too literally. He sees the Romans as muscular, the Saxons as wild and slaughtering and the Normans as wine-bibbing castlephiles, but he would be the first to admit that he is a bit hazy on detail and might simply be expressing his own prejudices.

After a good morning's work, he called the local taxi firm and asked for a ride up to Pevensey Castle, which Alice had said was well worth a visit.

'You still here, mate?' asked the driver when Michael climbed into the back seat. 'I'd put you down as a weekender, in spite of all your gear.'

Michael nodded and spent the short journey silently wondering what had marked him out as such. He didn't dress the part, surely?

Once through the castle's outer entrance, he began to feel more connected to his surroundings. The walls created a sense of both enclosure and space. Here and there he caught glimpses of the flatlands beyond, and their rim of encircling hills. He sat in the grass, drifting with his thoughts until disturbed by a party of school children who arrived like chattering starlings under the watchful eye of their teacher, a large woman with a voice like a French horn who kept order as best she could and even managed to impart small gobbets of information. Intrigued, he followed them into the inner bailey, paid his entrance fee and watched the children swarm like ants over the cannon and the piles of catapult stones, dislodging pebbles into the oubliette, and scampering up and down every available staircase.

The history of the place refused to speak to him, however, so after a cursory inspection of the Norman keep and the postern gate he climbed the north tower to the castle's small museum where the children caught up with him, jostling him against the wall as if they had failed to see him. Even their teacher seemed unaware of his presence as she gathered the children around her, talking of how the Romans had built the first fort here, one of a string of fortifications designed to defend the Saxon shore against the pirates.

'Now what's strange about that, children?'

Short silence, then one of the girls shot up her hand. 'Yes, Gemma?"

'It's not on the sea, Miss.'

'Well done. But it was in those days. All the land we know as the Pevensey Levels was covered by water at high tide, apart from a scattering of islands or "eyots" as they were called. You can hear it in the place names. Think of Horse Eye, and Chilley, and Northeye. Who knows Chilley Farm? Of course you know Chilley Farm, Gemma, you live there. What about any of the others?'

None did, it seems.

'When the Normans landed here in 1066 – at Normans Bay, although of course it wasn't called that then – the land all about was still mainly water and the Normans used the Roman stones to build their own castle inside the Roman walls.'

'So when did the land stop being water, Miss?' asked one of the boys.

'Good question, Ben. They may have begun to drain the marshes in the time we call the Dark Ages, but when the Normans wrote their Domesday Book – we covered that last week, remember? – the land was still regularly flooded with salt water. The real work to drain the marshes began later, in the Middle Ages.'

A small commotion broke out among the boys next to Ben, which the teacher moved immediately to quell. 'If you wish to make an observation, Lance, please share it with the whole class.'

'Well Miss ...' the boy began in a sly, insinuating sort of voice. He was clearly not one of her favourites. 'What if they stopped draining the marshes, or the pumping stations blew up? Then the sea could rush in again and we'd all be dead.'

'And who might wish to blow up the pumping stations, Lance?'

'Dunno Miss. How about terrorists, you know, like the ones who blew up them towers in America? They're always showing that on the telly. It could maybe happen here.'

'The targets are hardly of equal importance, Lance. But you're right to bring in the pumping stations, because that's how the land stays dry – that and the shingle ridge, which keeps out the sea and allows the land to be permanently grazed. Who knows how many pumping stations there are in the Levels?'

Gemma's hand shot up again. 'Ten,' she said, without waiting to be asked.

'Actually there are only eight,' said the teacher, with the tiniest hint of a smirk.

Gemma looked momentarily deflated. Pretty and sharp, her dark hair cut into a bob, she radiated cleverness even at this young age. The other girls were standing in a clump near the front. All had beautiful skin, including the plumper ones, before adolescence ravaged their bloom. Michael imagined them grouped into a chorus on stage, dressed in simple shifts tied around the waists like the children of serfs. A boys' choir would have been the more obvious choice, but Michael wanted girls whose experience of the land was more rooted, more of a drudgery against which the drama of his piece could play itself out. He heard the sounds they would make, a melody of clarinets in A major verging on the Mozartian, the chords of innocence before their inevitable corruption. By now he was swaying to the music in his head. A few strains may have escaped as a low humming noise, and he was making stroking movements with his hands, as if to ease the girls into their dresses.

The room fell deathly silent.

He opened his eyes.

The teacher was glowering at him indignantly, and all the children were staring at him.

'Excuse me,' he said, 'I'm so sorry - I didn't mean to disturb you.'

Without taking her eyes off him, the teacher searched in her bag and brought out a mobile phone.

'Don't worry, I'm leaving,' said Michael.

He hurried outside and down the stairs then walked swiftly towards the gatehouse, where a small queue was waiting to buy tickets. Stumbling past a woman in a wheelchair, he ran across the moat and out towards the east gate, imagining himself pursued by hordes of schoolchildren and their harpy of a teacher. He heard a cry at his back but didn't stop to investigate.

Once through the gate, he ran past the church and on through a small housing estate, which led him round to the main road. To his intense relief, he spied Nancy and Stas leaning against a car parked in the roadway. Both looked startled as he bounded up to them, glancing every few seconds over his shoulder, and asked if the car was theirs. If so, could they possibly drive him somewhere, anywhere, home would be perfect but absolutely anywhere would do.

'Jump in,' said Nancy, looking amused. 'It's Derek's car. He doesn't know we've got it but he's off in London again, so that's his problem.'

'Are you sure?' asked Michael, bundling himself into the back before she could change her mind.

With Stas at her side, Nancy took off like a rally driver, shooting through the traffic lights several seconds after they had turned red and heading straight for the main coast road. Michael shut his eyes. He felt the car careering once round the roundabout, and quite possibly a second time as Nancy calculated which exit to take. Other drivers hooted their annoyance.

Fuck you, said Nancy, winding down her window.

They were travelling at speed on the back road to Normans Bay. Michael thought he spied a field full of concrete blocks (they were actually hayricks) and asked Stas if this was the place where Nancy had first found him. Nancy said no, that was over on the other side, where the old RAF stations used to be. Edie had talked about them on their last visit. Uncle Arthur had worked there during the war, and stayed on afterwards.

'Good heavens,' said Michael. 'Weren't they linked up to RAF Bawdsey on the Suffolk coast? I stayed there as a boy. My grandfather had a place there – it's what I'm writing about in my music. Could we go there please, if you've got time?'

'What, now?'

'Now would be great but any time would do. If you don't mind.'

Nancy braked sharply and swung the car into a three-point turn executed – or so it felt to Michael – on two wheels. Riding with Nancy was as exhilarating as sex. They were now heading back towards the roundabout, which Nancy negotiated with the same verve as before. A police car crossed smartly in front of them and Michael ducked his head instinctively, re-emerging only when they had reached the other side and were driving north towards the Observatory dome. Nancy was watching his every move in the mirror. Their eyes met and he felt a stab of complicity, grateful that she showed no interest in what had happened at the castle. That was history. This was now.

They left Derek's car by a bank of red earth, climbed over a stile and took a wide track that skirted a drainage channel he could hear rather than see in the splashing of waterfowl beyond the reeds. Nancy went first, then Stas, then Michael, who felt peculiarly attuned to the landscape, as if he had been here before. Walking away from a line of blue hills they soon reached another gate and a clearing littered with junk: car seats, a smashed microwave, the frame to a burnt-out sofa. After this the track narrowed to a virtual tunnel just as Stas had described, blackthorn encrusted with a thick fuzz of lichen, dog roses, elder, hawthorn and bramble. Away from the main road, the traffic noise had reduced to a distant drone, several notes below the swishing of wind through the reeds.

The tunnel disgorged them at the back of a farmhouse, Pylons Farm, Nancy said. More junk but this time agricultural machinery, threshers, drills, rotavators, an antiquated reaper baring its massive jaws. And there they were, anchored to a field: huge concrete feet arranged in groups of four, all that remained of the giant structures that had once listened in on the Germans, then the Russians.

He could have been a boy again, cycling with Dickie along the Bawdsey road, cowed by the metal masts that soared into the wide East Anglian skies. You could hear them humming their secrets, everyone said that, and the few cars that drove this way often stalled and sometimes broke down. Dickie said that all the calves born for a mile in every direction had something wrong with them, two heads, no head, heads coming out of their bottoms. You wouldn't want to get too near, that's for sure.

Stas had taken him by the arm and was leading him into the field, to the place where he had recovered consciousness. They were acting like boys, fearful and brave in the same breath. In the next field he spied more concrete structures, pillboxes and gun emplacements like the ones he remembered at the bottom of East Farm lane, nasty places that stank of piss and slime, absolutely out of bounds on pain of a bollocking from his grandfather.

Still Stas wanted to show him more.

Black and white images flicker subliminally into view: a trio of giant 350-foot transmitter masts and a further block of four receiver masts at RAF Pevensey, built in 1939 as one of the twenty original Air Ministry Experimental Stations to provide early warning of attacks from enemy aircraft. Near identical transmitter towers (four in number) at RAF Bawdsey, which opened in 1937 as the world's first fully operational radar station. An interior shot *c*.1943 of RAF Wartling's Happidrome, as its brick-and-concrete operations building is known. Somewhere between the three sites, two hyped-up figures in a smelly underground shelter are poking their sticks into the slime of a shared memory in which each listens to the other, without ever grasping what he has to say. A girl hangs back, Nancy Flight of the tartan knickers and fuck-you attitude to authority.

Raking radar sounds pick up intermittent chatter, the number codes he has already written in to his music in the clipped tones of his childhood. *Three – zero – nine – three - one – three – zero – nine – three – one – three – zero – nine – three - one,* radar crackle raking the skies in a circular sweep, breaking like waves upon the shore. *Three – zero – nine – three - one – three – zero – nine – three – one – three* ... It sends shivers down his spine, to hear these sounds out in the marshes, no longer simply in his head.

In that moment he held the two landscapes together, the one superimposed on the other in space and time. Suffolk was come to the Pevensey marshes and not through any Shakespearean trickery. This was real. This was now. He grasped Stas in a bear hug, then Nancy, who smelt sweet as honey. Stas did too, Russian bear, Russian honey. Without the pair of them his piece would never have got this far.

The telephone was ringing as he climbed the steps to the beach house. Fumbling for his keys, he heard the answerphone click in as he tried first one key then the next. When he had finally opened the door he went straight to the bookshelves where he had left the phone but the caller rang off a second or two after he had picked up the receiver. It was Maddy, as he suspected, who had called to tell him that she had changed her cell phone number, so he couldn't call her even if he wanted to. She hoped this wouldn't inconvenience him but she really needed to spend time in a place where she was quite alone. Knowing that he could theoretically reach her on the old number had forced her to jettison it for this new one, which of course she couldn't reveal. Had he spoken to her he would have pointed out that if she didn't

want to speak to him, she didn't have to answer his calls, but then he realised that she didn't even want to know that he *might have called*.

'Have patience,' she said, 'I hope your days are good ones, and I'll call again one day soon.'

Maddy's voice sounded more American than ever. He replaced the receiver after first erasing the message. If he couldn't call her, there was nothing he could do to reach her, and he wondered why he didn't feel more aggrieved.

12

'You're looking well,' said Geraldine, unusually the first to arrive. 'If I didn't know you better I'd think you had a new lover.'

'And why do you think I haven't?'

'Come on, Alice, when did you ever stay silent about a love affair? And in case you're wondering, Bill's just stopped off at the off-licence. He'll be along in a minute.'

Panting after the sharp climb up Alice's front steps, Geraldine flopped into the hall. Alice smiled to herself. If Geraldine assumed she was manless right now, she was in for a shock. 'Things going okay?' she asked in what she hoped was a neutral voice.

Geraldine shrugged. 'Bill's an absolute sweetie but he's not exactly God's gift, you know.'

'I thought you and he were an item. You seemed to be getting along fine in New York.'

'That's New York for you. But listen honey, don't mind me, I'm having a filthy day.'

'Sounds interesting.'

'Filthy as in total crap. My Edinburgh gallery has cancelled my autumn show. We've just heard the studios are to be sold off some time next year to make way for fancy apartments. And despite working my socks off, I haven't produced a decent picture in weeks.'

'I don't expect you took many socks to New York.'

'That was business, too. Bill had some SoHo artworld friends he thought I should meet and anyway, you've got to allow yourself a little R&R from time to time.'

'You should know,' said Alice carelessly. 'I'm never happier than when I'm working.'

'In my line of business,' said Geraldine, 'it's important to draw the line between life and art. Otherwise you end up in the stew.'

'Is that so?'

Geraldine produced one of her hooded looks, as if she couldn't quite gauge Alice's mood. 'I don't want to argue with you,' she said, 'so let's just say that I know what I'm talking about.'

Alice took her friend's arm and ushered her into the sitting room where she had laid out drinks on a small table next to the window looking down to her back garden. Chez Alice you were always changing levels: up the steep stone steps to the front door, up again to her bedroom and – if you were very honoured – one more flight into the attic where she kept her treasured first editions, or down into the basement kitchen and the sweetest of London gardens, despite its cramped proportions and easterly aspect. Geraldine looked ragged and she had only just arrived.

'What'll you have?' asked Alice, pointing at the row of glass jugs containing pastel-coloured liquids, some frothy, some still, most with scummy bits floating on the top.

'What's all that muck?' asked Geraldine, pulling a face.

'Oh, just some cocktails I rustled up, to keep us amused.'

Her friend took a closer look. 'I'll have that one,' she said doubtfully, 'what's in it?'

'You tell me.'

'Never touch anything unknown. Rule of life, honey.'

'Gosh, you really are having a bad day, aren't you? I've planned a little Futurist evening, you know, Filippo Marinetti, there's a whole menu -'

'The *Futurist Cookbook*? But honey, you're not supposed to *eat* any of that shit.'

Alice felt her face flush. Geraldine could be such a put-down;

she wondered why she bothered sometimes. But some of the cocktails she had tried before making her final choice had been, well, mildly disgusting. One in particular lingered still on the tongue: two egg yolks, half a glass of sparkling white wine, three toasted nuts and three teaspoons of sugar, all whisked together in her ancient Moulinex for ten whole minutes then served in a glass with a garnish of peeled banana. Even diluted, the raw egg tasted slimy and the pulverised nuts left a gritty residue. She had manfully swallowed a couple of mouthfuls before sloshing the rest down the sink.

'Try this one,' she said, steering her friend towards the least offensive jug. 'It's got equal parts Asti Spumante, pineapple liqueur and chilled orange juice.'

'What's wrong with plain old Buck's Fizz?'

'This one has hidden depths,' said Alice.

The doorbell saved her from further explanations. Bill had arrived at the same time as her friend Paul and his partner Heather, a slim little thing hiding under a great bush of Pre-Raphaelite red hair. After they had kissed and presented their bottles, she took them into the sitting room to join Geraldine who was talking to the cat. Well, Lark was growling and Geraldine was mouthing a reply. Thank goodness the cat had never learnt to lip-read.

Leaving Bill to play surrogate host, she disappeared downstairs to finalise the antipasto, a word she infinitely preferred to the more common *hors-d'oeuvre*, although Marinetti would doubtless have banished it from the menu along with pasta itself, which made men heavy, brutish, deluded, sceptical, slow and tiresomely flaccid. Give us patriotic rice and absolute originality, she thought approvingly.

Her guests appeared to be amusing themselves famously without her. Through the floorboards came the sounds of Geraldine in party mode, evincing much mannish laughter and the odd squeak from that Heather woman. Bill's laugh was generous and warm. It was one of his best features second only to his build, which was just how she liked a man: tall, heavy-chested, good strong thighs that were destined to remain no more than a fleeting memory. At least she had learnt her lesson that night and a very good lesson it was too. Never give in to a man on your first encounter or he'll think you cheap ever after.

The food was just about ready but where was Jeremy? His status as a defrocked priest appeared to excuse him from ordinary civilities, like the time he arrived for supper nearly two hours late and brought another woman with him. The faux pas went beyond embarrassment. It humiliated her utterly – all that rushing around re-arranging the small table prettily laid for two. None of the chairs would fit and she had already downed a pint of white Beaujolais, convinced that her new friend had muddled his dates. Trying to make two charred chicken breasts stretch to a third would have been equally problematic if the other woman had displayed an appetite larger than a quail's but only Jerry ate with any gusto, pronouncing her cooking quite as good as he had hoped. Trust dear Jerry to open his mouth to express a compliment and put his foot right in it.

But she wasn't a hard woman. He said later he thought she'd said a party, not a dinner party, and after a suitable time in the wilderness she had welcomed him back into her circle of friends because – let's face it – he was witty and presentable and frequently available at short notice. He was a spare man, dammit, and you didn't get many of those floating around north London where the women took to hunting in shoals and any half-way presentable bachelor got himself instantly ripped to shreds. Talk about piranha teeth. Alice thought: what you have to remember with Jerry is to make the terms of his invitation absolutely plain as she had done this time: I'm entertaining friends on such-and-such a night at such-and-such a time, nothing fancy or formal, please come to supper *on your own.*

She opened the fridge and poured herself a large slug of cold white wine. Pineapple juice was all very well but it left a corrosive aftertaste, like fish from a tin.

Just as she was unloading the chilled starters she heard the roar of Jerry's motorbike in the street, footsteps running up the steps and an urgent pounding on her front door. Why couldn't he ring the bell like mere mortals? She waited several seconds, hoping that one of the other guests might think to let him in but Geraldine was launched into one of her interminable performances and it was obvious that none of the others could tear themselves away.

'I'm coming, I'm coming,' she called, removing her apron as she puffed up the stairs. The man on the other side of the glass-panelled door was swaying rather dramatically. Alice took a deep breath then opened the door. There he was, arms outstretched, smelling a bit rank and winey. No wonder he had quit the church. Who could imagine a priest with a dirty dog collar?

'Come down into the kitchen,' she said, 'I need a hand.'

'Snap,' he said with a damn-fool grin.

'Behave yourself Jeremy.'

'I'm not drunk, if that's what you think.'

'Then what are you?'

He thought carefully. 'How about happy?'

'Do you mean "happy" as in "merry" or "happy" as in …'

'Christmas?'

'"Happy" as in "joyful"?'

He held out his arms and gave her an enormous bear hug. 'Happy as in joyful, my little chickadee.' Then he thrust his tongue deep into her throat.

With Jeremy's help, she got the food off to a flying start. He went in first to activate the sounds and smells. Her original idea of substituting the Futurists' preferred Wagnerian opera for one of Michael's compositions ('Just something by a very dear friend') had fallen by the wayside as she couldn't find anything that struck the right note. His *Composition for String Theorists* came closest but even that wouldn't quite do – stridently original, perhaps, but Wagnerian it certainly wasn't, at least not in the sense of an all-consuming emotional force that enveloped you like Leda's swan, lifting you clean off your feet so that you wanted nothing less than to fuck with a goose. No, Wagner's *Tristan und Isolde* was a safer bet.

For smells, she had stuffed incense cones into a pair of Russian Orthodox censers picked up for a song in the Paris flea market and intended eventually for garden lights. (Oh, she would get around to it one of these days.) Although the Futurists were rabidly anticlerical, she hoped they might accept her gesture as ironically post-modern and of course having the censers swung by a defrocked priest was quite a coup, not least because his High-Anglican training had given him a certain panache. Even Geraldine looked impressed.

Once she had sat everyone down at the large dinner table

(she and Jerry at either end, which eased her nicely between Bill and Paul and meant she could keep an eye on Jerry's drinking at the far end) she handed out brown paper bags.

Geraldine took one look at hers and exclaimed, 'What, doggy bags already?'

'No,' said Alice. 'These are tactile devices. Put your hand in and guess what they contain.'

Heather, the red-headed mouse, was holding her bag by the throat and prodding it cautiously in case it might bite.

'Go on,' said Alice to Bill, 'show her what to do.'

'Why me?'

'When did you ever hesitate to poke your fingers into something new?'

'*Touché mon vieux.*'

'*Ma vieille* I think you mean.'

'What's a little grammar between friends?'

Wagner was just getting into his stride when she left the room, so she signalled to Jerry to turn the volume down a mite. She thought: a belting of Germanic emotion certainly gets the juices flowing but what was wrong with home-grown Verdi? Too popular with the shop girls, even then? Or were the Futurists as fascist as everybody supposed? Must make a note to check it out before they get a whole chapter to themselves. Maybe a passing reference would be safer?

Still trying to puzzle out their politics, she got the antipasto plates out of the fridge and carefully removed the cling film. On each plate she had arranged a quarter of a fennel bulb, an olive, a candied fruit, and a kumquat. Of course it looked odd but that was the point, wasn't it?

There's plenty of bread, she thought, and if it gets too awful

I can call in a takeaway.

Lark was scratching at the door. 'No sweetheart,' she said firmly. 'You know the rules. No cats while we're eating, not even you.'

Several deep breaths later, Alice sailed upstairs towards the sounds of laughter and Wagner, bearing her plates aloft. Jeremy and Geraldine had their heads locked together in conversation, Bill had his hand in Heather's paper bag, and Paul was on his feet inspecting her bookshelves.

There was an awkward silence as she put the plates down on the table.

Geraldine was the first to speak, sounding unusually kind. 'You okay, honey?' Heather gave an embarrassed titter and Paul said, 'What's that orangey thing?'

'That's a kumquat.'

'Now I see why you gave us the paper bags,' said Bill.

'Excuse me?' said Alice icily. 'This is not an airline.'

'No, I mean what you put in them. That velvety stuff and the sandpaper. Kumquat ... come twat ... oh forget it.'

'I think you'd better.'

'Honey,' said Geraldine from the other end of the table. 'The joke's gone far enough. What's for afters? More of the same, or is it something we can actually eat, you know, something good and wholesome like spag bol?'

'There's loads of stuff,' said Alice defiantly. 'Risotto and calf's tongue and prawns and vegetables. There's even a bit of chicken.'

'Sounds good to me,' said Paul. 'I like risotto.'

'Uh uh,' said Geraldine shaking her head. 'What've you put in the risotto?'

'Cape gooseberries,' said Alice. 'I got them at Sainsbury's.'

140

'Is that all?'

Alice nodded. 'A bit of parsley and onions and a smidgeon of garlic. And there was stuff I was going to read, about the Cape gooseberry being winged like an aeroplane.'

'Save the poetry for later,' said Geraldine. 'Come on Bill, you and I are going downstairs to rustle up something quick. I reckon everybody's tongue is pretty damn hanging out.'

Alice sat down in a cold fury. What were friends for if they couldn't enter into the festive spirit? No wonder Geraldine's work wasn't flowing. All that posturing when really, she couldn't paint her way out of a paper bag. I might be the hostess, she thought, but oh, don't mind me. Come round and cook your own dinners, why not, that's what the smart people are doing these days. If you don't like the fare that's put before you, hey ho, raid your hostess's fridge and start again. Much more fun. And don't worry if your hostess feels a little *put out* because you've turned your nose up at something she's slaved over for hours. No, make that days when you add in all the planning and the shopping and the trying-things-out because some of these recipes would really make your stomach churn, like candied citrons stuffed with chopped cuttlefish. I think Geraldine and cuttlefish are pretty much the same rubbery consistency so yes, I might well cook that one for myself later, when Miss Flouncy Pants has rustled up some dinner for *my* guests, in *my* kitchen, using *my* ingredients and *my* bloody Aga.

Paul said, 'You're looking well these days. Alice. How are things?'

'Oh just dandy,' she said. 'But listen, I'm so glad to be able to catch up with you. You never normally get the chance when you're the host but now that *Geraldine* has taken charge I can sit back and relax. I hear that book of yours is doing very well. Weren't you on Radio 4 the other week? *Start the Week* or maybe *Analysis*, I only caught the end, I'm afraid, which is me all over. Always rushing from one thing to the next. One of these days I'm going to sit down with *Time Out* and really plan my listening. The way I listen, I'm sure I miss all the best things.'

She smiled warmly if a little guiltily. She had actually listened to the entire programme while she did the ironing, so it must have been *Analysis* as she never ironed in the morning and, as far as she knew, never caught the repeats. While she could distinctly remember how impressed she had been by Paul's radio voice – mellifluous and gravelly, he spoke in undulating sentences that wound themselves around her head and landed her somewhere quite unexpected, with all the verbs and participles still miraculously in place – she couldn't recall a single thing he had actually said. What was his book all about? Drugs, that's it. Pharmaceuticals. Not the hippy stuff or crack cocaine. Something frightfully well-argued involving the poor in Africa (or was it India? Same grinding poverty, much the same diseases, undoubtedly a stitch-up somewhere.)

'So is the book … doing well?' she ventured.

'It depends what you mean by "well".'

'Is it selling?'

'Oh, it's selling all right. It's into its third reprint already and it's only been out a couple of months.'

'That's terrific. I'm not sure I've ever been reprinted. You must be pleased.'

'But is it making a difference, that's the real point, surely? We write these books. For a time they stir the pot, attract banner headlines and all sorts of media attention. You do a few talk shows, give some interviews, pontificate all over the Sundays, and for what? The villains pass a few uncomfortable weeks but they know and you know that if they sweat it out for however long it takes they can go back to buttering their bread in the same old way.'

'That's being cynical, surely. You must believe you can make a difference or you couldn't go through all that effort. I mean, writing a book's so jolly hard.'

'Lots of other things are a damn sight harder. Like being a coal miner, or living on the dole. Trying doing that day after day and see what happens to your soul.'

She glanced up the table at Jerry who looked as if he was half listening to their conversation while trying to get his teeth into Heather. Jerry winked. She hoped he hadn't heard the bit about souls - in her experience Jeremy was forever trying to rub your nose in some moral issue as if you were as biddable as a puppy.

'Anyway, enough of that,' said Paul, pouring himself some wine and passing the bottle down the table. 'Are you writing anything yourself at the moment?'

'Yes I am. Or I would be if Geraldine would let me. It's about food, you see, *The Joy of Food,* buying, cooking, eating ...'

'Excreting.'

'Thank you Jeremy. Trust a priest to bring us down to earth.'

'Is that what you are?' asked Heather in surprise.

'*Ex*-priest,' snapped Alice. 'He actually re-trained in computers.'

'Same thing,' said Jerry. 'They both move in mysterious ways and have a habit of crashing on you when you have the world on your shoulders and a deadline to meet.'

Paul and Heather laughed. Alice didn't. That's how she had met Jeremy, of course. She had phoned him late one night on the recommendation of a friend who swore he was the only computer man who wasn't a geek. Alice's computer had gone down hours before she was due to hand in a book she was copy-editing and for once she had been less than diligent in making a back-up copy. Maybe God would have sorted her out just as well. At least he wouldn't roar up to her door in the middle of the night, antagonising the shit out of the neighbours.

The food rustled up by Bill and Geraldine wasn't bad (curried eggs and basmati rice, not the dreaded pasta at least). Even Alice pronounced herself happy with their efforts and the others had drunk enough by now to eat whatever was put before them.

'What a gas,' said Geraldine to Alice. 'I saw the cookbook down in the kitchen. I wish you'd given us Carrot Plus Trousers Equals Professor.'

'Tell me more,' said Jerry, raising his glass.

Geraldine hooted with laughter. 'You take a raw carrot, still with the sprouting end on top, and attach it to two boiled aubergines.'

'So where does the professor come in?'

'Oh Alice, you explain if he can't get it.'

'You mean you can't remember. The effect is supposed to remind you of professorial testicles marching in pursuit of a pension. That's what the book says, anyway. I think Carrot Plus Trousers could just as easily equal computer salesman.'

'Now don't get mad at me.'

'Why on earth should I bother? I'd like a pension too.'

'Except you don't have balls,' said Geraldine, 'not the aubergine sort, anyway.'

Alice smiled across the table at her friend. She was beginning to enjoy herself, in spite of everything. Bill was drinking far too much and had turned as silent as a goose.

When they had finished eating and talked themselves into a lull, Alice went down into the kitchen to make coffee. Someone else could clear the plates, if anyone could be bothered. Melting in the pantry sink she found the remnants of her desert: two mounds of ricotta cheese dyed pink with Campari and chilled for a time in the freezer. Strawberry breasts, it was called. She wondered whether Bill or Geraldine had sucked off the candied strawberry nipples. Whichever the culprit, she tossed the dish (plate and all) into the bin.

As she came back upstairs, she caught the tail end of a joke related by Heather, which stopped her dead in her tracks. Heather had struck her as meekly colourless, apart from her flaming Janey Morris fuzz. Of course she hadn't heard the beginning but the joke seemed to involve some nasty pervert in a car with a little boy dressed in a welder's helmet. The man appeared to be probing the little boy's knowledge of sexual practices, the sort you didn't talk about in public. Each time he posed one of his horrid questions, Heather lowered her voice to a deep-throated growl. It made your skin creep. The story came to an end just as Alice reached the top step.

'*'Ere little boy,*' said Heather in her bad-man's growl, '*d'you know anyfink about fellatio?*'

The little fellow lifted his visor. 'I think I ought to tell you,' warbled Heather in her little-boy's voice, 'I'm not really a welder.'

Jerry was the first to laugh but the others weren't long in coming.

Well really, thought Alice, pushing open the door with her foot and hoping it wouldn't crash back into her tray. Now that even the dormice among us have sunk to this level, what hope is there for the rest of us?

Paul and Heather left soon after, trailing Jerry, who remembered suddenly he had double-booked himself. 'Sorry old girl. Got to dash. Can't keep a good woman waiting now, can I?'

'What woman?'

'No one you know. Probably no one you'd care to know, either.'

'Not one of your hostesses again?'

He grinned. 'Just one of those cat-and-mouse affairs, you know.'

'Well actually, I don't know.'

'Best keep it that way,' he said, squeezing her waist and depositing a dollop of spittle on her cheek.

'You must come to us some time soon,' said Heather to Alice, without looking particularly sincere.

'Thanks for a terrific meal,' added Paul.

'You should really thank Geraldine.'

'No honestly,' said Paul. 'We've all had a great time. Who gives a shit about food?'

Well I do, actually, thought Alice, w*hy else would I write a bloody book about it?* She smiled nicely and proffered the other cheek.

When Alice went back into the room, Geraldine was sat in her chair over by the tall windows, a dreamy smile on her face. Bill stood right behind her massaging her neck and shoulders, his strong hands pressing hard into the fleshy parts above the shoulder blades. Alice couldn't help feeling *de trop* in her own home.

I would like a man who'd do that to me, thought Alice with a pang, a man who can tell when I need solace. Sex is all very well but it can get a bit, oh I don't know, *confrontational* at times.

Feeling dizzy, she sat down. Too much alcohol? Something she had eaten? Or was it what Bill was doing to Geraldine, right before her eyes? Seasick, that's how she felt, like a cork bobbing up and down in the ocean. Fanning the nausea was a great waft of maleness, tobacco breath, sweat, the unmistakeable pheromones of male skin. I could weep for the longing of it, she thought, that great enveloping warmth of a man's arms folding me into the crook of his heart.

Bill caught her eye. For a moment they connected above the slumped body of her friend. He raised one eyebrow. She tried to smile. Geraldine stirred and the moment passed, she couldn't read his mind. Now they were bustling into a leave-taking of sorts, Geraldine trying to remember where she had left her bag and Bill saying he couldn't possibly drive, they should maybe call a cab.

'They'll make us wait for hours,' said Geraldine briskly, 'come on, we can't hang around forever. I'll drive. I'm okay. I drive better when I'm pissed, anyway.'

They said goodnight on the steps. The night air felt strangely cold. Lark was growling at Alice's feet. That's funny, she thought. I don't remember letting you out. Maybe Geraldine did when I was down in the kitchen. She doesn't like cats much.

The cat rubbed against her legs.

Bill was reaching down to kiss her goodnight. Did she move

at the last minute or had he meant to kiss her on the lips? His eyes were half shut. Sod it, the man was drunk, that's all.

Now it was Geraldine's turn. A kiss on either cheek, and not so much as a thank you.

'I'll call you in the week,' said Geraldine, holding Bill by the elbow and steering him expertly down the steps.

'Careful,' said Alice, 'they're very steep.'

'Nothing that I can't handle.'

Alice shut the front door and turned off all the lights. Instead of going up to bed she went back into the living room and stood by the window looking down at Bill and Geraldine haloed under a street lamp, locked together so tightly you would think their two heads came from one sinuous body. He was practically fucking her in the street, which was probably just as well for Geraldine since he would have passed out on her by the time she had driven him home and manhandled him into the six-foot bed she had had made to order for men like him because that's how Geraldine liked them too, big and brawny, and who cares a bugger about brains?

Slowly Alice mounted the stairs, washed her face in the bathroom, cleaned her teeth, had a last quick pee then went into the bedroom where she stripped and folded her clothes neatly on the Lloyd Loom wicker chair that Lark was always using to sharpen his claws.

The evening's one achievement that really pleased her was the way she had stuck to her resolve to keep Michael out of the conversation. Now she could will him to appear unsullied in her dreams.

13

Locked in his own thoughts most of the time, Michael was at last making progress. That sorry episode at the castle put behind him, his days had settled into a rhythm of work, sleep, walk, more work and more sleep, interrupted only occasionally by the telephone (mercifully short calls from Alice and none from Maddy) and breaks for food, which he took when he remembered. When work was going well, he invariably lost weight, especially if he extended his walking time and cut down on his sleep. On his walks he rarely took note of his surroundings and if he were questioned about where he had gone he could tell you only that his feet had walked over pebbles, or grass, or a boggy track, or sometimes the edge of a tarmacked road. Once he had found himself walking into a willow grove as if into a cathedral, still and darkly green; he raised his head but couldn't for the life of him recall how he had got there.

Now that he had mapped out the opening to his piece with its snatches of radar chatter and the footfalls of invading armies he could concentrate on establishing the soundscape of a land that was gradually emerging from the brine. He had no wish to translate the individual elements in any obvious sense but rather to mould his piece according to the lie of the land. This was a working landscape, used first for its salt pans, then for summer grazing, then for more permanent agriculture as man became progressively more confident and more skilled at holding back the waters. The music he envisaged was necessarily in the lower registers with plenty of double bass to signify the sunken nature of the flat marshlands; and for the lowering skies and magical cloudscapes he turned to the violins' bright overtones with a dulling of flutes to bring the tones down to a very English earth. As for the watery light, he experimented with Apollonian A naturals on pizzicato strings piercing the gloom like rays of light on water. If you listened carefully, you could catch a glimmering of straight drainage ditches that disconcerted expectations with sudden right-angled bends as the tuba took over mid-phrase from the bass clarinets, and the cry of the birds that Nancy had enumerated for him, the seagulls, lapwings, snipe, redshank, golden plover and yellow wagtails, which in his music coalesced into flourishes for clarinets and violas that you could equally read as the breaking of waves against the shore. When he realised where his music was taking him, he added a deliberate homage to Elgar's quintessential bombast and to the Englishness of Vaughan Williams' Fifth Symphony, its major scale with flattened seventh echoing the pitch of English folk music.

The shingle dyke holding back the sea gave him more of a headache. He wanted to convey a sensation that was at once solid and impermanent, of feet scrunching through a sliding mass of stones, made smooth by the pounding of the sea, and of the sea's relentless probing for the dyke's weakest point. His eventual solution was to combine the gentle heaving of low strings and woodwinds with a cascade of unstable horns and brass sliding across a treacherous scree of chords in C♯ major.

The further into his music he worked his way imaginatively, the more signals of unease he detected, as if the land was using him as its mouthpiece and he was merely the medium that transmitted its anxieties. In musical terms, this unease revealed itself in a loss of balance, a slight and unexpected dragging of the tempo and a more invidious muddying of its original clarity of tone, just as the native flora was at risk from foreign invaders such as floating pennywort from North America and the choking red algae that Nancy had pointed out as they walked the Manxey Levels close to Pylons Farm.

There were ugly intrusions, too, from the tuba and timpani as the land sank beneath a detritus of obsolete equipment and discarded consumer durables: rusting farm machinery, joy-ridden cars, old sofas and refrigerators, the scrap metals once picked clean by the rag and bone trade but for which the market – and the energy required to reprocess them – had disappeared. As well as the lumps of discordant sounds, he added a rustling of reeds along the drainage ditches, which came to him in the form of a Biblical chorus presaging some distant retribution for the sins of the fathers, and of the fathers' fathers, even unto the seventh generation. And through the re-emergence of the opening sequence's radar chatter, amplified by the hum of electricity carried by brutish pylons marching across the landscape and caught on sound and camera by proliferating surveillance equipment, he succeeded in welding a unified structure that contained within itself its own vulnerabilities, the first pinpricks of metal fatigue indicating that all was not well in Eden - a very English Eden admittedly, but he hoped Per Woudstra and his fellow New Yorkers had the musical nous to read their own geography into his score.

A fundamental problem remained, however: how to work the angel into his music in a way that made it central to his creative intentions rather than simply an add-on designed to attract attention. While he remained convinced that it *was* central, he couldn't fathom why, beyond his conviction that each landscape has its own iconography and the angel belonged here, in the Pevensey marshes, even if he had glimpsed it a hundred miles around the coast; same terrain, different latitude, but what did it *mean*?

So far, the disparate elements did not cohere into a persuasive argument. He had Nancy Flight singing a pop re-working of Walter Benjamin, and he had his Blakean memory of the angel at Shingle Street, which had appeared the day he had stumbled across Fairground Jim and his girl doing God-knows what in the Suffolk marshes.

It was the girl who put the angel notion in his head, the way she had crouched over the body of the man, flapping her great white wings like the angel of the Apocalypse and shouting her triumph at having so unmanned him.

He remembered the day with unnatural clarity, as if he were experiencing it for the first time. After the girl with the short pants and slinky voice had interrupted their roller-skating, he and Dickie had cycled down to the end of the lane, intending to push their bikes along the coast path to Mad Uncle Jack's at Shingle Street. Dickie had dared him to climb up the abandoned watchtower and they had played their usual warfare games in the forbidden gun turrets sunk behind the sea wall, so it was already late when they set off for Jack's shack.

Gun metal skies and a fudge-coloured sea lapping sluggishly at the granite boulders piled in a thick band to keep the sea at bay. Sea to his right, ponds then marshland to his left, all held together by a line of Martello towers strung like washing across the landscape.

Dickie had gone on ahead by the shortest route, but something made Michael turn inland, taking the raised path by the stream. That's how he had seen them, lying down below in the reeds; Fairground Jim flat on his back, the girl riding him like an angel might, her sinuous motions lighting a fire in his belly and a thundering excitement in his head.

Leaving his bike on the path he had slithered down the bank intent on creeping closer but Fairground Jim had suddenly reared up from the ground, hollering at him to keep his filthy eyes to himself.

Instead of heading back the way he had come, he had taken fright and pedalled on to Shingle Street and then – because he daren't risk another encounter with Fairground Jim, who would flay him alive – up by Hollesley and Alderton and the long way round to Bawdsey, pedalling like crazy but still arriving very late indeed.

Shocked and enflamed, Michael had invented a whole posse of avenging angels for his grandfather to excuse his lateness and the mud slathering his plimsolls. *Feet like pillars of fire they had, Grandad, and flaming trumpets. Choirs of them. You should've heard the racket they made – scared us both to bits.*

Grandfather, who didn't know whether to exorcise the devil out of his raving grandson or to wallop him as an arrant liar, forced him to his knees on the kitchen floor to ask God's forgiveness and then beat him till he bled. Even his normally supportive grandmother failed to intervene.

The episode represented a breach with his past. Before the angel he had been like any young boy, albeit one marked by his mother's illness and absence. After the angel he felt different. He saw things that other people didn't see. Even Dickie, his companion in crime, never saw the angel on the marshes and pestered him continually about why Fairground Jim had turned so nasty. 'Waddya see, waddya see?' he had asked again and again, but Michael never told him because he frankly didn't know, or know what it might mean; only that he was marked out as someone with the gift of seeing into the heart of things.

But the angel business taught him another lesson that became a guiding principle to his creative life. Keep quiet about your visions until you know what to do with them. Grandfather beat him not because he was late but because he had spoken of the angel. Had he kept silent, the worst that might have happened to him was to be sent supperless to bed. Yet because he talked, the angel had flown away. Even now, he felt its message was eluding him. Without it, his music might work as a melodic exploration of Englishness, but as a work of art it would fail.

Experienced enough to know that problems can sometimes solve themselves if you put them to one side, he concentrated on his other dilemma: how to resolve the conflict of the two voices, Maddy's and Nancy's. At the centre of his piece, he had decided to orchestrate Benjamin's text as a way of prefiguring the storm blowing in from Paradise, and to have it spoken by two overlapping voices. But the voices continued to rebel against his intentions: Maddy's soprano, which he imagined as the voice of the future, ushering in the promised new dawn, and Nancy's more problematic alto, which continued to slide this way and that.

In the early part of the storm, a young woman leads a procession of all ages across the Levels as the waters rise and the seas swirl behind the just-holding dyke, the dangers of the thudding waves expressed in booming brass chords kept – only just – at bay by tripping strings. As he worked his way through the notation, Michael kept in his head Samuel Palmer's tiny jewel of a painting, *Coming from Evening Church* of 1830, in which a married couple (himself and Maddy, evidently) lead a procession of children, grandparents and other families away from the black-robed pastor in front of the Saxon church, their path illuminated by a giant moon that makes the whole painting glow in the dark. As well as divesting the image of its Christian content, Michael wanted to excise himself from the action and to give Maddy the leading role as the community's saviour. But Maddy's soprano voice refused point blank to have anything to do with it, leaving him with a choice he wasn't yet ready to make: either to drop the salvation theme from his score, or to find another voice to perform the role.

Several times Michael found himself staring at the portrait of Maddy he kept on his desk. Taken on their wedding day some eight years previously, it showed his bride-to-be wearing a simple shift in oyster silk, her auburn hair hanging in lustrous curls around her fine, intelligent face. She was smiling gaily towards someone to the right of the photographer, while he stood on the other side of her, half out of frame, dressed in his brother's grey morning suit. Maddy had insisted on the old custom of wearing something old, something new, something borrowed, something blue, which he had translated prosaically into a pair of new blue underpants, the borrowed suit, and an old dress shirt. Maddy trumped him creatively by telling him the day before their wedding that she brought the blue of her occasional melancholia, the old of her unreconstituted self, the new of their future together, and a borrowed belief that all would be for the best in the best of all possible worlds. Everyone said what a handsome couple they made, and naturally all eyes were drawn to the radiant bride.

But Maddy today was in more recalcitrant mood, and when one of his neighbours began hammering at some loose weatherboarding in the small passageway between the two beach houses Michael knew that his inspiration had flattened and he would write no more music without a change of scene. He needed air, and he needed help, if he could only drop his guard and ask for it.

It was inevitable that Michael should find himself walking towards Edie's house beyond Normans Bay, which Nancy was sharing with Derek and George and other sundry stragglers from their world. Nancy had described it for him as a gaunt, twin-gabled house with bow-fronted windows right at the end of a row of coastguards' cottages, close to the railway line. He found it without difficulty. Seagulls clustered on its gothic chimneys, and on the adjoining house he picked out the words 'Hovis', 'Teas' and 'Stores' faintly embossed in the grimy walls. These were the only two properties sinking into decline; several of the others showed signs of holiday occupation.

Even now he wasn't sure whether to knock. Twice he opened the gate and twice he turned away but each time a memory of Nancy's teasing, sliding voice dragged him back. The third time he spotted Derek staring down at him from a first-floor window. It would be rude, now, to hurry away.

Someone had recently hacked the thicket of a front garden into some kind of order. The door swung open before he had time to knock, and Derek stepped aside to let him enter. The dark hall smelt of Jeyes Fluid and a lemony essence of pine.

'I'm sorry,' said Michael. 'I would have come to hear the band last night but I lost track of the days.'

Derek shrugged. 'We cancelled. I was busy in London, should have stayed on, point of fact, but we'll be playing next Saturday for sure. How's the piece going? I expect you want to see Nancy.'

'That's right. Is she in?'

'Not sure. But listen, now that you're here – '

Michael had already turned towards the door, wishing he hadn't come.

'Nancy tells me you're having a spot of trouble with the piece.'

'I wouldn't say that.'

'I'm not thinking terminal, more a ... hiatus. No? Well anyway. I've had an idea. We've got plenty of space here – Nancy's always hoping her aunt will come back home but there's not a cat in hell's chance of that happening. Edie is on her way out, and not before time. She's been ailing for years. I could offer you her room as another space to work: you'll have Nancy on tap and I'm sure you'd like that. You could bother her at all times of the day and night, she wouldn't mind. Nancy is very *accommodating,* if you catch what I mean.'

Michael wasn't sure that he did. Aware that he should decline the offer without further consideration he felt himself nonetheless sucked over the threshold. Derek ahead of him was opening doors to either side of the hall. 'I store my gear in here,' he said, 'and we rehearse in here ... '

Heavy curtains blocked out the light. He saw drums, amplifiers, an enviously large keyboard, and other kit he couldn't distinguish.

'The house next door is empty,' said Derek, 'so there's no one to complain about the noise. Well, the Major from a few doors down has threatened to call the council on a couple of occasions, but nothing that a little reciprocated goodwill can't cure.'

'Why are you doing this?' asked Michael. 'I mean, why are you prepared to help me, when there's nothing I can offer in return? I'm renting a place already, as you know, and can't stretch to another.'

'Like I said, I admire your music – it can't hurt me to help you, just as it can't hurt you to accept my help. Agreed?'

In the half-light of the hall, Derek's expression was remarkable only for its blandness.

'Come on up,' said Derek. 'I'll give you a key. Whether you use it or not is up to you.'

The first-floor room ran across the whole of the front of the house. He liked the pot-bellied feel to it, and its wide sea view over the hump of shingle. Dust covered every surface. A kidney-shaped dressing table to one side bore a muddle of old woman's things, and the door to a heavy mahogany wardrobe hung open to reveal a thread-worn rack of clothes.

'Don't worry, we'll get rid of all that. I could lend you the keyboard, if that would help. Just tell me what you need and I've probably got it. There's a couple of harps in there somewhere, any use?'

Michael shuddered. 'And Nancy? What would she think about my coming here?'

'Nancy does what I ask her, I promise. Look, there's something I wanted to show you.'

He followed Derek down the landing into a pokey room at the back of the house, overlooking the railway line. Nancy's tartan pants crowned a pile of dirty washing.

'I'm not sure we should barge in here without being asked...'

Ignoring his objection, Derek pointed at some large, black and white photographs sellotaped to the wallpaper. Michael's heart stopped still.

Pevensey Castle scanned the marshes through a horizontal slit cut and concreted into its ancient walls. The barnacled throat of the outfall to Pevensey Haven. A maggoty swan, its outstretched wings attached to a skeletal body that looked too small to bear their weight.

'Nancy's own?'

Derek nodded.

Nancy could pick your bones clean, if she felt like it.

Snared by the strange beauty of Nancy's photographs, Michael didn't hear the front door opening, or the sound of two people climbing the carpeted stairs, or even the muffled noise of Derek retreating from the room and leaving him to face the full fury of Nancy, who wanted to know what the hell he thought he was doing, stealing into her house, her room dammit, and rummaging through her things when he had absolutely no business to show his face anywhere near the place. Michael's immediate instinct to blame his presence on Derek only made matters worse.

'I'll fucking murder him,' said Nancy. 'Nobody comes here without Edie's say-so. It's not a fucking doss house.'

'If it bothers you, I don't have to come.'

'Too fucking right.'

'But these are good, Nancy, really good.' He pointed at her photographs on the walls. 'I could use them, if you'd let me. I ask you to be my guide, my angel, if you like.'

Nancy's rolled her eyes. 'I'm not the angel kind,' she said, half turning towards him. The Chalkhill Blue looked set to fly away.

'I'm not explaining myself very well, I know. But here, between us, I think we hold the key to my piece.'

She looked first at Stas, then at him. 'What is it about you guys that puts _your_ ideas, _your_ concerns before everyone else's?'

Stas looked stung. A telephone rang deep within the house. He heard Derek's answering voice.

'Look at it from my perspective,' she said, her anger ready to spew in their faces. 'Derek asks me to keep an eye on you, make sure you have everything you need. Maybe he wants to pimp me too, God knows, he's devious enough, but the fat lady gets there first. I listen to you droning on about your music and your marital difficulties. I take you guys out into the country for a spot of memory bashing. I coax you through your creative black holes and what do I get in return? I get you, Mister Fucking Great Composer, coming in here uninvited and asking me to be an angel. Well let me enlighten you, Michael whatever your name is. I don't do angels. I might do virgins at a pinch, maybe even nuns, and ghosts, no problem – ask Derek. But I most emphatically do NOT do ANGELS. Angels suck, is that clear?'

He nodded as best he could. He really hadn't explained himself very well. If he gave her more time, perhaps she might grasp what he wanted from her.

'And there's another thing –' she started, then stopped. Stas had pulled her close and was saying something very quietly in her ear. It sounded Russian. Not English, certainly. She buried her head in his neck. The gentleness between them made him ache. He wanted to touch her hair, her face, her naked shoulders, to convince himself that she really was of this world. He wanted her to be his angel, and that was only the beginning.

He moved towards the pair of them with his arms outstretched in an unfortunately Christlike pose.

She looked up at him aghast.

'Please, I mean you no harm.'

She pushed him away without another word and ran out of the room.

He was left alone with Stas, who raised his hands in resignation, but which to Michael looked more like a blessing.

14

Nancy's rage took some time to calm. Hoping to confront Derek, she looked in the kitchen but found only George eating beans on toast, and Derek's car keys on the kitchen table. These she took, saying to George that she might be gone for some time. Her phone was switched off and if Derek wanted his car back in a hurry he could go fuck himself or call a cab. George nodded and went on reading the newspaper.

The late commuter traffic along the road into Eastbourne was swollen with holidaymakers, switching lanes at the roundabouts and generally dawdling. She turned on the CD player. An irritating whistle formed a perfect ellipse of sound in its repeated crescendos and decrescendos – the sort of music that would very quickly drive you nuts, she thought, so she switched it off and felt in the glove compartment for something with more guts. Among the CDs she pulled out were Michael Anders' *Lighthouse Blues* (empty) and a Howlin' Wolf compilation that included the gloriously bluesy *Smokestack Lightning*, wailing like a freight train in the night. Keeping one eye on the road she checked its place in the running order then played it again and again, hitting the back switch before it ended and closing her eyes from time to time when the traffic along the seafront advanced at the slowest of crawls. As she passed the Bandstand she broke into song, letting the Wolf's howl of anguish from the little bitty boy banish the remnants of her anger. Michael Anders, bless his soul, would have said that she sang with the voice of an angel.

Nancy's plan was disarmingly simple. She was going to

march into Mr Jones's office and tell him she was bringing Edie home. Edie wasn't a prisoner and from now on she, Nancy, was taking charge. She'd stop fooling around, get a job and hire some help if she had to, but Edie had taken her in as a child and she was now going to repay her in kind. It wasn't right to leave her aunt in the company of strangers. She'd talk to the council, see what help they could give her. Somebody was paying for the care home. If it was Edie's money, they'd spend it on themselves and if it was the council's, she'd find a way to wheedle it out of them. With Edie home, she would send Derek and George packing and life would return to ordinary, decent normal. That's what she wanted: to go back to the time when Edie and Arthur had kept her safe in a world where bad things happened to other people, until Arthur went and died in a freak accident, electrocuted by his work's mower and drowned in a ditch just a few months short of his retirement. Arthur was working for the Water Board at the time. The irony of it made her weep. She and Clive hadn't even made it to the funeral. She was sitting her GCSEs in London, and her mother wouldn't let her go.

Well, she'd make up for it now. Clive might too, if she could track him down. They'd make a family again, a proper one with meals on the table at the proper times, and each looking out for the other.

The traffic eased as the road climbed up towards Beachy Head, and soon she was turning off to the right, and right again, before pulling into the small car park at the side of the care home. Howlin' Wolf had colonised her head.

At the top of the steps she jumped over the fat dog's head and ran into the day room. No Edie. She knocked on the downstairs toilets, put her head round Mr Jones's door (he was talking on the telephone, as per fucking usual), searched the kitchens and the walk-in pantry, even trawled the garden, where the young lad was dead-heading the roses. No sign of Edie anywhere, and the only nurse she spotted was the one she couldn't stand.

In mounting alarm she ran up the stairs three at a time to the bedroom Edie shared with three other women, each with a bed, a small cabinet and a chair for visitors.

Edie's bed was empty, and the bedding stripped bare. At least her things were still on the bedside cabinet: a water jug of stale water, a bunch of wrinkled grapes, a hairbrush and two small photographs in silver frames: of Nancy and Clive in their teens, frowning at the sun, and of Edie and Arthur framed by roses.

Out on the landing she called for help. When none came, she ran down to Mr Jones's office and this time caught him between calls. He hastily put away his magazine.

'Where's Edie, Mr Jones? What have you done with her?'

He looked surprised. 'Didn't you get the message? I asked Jenny to call you an hour or more ago.'

'What message? I never spoke to anyone.'

'Well she told me she'd telephoned, and Jenny is very reliable. I would trust my own mother with her.' He looked at his watch. 'She'll still be on duty. Let's call her now and see what she says.'

He rang for Jenny, who appeared almost immediately. Faced with the manager's questions, she explained defensively that she had done exactly as she was asked: called Nancy at home and spoken to a man who sounded slightly foreign – American, or Australian, South African at a pinch. She hadn't asked his name as she hadn't expected to be grilled about his identity, but he had promised to pass on the message to Nancy: that Mrs Fisher had been taken in to Eastbourne General after a suspected stroke, a much bigger stroke than the last one, and that Nancy should contact the hospital straight away.

'And the … slightly foreign gentleman agreed to pass on the message?' 'Yes, Mr Jones. I got the impression that Nancy was in the house but not able to come to the phone. I mean, I could have insisted, I suppose, but the man sounded perfectly okay, a bit foreign, yes, but not a lunatic or anything.'

'Thank you Jenny, that's fine, very helpful in fact.' The manager turned towards Nancy, unctuously clasping his hands. 'So you see Nancy, we did all we could.'

'And Edie?' she asked, trying to keep the panic out of her voice.

'Dear me, yes. Poor Mrs Fisher. Do you want me to call the hospital now? We were rather waiting for you to call us, keep us informed about … you know, because we'll keep the bed open for as long as it's wanted but there's no point paying for … well, you know, an empty bed that somebody else might just as well be using.'

Nancy ran back to Derek's car in a state of suspended panic. The hospital had said that Edith Fisher was holding her own but that was all they were prepared to divulge over the telephone. She should come and see for herself as soon as she possibly could.

The hospital smelt of stale antiseptic, and fear. Edith Fisher was in Pangbourne Ward, second floor. Take the lift. No, not that one, that's for theatre patients. Are you a relative?'

'Yes, she's my great aunt.'

She found Edie lying on her side in a large cot with metal sides to stop her falling out. The ward was squarer than most, the beds pushed to the side leaving lots of dark shiny floor space in the middle. Edie was wired up to several machines. So were most of the other patients.

Nancy poured herself some water and pulled out a chair. Nurses came and went. Footsteps pattered about the corridor outside. An orderly appeared with a tea trolley. Other visitors hovered out of sight. Two nurses, one black, one Chinese, stopped by Edie's bed and expertly flipped her on to her other side like a turtle. They smiled briskly and were gone before she had formulated the questions she wanted to ask. There wasn't anyway much point. Only Edie knew the answers and Edie wasn't telling. Nancy reached for Edie's hand: it felt strangely heavy, as if the will to live had already departed Edie's body. All that remained was deadweight.

Not many people had got as close to her as Edie, only Clive and maybe her mother but that was a relationship complicated by resentment on both sides, whereas her love for Edie was unconditional.

Now that Edie was letting go, Nancy had the terrifying sense that Edie had already become the other, and that she herself was locked into the present, a cold hard place whose only virtue was that it kept her demons at bay. As long as she stayed here, trapped in the moment, she was saved from thinking about before, when Edie had given shape to the fabric of her life, and after, how the world would be when Edie was gone.

Sometime in the night, Stas appeared by Edie's bed. At first she thought he was a ghost, or the dream of a ghost conjured from her desires, but when he touched her shoulder she knew he was real. In the ward's fitful illumination his face looked mournfully comic; in other circumstances she would have laughed and nearly did, even then. She asked how he knew where to find her.

'We were speaking,' he said. 'You remember?'

She tried to think, and couldn't. No matter. He was here and that felt right. They sat side by side, Nancy holding Edie's hand and Stas holding Nancy's.

Edie opened her eyes at one point, blinked in surprise, then stared hard first at Nancy, then at the man by her side.

Nancy leant forward. 'It's Stas, Aunt Edie. Remember Eeyore? He's here with me, as you hoped he always would be.'

Edie might have smiled – she couldn't be sure, but she read a flicker of recognition in Edie's face, or maybe she just willed herself to see it, for Edie's sake – then Edie's eyes snapped shut.

The three were still holding hands when the monitor began to beep loudly and nurses came running. Edie's hand felt the same as before, inert as a pudding. Shouldn't it have given her a sign? She felt suddenly unplugged.

A nurse swished the curtains around the bed. Another asked them to leave. It happened in a blur of activity, of controlled movement, no panic, each with an allotted task, except she and Stas who cared more than anyone about what was happening to Edie, but whom protocol demanded should be swept aside.

They sat in the corridor, holding on to each other wordlessly because nothing they might say would make any difference, not now. And when she saw the serious face of the Chinese nurse come to usher them back inside, she knew that Edie was dead.

It was long past dawn when they left the hospital, after Nancy – as next of kin – had formally identified Edie's body, and they had hung around the main reception, waiting for the hospital's administration to hand over Edie's things.

They didn't amount to much: a stained nightdress bearing another woman's name, a pair of worn pink slippers, a spongebag, and a small envelope containing a watch and two rings, one gold, one sapphire. Nancy asked what had happened to Edie's handbag. Edie never went anywhere without it. The nurse went to check, returning with the information that according to hospital records, when the ambulance people brought her into the hospital, she had no handbag with her. Nancy could call the ambulance service, or lodge an official complaint, but as far as they could ascertain, Mrs Fisher came in without her handbag.

'Edie was lost without her handbag,' said Nancy. 'No wonder she fucking died.'

15

Friday for Alice was a difficult day, which she blamed partly on missing Michael and partly on the problems she was having with the chapter she had decided to tackle next, one she had provisionally entitled 'Darkness and Light' to convey her point that food has its evil side as well as its good, and its joys feed necessarily on pain. *The horror! The horror!* Had Conrad added cannibals to his darkness, she wondered, or did anyone accuse Kurtz of eating his brutalised populace? They were surely lurking somewhere in the wings, and even if they weren't, cannibals inhabited a space she felt constrained to investigate. Okay, so her publishers might not like it, and she wasn't sure she would like it herself; nowadays everybody wanted you to be so resolutely jolly in the face of impending doom but somewhere in the book she was determined to take a stand.

The lightness of food was a given. She planned an illuminating probe into the properties of manna, the bread of angels, which rained like dew upon the Israelites in the wilderness and dried into flakes as small as hoar frost, to each according to his eating. She liked that bit, and the fact that you weren't supposed to leave any of it uneaten or it would turn maggoty, and stink. Otherwise the Bible was a bit vague on detail. All she knew was that manna was white like coriander seed and tasted variously of honey and oil. Some kind of honeydew, perhaps? Unlikely in a desert. A Levantine lichen? Or maybe a kosher locust? She had read somewhere that manna could never be excreted, so throughout their forty years' wandering in the desert, the Israelites never needed to pop behind a rock. Imagine that.

It was Jerry in fact who had given her the whole idea, Jerry with his dinner-party talk of bodily functions and his split personality, devilishly leering on the outside but at heart a good and decent man. Perhaps that nice librarian at Lambeth Palace could enlighten her further.

But the darkness part of the chapter was giving her real trouble; it was all so *disjointed,* and horrid. There was that gruesome case of the German who had willingly given himself up to be eaten by another. The pair of them had sliced off his penis and eaten it together, before the butchered victim bled to death. The penis was apparently quite unpalatable, stringy and tough like chicken neck without the bones. Alice found the observation interesting. The police must have asked the cannibal what the different body parts tasted like – a promising line of enquiry for her to take. She was, after all, writing about human flesh as food.

And anthropologically, cannibalism demonstrated beyond question the potency of food. You eat your Gods just as you eat your ancestors and your enemies, and that way gain power over the universe. Come come, Bishop, she thought, we're still doing it – what else is that pathetic little wafer you give us that sticks like rice paper to the roof of your mouth and can only be swilled off by a large slug of cheap cooking sherry? I know it's a symbol but peel off the symbol and what do you get? A religion that is every bit as primitive as those that have gone before. You see? You might dress up in fancier clothes but you are still rattling your bones like a shaman.

Alice got up from her worktable and went over to the window. The street outside was lifeless, as it always was at this time of day. Working from home had its downsides. You needed boundless enthusiasm just to get started and sometimes even Alice felt her store was becoming a little depleted. On a good day she would positively *devour* monsters like these but today … well, she wondered if she had the stomach for it.

The *Daily Telegraph,* for instance, had linked an upsurge of cannibalism in North Korea to a cut in international food aid. It was like that butterfly sneezing all over again, except the logic was chillingly clear. If your daily ration drops to nine ounces and the harvests have failed, what else can you eat? It's all very well the overfed West condemning the practice but we haven't been there. Take Lark here – if we were suddenly transported to a desert island with absolutely no food, no mango, no fish in the sea, no birds, no game, no manna, no grubs even, would it ever cross my mind to … eat you?

The cat, which had been rubbing against Alice's legs, started miauling piteously. She picked him up and cradled him in her arms like a baby. Skinny and sleek, Lark lay on his back, purring loudly.

No, thought Alice, hugging the cat to her breast. I could never go that far. But if an unknown child came paddling along in a canoe, a baby say, not really conscious of what life has to offer, would eating it be so very terrible if our lives were thrown into the balance? Of course it wouldn't be *nice* and I would have to go through a right old ding-dong with my conscience. Maybe in the end I wouldn't do it, not if I had to bring about its death, I don't even relish killing flies, but if a *dead* baby came along in a canoe – a baby that had died of sunstroke or malnutrition or just … fallen asleep, like babies do, and not woken up again, what could possibly be the harm in that? No point sending you a dead baby in a canoe if you weren't allowed to do something with it.

Simply wrestling with your conscience was pointless, like Simeon Stylites up his pillar.

While she was pondering her response, Lark started to struggle. The poor cat couldn't breathe. As it dropped to the floor with a soft thud she thought with a stab of surprise: I wonder what babies taste like? Nobody tells you that. Did any of the anthropologists try some? How can you describe a smell you don't know, or a sound you can't hear? All a bit of a puzzle, but babies ...? More like veal than chicken, I suspect.

'How's the work going?'

'Not very well, right now.'

'Join the club.'

'You always say that, and look at how productive you are.'

Alice swept her arm around Geraldine's studio, its canvases stacked around the paint-spattered walls like a furniture store where the decorators had run amok.

Geraldine followed her drift and shrugged. 'In my game, you don't measure productivity by the square metre. My star is pretty much on the wane.'

'Don't say that, Geraldine. I can't imagine you won't turn things around.'

'Oh, I'll do that all right, providing I go to the right parties, sleep with the right people, make the right noises – in bed and out of it.'

'Gerry.'

'Don't be a prude. It happens in my job same as anybody else's.'

'I don't think of you as having a job.'

'Why else would I paint these bloody things?'

'Because you're an artist. Because there's something inside you that says you must do this and not anything else, I don't know, make handbags or work on the Stock Exchange.'

'Bullshit. I paint because I'm marginally better at painting than I am at anything else. If I found some other way of paying the bills, I'd shut up shop straight away.'

'That's not how I look at things. I write because I … because I, well, I like writing, it gives me a buzz. You've got to do something that gives your life meaning.'

'Come off it, Alice, there are plenty of other ways of giving yourself a buzz, damn site quicker, too, and as for meaning … let the young bother about crap like that.'

'And now that we're older we don't need to make sense of our lives? I don't believe how cynical you've become.'

'I'm more of a pragmatist myself. Meaning isn't lying there like some great slug, waiting to be discovered. You have to go out and make your own. My approach is more hands-on than yours.'

'That's because you're an artist. I live more in my head.'

'And we know where that gets you, sweetie.'

'But Geraldine, I'm not sure I believe you. Look around your studio – it's all stuff I'd like to live with, sort of upbeat and jolly, even if I don't quite get what the shapes mean.'

'There you go again, meaning, meaning. But you know Alice, that's the first time you've ever said you like my work.'

'Heavens, is that true? Of course I like your work, that's why I don't believe it when you say you only paint because there's nothing better you can do.'

'No – nothing that I can do better, there's a difference, you see.'

'I suppose I haven't said anything about your work before

because I don't quite know what to say. If you painted trees, or people, or landscapes, or flowers, things I can recognise in the world around me, then I'd know how I felt. But these are just, well, shapes.'

'And colours and textures and *tension*, can't you see that? That yellow square....'

'Well it's not quite square.'

'Nothing is, honey, fact of life. Can't you see how it's trying to escape that crown shape down there -.'

'It's a bit like a picture book I read once to my cousin's little girl, about potty training. The king had a crown just like that.'

'Whatever you bring to a painting is fine by me.'

'And what about that sludgy green triangle up there?'

'You're getting the hang of this, aren't you? That's … mediating between the other two.'

'Like a relationship counsellor?'

'I hadn't thought of that, but okay, that'll do. So when you look at this painting, you might think it's just a flat piece of canvas stuck to the wall but the whole picture is dancing, moving, right in front of you and you're part of it, can't you see, you get sucked in and join in the dance. You don't just stand there like a pudding, well, lots of people do but they don't get it, never have and never will. I'm not presenting you with something that's final, finished, but something you … take over and dance with, like some incredible Cuban who just *knows* you're going to love this number.'

'So when you're working on it, I mean, how do you know which bit goes where? I'm sorry, this'll sound really stupid, but when you're painting a tree, you know it has a trunk and branches and leaves, if it's summer time, and you know roughly what colour it is though you obviously don't have to stick with that but with your sort of art –.'

'Call it painting, honey, I'm happier with that.'

'Nothing is given. You don't even have a starting point, unless you start with a title. Like this one here, what have you called it?'

'Names come later, when I'm about to hand the stuff over to a gallery, or someone is snapping at my heels because I've got a show coming up and they need to get the catalogue printed. If you like, I'll call that one "Diner".'

'*Diner*? Sorry Geraldine, I don't get it.'

'Alice's Restaurant, remember the film? You're here and you've made me look at the painting again so I'm naming it in honour of you, restaurant, diner, same thing but you can't really call a painting "Restaurant" can you?'

'I don't suppose you can.' Alice giggled. Standing in front of 'her' painting in Geraldine's disorderly studio gave her a glow. 'Thank you, Gerry,' she said, 'I'm honoured.'

'Honour's all mine, honey. If I were feeling flush I would give you the damn thing but I'm not so I won't. If I sell it on the other hand – and I bloody hope I do – I'll tell the buyer a little bit about you. Punters like a bit of back-story, they feel they're getting something extra for free.'

'You know Gerry, I don't believe what you were saying earlier about painting being just something you do. You're good at it, you really are. One of the best, I'd say.'

'Don't let's get carried away. But I suppose deep down you have to believe in yourself, or you wouldn't be able to continue. The world might be full of crap but you have to make exceptions for your own work or you really might as well stick to knitting.'

Still glowing, Alice proposed supper at a Turkish place quite close to Geraldine's studio. Or was it Greek? Then they could celebrate the naming of her painting. Geraldine declined – said she was meeting Bill later in town – but she had time for a drink. How about that bar on the corner? Okay, so it got a bit noisy at times with the influx of art-tourists but they did a mean tequila and she had heard they had started serving absinthe. Ever tried any? No? You should learn to let your hair down, Alice my friend, and by the way, how's that musician getting on down at the coast? The one you thought might need a little *helping hand*?

Alice said: 'I'll tell you later but if you want a seat, we'd better hurry – the place looked heaving when I passed by earlier.'

In the bar they grabbed the only spare seats in the whole place, half a leather sofa jammed up against a low fifties-style coffee table (Charles Eames, Alice thought, clearly pastiche). Geraldine went to the bar for drinks while Alice spread out over their half of the sofa to ward off the competition.

'You were asking me about Michael,' she said, after Geraldine had fought her way back through the crush. 'It's going very well, actually. I would love you to meet him, he's so – dedicated and serious. I couldn't imagine him classing his work as anything but art.'

'That's because nobody else has a clue about modern music.'

'I wouldn't dream of saying this to him but even I've had trouble with some of his latest pieces. He's working pretty hard at the moment, flat out in fact, so it's pretty hard getting him to relax. I do what I can but -.' Alice broke off coyly. It wasn't always wise to let Geraldine in on your secrets. In company – especially when she had a drink inside her – she could be horribly indiscreet. But what were friends for, she thought, if you didn't share with them your triumphs and your joys, even if you had to shout them out in a noisy bar that was getting quite horrendously crowded, and now some young man in a black shirt and tight black jeans had decided to park his bottom on the sofa's arm. Braying away to his friends, he might just as well have sat on her lap. She looked at Geraldine then down at her drink. 'I mean, we … slept together last weekend, and I'll be going down again Saturday next.'

'That's more my kind of speed,' said Geraldine. 'What's the rush? Is he married or something?'

'Well, yes, there is a wife in the background but I get the feeling she's pretty much out of the picture. I mean, she's over in America, has been for months, and she's a bit of a monster by all accounts.'

'Have you met her?'

'No but I … well, there's a photograph -'

'He shows you a photograph of his *wife*?'

'He didn't show it to me exactly. But I saw it, down at the house. She's some kind of academic at Princeton. Shrink-stuff, you know – psychoanalysis. I expect she's a Freudian. She looks pretty screwed up to me.'

'Has he talked about her to you?'

'Not really – we have so much else to talk about. And you know me, I don't like to pry. Besides, she really doesn't seem very present in his life. I gather they've been married for eight or nine years but really, you don't understand what it's like. When I'm with him, it's as if she doesn't exist any more. She might as well be wiped off the planet – does that sound awful?'

'Alice my dear, I want you to listen to me very, very carefully. Just because a guy doesn't talk about his wife doesn't mean she isn't present in his life. Believe me, I know. I've been there. I've done all that shit and discovered it for myself, the hard way, which is the only way that counts. What I'm telling you is way below rocket science. Fact of life, honey. Man on own. Woman on own and willing. Man and woman in bed together fucking – okay, I know you hate that word but that's what it is. Even good sex is just plain fucking. Long marriages do things to people – and in my book, anyone who goes eight years deserves a cuckoo clock. They become intertwined like the rose and the thorn and Jesus, don't we know which one has the pricks. It's okay, honey, calm down. I'm not trying to upset you. No, this isn't about me and Bill, you and Bill, Bill and his best friend's mother, this is about *you*, my dear friend Alice Pearson, and how I'm asking you, begging you to take better care of yourself. Don't go planning a future just because some guy drops his trousers. That's what guys do, that's what they're there for, honey, and if they weren't we'd have to find something else that would do it just as well. Okay, I'm sorry I spoke out of turn. Please Alice – stay and have another drink. I'm not meeting Bill for at least another hour. You don't have to rush. No really, Alice. I'll not say another word about him and yes of course you're right – I don't even know the guy so how can I possibly judge. Please honey –.'

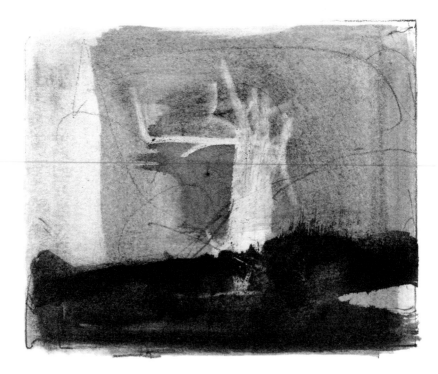

16

Nancy's explosion of anger at Michael's intrusion – and by implication at Stas, too, guilty merely by his maleness – bound the two men in a common cause. After she had fled the house, the pair walked back along the coast road, skirting any mention of Nancy and talking instead of the strange confluence of radar in their separate spheres.

'What you mean, confluence?' asked Stas.

'A coming together, a coincidence, if you like, except I don't believe in coincidence.'

'She is ... mmm ... mathematically possible,' said Stas helpfully.

'Perhaps. But I think we came together for a reason, a purpose, does that sound crazy?'

'To me, no. What reason you are having?'

'Both our beginnings here start with radar, you in your field, me in my music. I find that curious. I remember that radar sends out electromagnetic waves, but is it possible that my receptors could pick up stray radio waves that had, well, hung around for years, for centuries even?'

Stas laughed. 'You hear about George Smoot? He pick up cosmic microwave background radiation that hang around for billions of years, from when universe is first beginning. They give him Nobel Prize for that. He is also winning million-dollar prize on TV quiz show. Lucky man, in right place at right time.'

'Okay. And in our world, how do you interpret what radar tells you? Your readings give you a series of pulses, I imagine, which you can plot graphically. But how do you know whether you are seeing a plane, for instance, or an unidentified flying object?'

'That ... mmm ... depends on what you look for, and where you are. Radar, she have many applications, not just planes or wars. Radar tell you of storms, and what is under ground, or under water. Or when you drive too fast, and what is wrong with body. In astronomy, radar tell you of star speed – many things. Radar very useful, when you know what is normal.'

'What if radar picks up something that you hadn't expected to find. Something completely unknown?'

'You have pattern made by waves, then you use imagination to find what you look at. Same as all things unexpected.'

'What about angels? Could radar pick up an angel flying through the skies, or the burst of an angel's trumpet?'

'Angels go with God, and God is ... ,' he seemed to be searching for the right word, 'God is consolation. I am sorry. You have religion? I upset you?'

'Not at all.'

'I give you angel, if you like. Angel Gabriel with hair like gold and eyes like woman. Icon, you know, in Russian Museum at Petersburg, very old angel, older than Andrei Rublev.'

'I've got my own angel, don't worry.'

'Okay, this is what you do. You construct experiment to plot pattern she make, and then you test to see if experiment is .... mmm ... repeatable, if it is falsifiable. That will tell you whether you are having angel, or not.'

By now, they had reached Stas's caravan site, and Michael happily accepted his offer to continue their discussion over a drink. The caravan was in some disorder, its bed not yet stored away and the bedcovers wound into a tangle. Michael sat on the edge while Stas produced a half bottle of vodka from a cupboard and squeezed himself onto the red plastic banquette beside a cache of empty bottles and an old sock. The talk turned from radar to wives, and to Stas's Russian wife Elena, a radiologist by training but currently staying with her cousin Yana at Novorossiysk on the Black Sea. Stas hadn't managed to speak to her yet about the delayed arrival of his colleagues, and he was beginning to worry that all might not be well. He was missing her, too, no doubt about that, expounding on the blubbery comfort of her arms and her voluminous cotton dresses that could swallow the pair of them.

Returning the confidence, Michael told Stas about Madeleine, who was, he suspected, on the verge of leaving him. Stas told him to take heart: he couldn't be sure what Madeleine had in mind. Women functioned according to their own laws, which was why he liked them so much. Sometimes they forgave you the most shocking betrayals – like sleeping with the daughters of their best friends, he said ruefully – and sometimes they turned against you not for what you had done, but for what you might one day do. Lena was always blaming him for future misdeeds and he couldn't wait to see her again.

'And Nancy?' asked Michael, a trifle more aggressively than he had intended.

'Nanc-ier is own person,' said Stas, 'I not mess around with that.'

Michael hadn't meant to stay long but every time he got to his feet, Stas poured him another drink. It seemed churlish to refuse, especially as Stas was explaining how unwelcome the English made him feel. Here at the campsite dogs barked at him, children jostled and the men mostly behaved as if he wasn't there. Some of the women were okay, especially the well-built ones who reminded him of his wife, but only with Nancy did he feel accepted for who he was. Women were like whales, he said, they swim into your soul. Stas said a lot more that didn't make much sense, much of it in question form, ('How world look without colour red? World very different place, and Nanci-er, you think, how she manage without red?') and Michael , who by then was lying back on the greasy pillow, must have drifted off to sleep because the next thing he knew, the caravan was dark and Stas was shaking him by the shoulder, asking for his mobile phone. He fished around in his pockets, having only recently started carrying it around, and brought out an antiquated phone, squat and chunky. Stas entered a string of numbers, held it to his ear, frowned, tried again. He was trying to call Lena, he said, in Novorossiysk. Michael said that was unwise as Elena his wife would surely be sleeping.

'Okay,' said Stas sheepishly, 'in marriage who care about time? I try Nancy instead.'

Between them they managed to remember Nancy's number, and Stas got straight through.

'Stas here,' he said, grinning.

The smile left him as he listened. Nancy's voice (if it was Nancy's voice) was barely audible. Michael hoped she wasn't still mad at him.

Stas got to his feet, pulling on his jacket. 'Where you are?' he asked down the phone, and to Michael, 'I go now. Please. Finish vodka, stay here if you like.' At this he ran out of the caravan, still clutching Michael's phone.

Wondering what had happened to Nancy, Michael finished the bottle in the dark (there were only two fingers left), tidied up the bed, and left their glasses draining in the aluminium sink. Then he walked unsteadily through the campsite, across the road and up the shingle ridge. To his right, the Martello tower loomed like a great concrete bucket turned on its end.

Disoriented, he shook his head. Beach and sea had tilted in the darkness and a giant vermilion buoy hung crazily from the sky.

When he looked again he realised it wasn't a buoy but a blood-red moon rising through the blackest of skies, its pathway splashed in silvery red slivers across the surface of the sea.

He felt his heart racing, and a sensation he could only describe as dread taking charge of his soul.

But the moment Nancy arrived on his doorstep, late on Saturday afternoon, Michael knew that his cantata was safe. Stripped of her trademark lipstick, looking pale and tired, she told him in a monotone that Edie had died early that morning, and if he promised to dedicate the music he was writing to her great aunt Edie, Edith Fisher by her proper name, she would do anything he asked of her, and do it gladly.

'I'm sorry,' he said, trying to keep his eyes away from the nipples of her boyish chest, dimly visible through the gauze of her sleeveless top.

'Not your fault.'

'Will you be singing tonight?'

'Derek cancelled the gig. Not my call, and if he had bothered to ask I would have chosen to carry on. Singing takes your mind off most things, Edie wouldn't want a fuss.'

'I'm sorry about yesterday. Derek said he had something to show me, and when I saw your photographs ...'

'Fuck Derek. I don't want to talk about him.'

'I had a drink with Stas afterwards, did he tell you?'

She shrugged, apparently unwilling to talk about Stas either.

'This is none of my business,' said Michael, 'but you know he's married, don't you?'

'To Elena, I know. He talks about her all the time.'

'I just wanted to warn you, in case ...'

'In case what?'

'In case he hurts you, I suppose. I'm sorry, that was wrong of me. I should know when to keep silent.'

'I'm perfectly capable of looking after myself, thank you. And please don't apologise for things you haven't done. It's driving me nuts.'

Nancy's tone was formal rather than aggressive. There was a blankness to her which he attributed to shock over Edie's death, but he was nonetheless galled that she should offer him anything he wanted while holding herself back. Unable even to put his arms around her, he said merely that having lost his own mother at a young age, he understood a little of what she felt.

'I don't expect it was anything like the same,' said Nancy. 'She was your mother, Edie is ... was ... something else.'

She was right, of course; it couldn't possibly be the same. He thought of his mother wandering out into the fields, and the weeks that passed before they told him she was never coming back. Death for him was exquisitely protracted like Schubert's *Notturno*, which played in his head whenever he thought of his mother dying alone in a frozen field. Whistler's *Nocturnes* worked on him in exactly the same way with their slow dissolve into grey. Edie's death, by contrast, was more like the linear devices Schoenberg used to liquidate his pieces, a kind of death by exhaustion, until only the inessential remained.

'If there's anything I can do ...' he said helplessly, and left it at that.

Alice called soon after Nancy had left, proposing to visit the very next day instead of waiting a whole week more. The weather promised fine, and she had heard there was a simply marvellous exhibition at the De la Warr Pavilion – Antony Gormleys all over the roof, rained down like manna from heaven. They simply had to go and see it. Michael declined as politely and as honestly as he could. Sunday was a normal working day. He had arranged a meeting with Nancy Flight to talk about her singing, he said, and to look at some photographs she had taken which he thought might help in his work.

Alice's intake of breath at hearing Nancy's name indicated that she well remembered who Nancy was. 'She's not coming to the house, I trust.'

'No, I'm seeing her at her home.'

'Well you *are* settling in. I'm glad about that, at least. Don't worry about tomorrow. There are millions of things I should do, and I shall look forward even more to seeing you next week.'

To put Alice out of his mind, Michael went for a short walk along the beach, willing himself to think of Maddy in her place. He tried to remember when he and Maddy had last spoken. The days were becoming so muddled he couldn't separate one from the other. When he thought about her rationally, he felt perfectly all right, but she had developed a habit of creeping up on him unawares – when he was making tea, for instance, or cleaning his teeth in the bathroom mirror, which hung awkwardly over the lavatory so that he was always banging his shins. She would appear suddenly behind his shoulder, shaking her beautiful auburn hair and looking at him so piercingly he turned cold inside. Sometimes he found himself wishing she would go away altogether, provoking alternate states of guilt and longing that left him limp.

As Alice had foretold, the next day dawned fine and after a late breakfast he walked up to see Nancy, whom he found on her knees in the front garden, hacking at the rose thicket. Michael asked if the roses could wait. He wanted to see her photographs, if that was okay with her.

They found a crate under her bed and took it into Edie's room, now cleared of its old woman's clutter. The ones that interested him most were close-ups she had taken of the dead swan's wings, stretched out and pinned to the rutted earth like a crucified Christ. He asked if he could borrow them and Nancy said sure, why didn't they nail them to the walls? Michael stared at the sea while she went to find tacks and a hammer.

When they were done, she left him alone for a time and he stretched out full length on Edie's bed, which was now covered with a bright red bedspread, patently new. Derek must have provided it, for reasons unknown. Surrounded by the memory of Edie's presence he felt cocooned and safe, protected from the marauding armies outside the walls. He heard the clatter and barrage of warfare over many centuries, which he narrowed to individual acts of slaughter, an arrow slicing into an eye socket, a man's body blown to bloody shreds by a mortar bomb. And he heard the girl's soprano voice – the Maddy voice – leading the community to safety like an English Joan of Arc, a barefoot Maddy in her oyster-grey wedding shift trailing a wake of men, women, boys and girls, their path lit by a golden moon.

But wait a moment. The red of last night's moon seeps like blood into the golden globe, which changes colour before his eyes. He hears a faint swishing of wings, then the voices of the people singing, so softly at first you think it's the night wind, and then the words which he strains to hear, sung first in German, then in English. Of course: this is how it must be.

They are singing the words that Walter Benjamin used for his backward angel, Gershom Scholem's *Gruss vom Angelus*. Now the English and the German overlap, each coming out of the other, sometimes one gaining the ascendancy only to fade into the other.

Mein Flügel ist zum Schwung bereit
ich kehrte gern zurück
denn blieb ich auch lebendige Zeit
ich hätte wenig Glück.

My wing is poised for flight,
I would gladly turn back.
For if I stayed in living time,
I would have little luck.

The voices continue into the night, weaving their plangent song to the accompaniment of tramping feet and swishing wings, *mein Flügel ist zum Schwung bereit,* turn back, turn back, *denn blieb ich auch lebendige Zeit,* in living time, *ich hätte wenig Glück.*

He feels his heart letting go as the song washes over him.

The voices were still playing and re-playing in Michael's head when Nancy returned and lay beside him on the bed without touching, and neither did he move to touch her. *I'll do anything you ask of me, and do it gladly.* Was Nancy a woman who kept her word? For the moment at least, he preferred not to put her to the test, however much he might want to touch her, feel her, make love to her, because that's what she seemed to be offering and because that's what he wanted, deep down, if he could only be honest with himself. But Maddy had taught him to be circumspect in his desires, and while he couldn't yet decode the signals he was receiving from Nancy he was happy to slip into her wake and see where it might lead him.

And so they lay side by side staring up at the ceiling, Michael mentally noting the words which a Jewish mystic had put into the mouth of the angel Gabriel, but which for Michael represented a quite different if as yet unformulated idea, Nancy thinking God knows what.

The pair were still lying stiffly on the bed when Derek slipped into the room to check that he had everything he needed. Embarrassed, Michael leapt to his feet and said that he really should be off. Nancy had been terrifically helpful. She seemed to communicate ideas just by being there. It was quite extraordinary: another week, ten days at the most, and his piece would be finished. If the others agreed, he would like to divide his time between the two houses. He was used to the beach house by now. Its closeness to the sea gave his work an underlying rhythm, a restless inevitability that had become integral to the work. But he would come to their house – sorry, Edie's house – for inspiration and to test his work in progress. Accustomed to working on his own, this would be a new experience, but he sensed his cantata was more collaborative than anything he had attempted so far. Derek looked pleased, and Nancy made no objections.

And so for Michael, a different work-life rhythm established itself involving frequent changes of scene. To aid his comings and goings Nancy lent him Arthur's bicycle, and most afternoons he would cycle up to Edie's to talk with Nancy, when she was there, and Derek on the several occasions when she wasn't. Derek seemed to spend most of his time on the phone but always let it ring unanswered when the two were talking, a courtesy he did not extend to others.

Maddy still hadn't called, or at least never when he was at the beach house, and no one had left any messages. Late one afternoon he heard the telephone ring just as he was wheeling Arthur's bike from under the house and he surprised himself by letting it pass. Whoever it was could wait until his return. If it was Maddy she would call again, and he wasn't convinced that he wanted to hear what she might wish to say.

The new regime required a way of feeding himself that didn't involve Nancy or the others. To his surprise, he found his small freezer packed with foil containers, each meticulously labelled. *Boeuf en daube à l'orientale. Prawn and Green Pepper Fritters. Pot Luck Salmon. Ratatouille with Caraway. Liver à la portugaise.* Of course – he remembered his landlady unloading them into the freezer before whisking him off for dinner at the pub. Now that he had no time to buy food, his only alternative was to eat in the pub or cycle on to the cafe in the village, which ran the risk of introducing extraneous sounds into his composition as so much background static, hissing espresso machines, knives and forks rattling around the cutlery tray, the clunk-clunk of money tumbling into the till. He risked breaking his concentration and he judged it preferable to stay clear-headed and focused, even if that meant eating his way through Alice's dinners and storing up trouble for himself at some future date. Anyway, as he couldn't help admitting halfway through the Portuguese liver, Alice Pearson was a quite remarkable cook.

How to deal with Derek was another problem that lurked on the periphery of his consciousness. At Edie's, Derek would often drop by the kitchen when Michael was making tea, slipping in a nonchalant 'Hi, how's it going?' or engaging him in pointed conversations about other composers, Copland and Tippett and once or twice William Walton. Whenever Nancy sang for him, or he tried out different melodic lines on the keyboard they had moved into his room, he sensed that somewhere in the house Derek was listening, memorising, judging, perhaps even recording the music he was in the process of making. When they talked, however, he found Derek extremely knowledgeable about the technical problems he was facing, and he couldn't help but be flattered by the close attention Derek continued to pay to his work.

One particular difficulty he was facing was how to orchestrate the radar chatter at the beginning of his piece. Orchestral equivalents sounded so banal, like Strauss's bleating sheep in *Don Quixote*, and he was tempted by Derek's suggestion that they should visit a recording studio in Brighton run by a couple of Derek's friends, where they could download what they needed from the internet and mix it with live sounds.

'If it doesn't work, scrap it,' said Derek. 'You'll have lost a day's work at most.'

'I'm not sure my funds will stretch to that,' said Michael. 'New York isn't being very generous.'

'No problem. This won't cost you a penny. The boys in Brighton owe me a favour so they'll be doing this for me, not for you. Everybody expects to pay back a debt at some point.'

'Does that include me?'

'Think of it as a long-term loan,' said Derek casually. 'No big deal.'

But despite Michael's misgivings about the enterprise, the sounds they achieved from their visit to Brighton were first class, no doubt about that. Derek's friends had scoured the airwaves for a multitude of spy noises, number codes, raking radar sounds, illicit communications, the whine of the Boeings' engines moments before they crashed into the Twin Towers and the Pentagon, the swelling drone of enemy aircraft, marching feet, bangs and more bangs and plenty of crackle. Cutting it all together was a joy and it came out sounding exactly as he had imagined.

Just one moment spooked him. He was talking to the technicians when he caught sight of a disembodied Derek in the control box. Derek's black shirt had made his torso disappear. All you could see through the one-way glass was Derek's shiny bald head and a pair of gesticulating hands.

Michael's unease resurfaced on the way home. However pleased he was with the finished results, he considered it was dangerous to let others inside his head where they might capture his ideas and generally mess up the wiring. So he tried to extricate himself from any commitment to use the material they had put together that day, saying that if it didn't flow into the piece itself he would cut the opening and use something else.

'Fine by me,' said Derek, who was driving with one hand on the wheel and the other holding on to the roof. 'If it doesn't work, bin it. No problem.' He leant forward and turned on the radio.

For a couple of seconds the car was completely driverless. Michael shut his eyes as an HGV flashed past in the opposite direction.

Nailing the angel in his two warring voices remained his single most pressing problem. Convinced that the voices were Manichaean in origin, the one representing light and the other darkness, he took a selection of Nancy's photographs home with him to see how they might look in the light of Alice's sunroom.

If there were a dark spirit to the marshes, he felt it had to reside in the black mouth of the Pevensey outfall, which he naturally envisaged (thanks to his grandfather's tub-thumping sermons) as the belly of a whale, dark, stinking, awash with filthy bilge water and sudden surges from either end, sea water pouring into the marshes and marsh water regurgitated out to sea. Nancy's photographs caught much of its evil sliminess, but he wanted to experience it for himself.

One evening at low tide he rolled up his trousers and paddled out to the end of the outfall, which was guarded on either side by barnacle-encrusted groynes. Watched by a straggle of curious onlookers, he reached the end and started to walk back between the groynes towards that black hole of a mouth, willing himself to keep on walking into that monstrous orifice which was waiting to suck him inside.

He couldn't do it.

When he reached the place where sand and pebbles gave way to slippery concrete his nerve faltered, and he turned back. Regaining dry land, he affected unconcern as he retied his shoes, aware that his face was flaming.

The next evening he went walking with Nancy, who claimed to have actually entered that stinking mouth and gone a little way inside. He was glad he wasn't with her at the time or he would have tried to hold her back.

He asked after Stas. Nancy said he was fine but worried about his wife. Although he had repeatedly called the number of Elena's cousin at Novorossiysk, she had never picked up the phone. The cousin didn't like Stas, said Nancy, so this could be her way of getting back at him.

She wanted to know if Michael would come to Edie's funeral, scheduled for 1.30pm on the following Tuesday at Eastbourne Crematorium. As he had promised to dedicate his cantata to her great aunt's memory, this seemed only right.

'Edie would have much preferred a waltz, or something she could dance to, but if it has to be your kind of music, that's better than nothing, don't you think?'

Having established the *Angelus* opening to his Benjamin text, Michael was now working on the text itself. Nancy suggested that Laurie Anderson's words were easier to sing than Benjamin's but Michael wanted to stick as closely as possible to an English version of the original. Not only did he favour its Teutonic weight but Anderson's re-working would cost him a fee he couldn't afford. Besides, the effect for which he was striving went beyond Anderson's brand of experimental pop.

Taking his cue from Benjamin, Michael began his angel text with reference to a Paul Klee painting, the *Angelus Novus*, sung by Nancy. He played her the simple melody.

'What's the angel looking at?' asked Nancy, after he had described the painting for her.

'I'm not sure it matters. But how about you imagine you are walking in the marshes and come across piles of junk and a dead swan – like the stuff in your photographs.'

He gave her the lines, taking her through the notes for each.

Its eyes are staring wide,
its mouth is open,
its wings outstretched.
The angel
of history
presents itself
thus,
glancing backwards
into the past.

Nancy sang the lines several times, until he was satisfied. Her voice had a range that thrilled him and he asked her to take it down as low as she could, to the E below middle C if she could hold it comfortably. He wanted her to sound like a man singing a woman's part, or a woman singing a man's. He could fix the notation later.

'My angel transcends gender,' he said.

'What about sex?'

'Not relevant here,' he countered.

The next part was giving him trouble, he had to admit, largely because he wanted the two voices to sing together, sometimes high, sometimes low, sometimes shifting between the two in a single phrase. The only way he could imagine doing this was to record Nancy singing one of the voices, and then to have her singing against herself. Derek had the idea of bringing a second voice into his rehearsals. He had just the woman in mind: a singer friend with an extraordinary coloratura voice and the widest vocal range of anyone he knew – wider even than Nancy's. She could shatter a glass at twenty paces and still hit a low tenor C. Why didn't they get her down to help Michael work through his ideas?

Remembering their excursion to Brighton, Michael immediately said no, and was beginning to regret his decision when Derek appeared at one of his practice sessions with Nancy, trailing a stick insect of a girl he introduced as Sophie, the singer he had mentioned the other day. Nancy looked as surprised as he did, and none too pleased.

'I told you Derek. I don't need any more help. Nancy's doing fine.'

'Sophie was coming anyway. You don't have to use her if you don't want to. But look at her. She'll be perfect for your rehearsals. What do you think, Nancy?'

'Not my call,' said Nancy.

Derek stepped back into the shadows, giving Sophie the floor. In her early twenties, she stood over six feet tall, wearing a full-length black T-shirt dress, which accentuated her body's angularity. Michael supposed that she was beautiful but in a way that left him untouched. Responding to a twiddle of Derek's fingers, the young woman turned on the spot to let him see her from all angles, then waited for his approval. When none came, she did an extraordinary thing. She went over to Nancy and gave her a hug, not a particularly warm hug, true, but one that seemed to ease the tension between them. Derek looked relieved, and Michael said that if both women were happy with the arrangement, he was willing to give it a try.

Sophie looked at Derek, who nodded on her behalf.

Nancy said that was fine by her.

Michael said: 'Good, but let's keep it to the three of us, shall we?' He didn't want Derek making any more suggestions from the sidelines.

Whatever differences existed between Sophie and Nancy, they worked well together and he was impressed by the way their voices harmonised perfectly. Sophie's voice was deep where it needed to be and clear in the higher registers while Nancy's contralto was necessarily muddier and her high Cs inherently more dangerous. Maddy was prophecy and air, aire and angels, that's it, even angels must brush their feet in the dirt. Sophie's crystal timbre was just right, and he liked the way she wove her voice around his head.

Over and over again he asked them to sing phrases from Benjamin's text, first Nancy, then Maddy/Sophie, then both together, higher, lower, fading sometimes so that all you could hear was the trilling of his fingers on the keyboard to indicate the chain of events which the angel sees as one single catastrophe, wreckage piling upon wreckage, hurled before the angel's feet. Here he indicated the orchestral sounds that signified a world that was inherently unstable: dissonant horns, snare drums, gongs, cymbals and occasional trombones, all flying off in different directions towards the void. Then the women's voices in their different guises, which Michael conducted with a sweep of his hands, bringing in now one woman, now the other, sending each one high, or low.

The angel would like to linger,
awaken the dead
and mend what has been broken.

202

But a storm is blowing
from Paradise;
it has snagged the angel's
wings
with such force
that the angel can close them
no longer.
This storm drives the angel
ever forwards
into the future
to which its back is turned,
while the pile of debris
swells to the heavens.
This is the storm
the storm
we call
Progress.

One final time he took them through the text, introducing subtle variations that looked back to the radar chatter of the opening and forwards to the as-yet-unwritten finale. When his hands brought them to a sudden end he felt exultant but also drained by the voices the women had dragged out of him. He hugged them both at the same time, the giant Sophie who was at least a head taller than he was and dear Nancy, shorter, stockier and infinitely more precious to him. He didn't even take offence when he saw Derek listening through the open door, Derek who was bowing his head and silently clapping the performance. Yes, thought Michael, I am ready to approach the end. I feel it cooking even if I don't know yet what it shall be.

17

That night Michael slept well, untroubled by dreams, and it was nearly 10am before he woke, unimaginably late for a workday. Instead of rushing back to his score he took a leisurely breakfast outside and decided to hold off for the morning. Something was building inside. He felt a tightening at a point just below his diaphragm, as he always did when he sensed a breakthrough was near. Maddy had queried the physiology but it felt real enough, as if his body had taken over from his brain.

He was restless nonetheless and decided to take a long slow walk up the shingle, past the Martello tower and Edie's and on towards Bexhill. The day was threatening a storm. Pressure was building on the horizon as it was inside him – no obvious black clouds but a concentration of sky towards the east. Looking west, the light still sparkled.

Anxious suddenly to hear Maddy's voice, he dialled '1471' to see if an overseas caller had tried to get in touch. Someone had indeed called in his absence the night before, a London number he didn't recognise but it can't have been important or the caller would have left a message. Damn, he thought, Maddy might have tried to call *before* the mystery caller but he would never know. Or was that Maddy herself? Might she have flown back to London on a whim? *Oh Maddy, Maddy. Are you out there waiting for me, wondering where I am?*

In a fever he re-dialled '1471', wrote down the number, which he started to dial until reason got the better of him. Maddy would never let him discover her number so easily. The mystery caller must have been someone else. He replaced the receiver and went out through the French windows to the beach, remembering to lock the door behind him. Plastic bags had caught among the tufts of sea kale and bugle in the square of shingle that passed for a front garden. He should clear them away on his return.

Looking at the sky, he realised that the storm might break sooner than he had thought. Rather than exposing himself to a long beach walk, it would make more sense to take Arthur's bicycle into the marshes, facilitating a hasty retreat if required.

★ ★ ★

Alice padded up and down the steps between her house and her car. Really, she thought crossly, I'm so disorganised today. Next time I'll write a list and tick things off as they get done – iron skirt, pack food and suitable clothes, feed and water cat, change answerphone message, choose book (any book will do – we'll hardly find time for reading), check window locks throughout the house, water pots. She had thought of telephoning again, and had even searched through her bookings file and found Michael's mobile phone number, but when she rang it she got some Russian mafioso and she daren't try again. Better to surprise him with the time of her arrival. Pevensey was such a small place; it wouldn't take long to find him.

Her last trip back to the house was for her landlady's key, which she kept in a bowl on her desk.

Lark had appeared in the hall and started to growl. 'Oh dear,' said Alice out loud, 'I'll not be away long, I promise you. Just one night – two at the most, and I'll cook you some fresh tuna when I get back. Or should I take you with me?' She thought of all the paraphernalia this would require: cat litter, food, bowls, litter tray. He might not even like cats. She couldn't remember if she had asked. 'Maybe next time,' she said.

The door clicked shut, leaving Lark – still growling – on the inside.

★ ★ ★

Michael turned right onto the coast road but instead of cycling past the caravans and on to Nancy's he turned left, crossed the railway line at the manned crossing and then turned right again, continuing past the pub and over the humpback bridge. Immediately after the bridge he came to an old wooden footpath sign pointing into the Levels. It seemed as good a place as any so he hoisted Arthur's bike over the style and continued on foot. If the bicycle became a hindrance he could conceal it en route.

After skirting a hayfield, the path led him to a metal gate held shut with orange twine then out along a narrow causeway overgrown with thistles and flanked by stagnant ditches.

The landscape looked more and more familiar despite his conviction that he had never been here before. The time he went walking with Nancy and Stas was in a different part of the Levels altogether, and he was certain that none of his solitary walks had brought him this way.

The horizon opened out and the briny smell grew stronger. Every step took him closer to a place he knew intimately yet couldn't locate. Round every turn he was sure he would come face-to-face with a familiar landmark: a line of wind-bent trees, a clump of tussocky grass.

Birds twittered all around and out of the marshes came the faintest of sounds: Muddy Waters singing *Long Distance Call* across the years, his voice sliding above the harmonica and electric guitar. Of course. Mad Jack's favourite track. That's why the landscape looked so familiar.

He was tramping the marshes of that childhood summer spent running wild in the company of his new friend Dickie while his mother sleep-walked into her grave. Same wide-open skies, same smell of the sea and the sense of living at the margins. He remembered pushing his bike towards Shingle Street, that day he had stumbled across Fairground Jim and his girl in the marshes.

Dickie was the one good thing that happened to him that summer, their friendship sealed by confidences exchanged over cigarettes filched from Jack and smoked in the churchyard across the road from his grandfather's, sheltering behind the Quilter family tomb. Dickie told him about the things he had witnessed at Uncle Jack's shack, which mostly involved whisky and women and a fair amount of song. Michael countered with the sobering tale of his mother's illness and how she had been carted off to the hospital for nervous diseases.

'You mean the loony bin?'

'Something like that. But she'll get better, I know. Promise you won't tell?'

'Course not. But you really should talk to Uncle Jack, he's pretty good at stuff like that.'

He should have taken up his friend's offer. Doubtless Jack knew many things, about life, and women, and how you mend things that have been broken. It wouldn't have made any difference to the outcome, but it would have given him the chance to discover more about what really goes on between men and women, out in the world that his grandfather stigmatised as wicked and his music teacher, Herbert Jones, held to be full of promise. Later he became aware of the stories that had circulated about what went on at Mr Jones's Saturday afternoon music sessions but despite all the whispering, the teacher never laid a finger on any of his boys, and you can't lock a person away just for thinking, can you?

Dickie had come to his grandfather's funeral at the Chapel on the outskirts of Woodbridge. That was kind. Not many others did apart from the Chapel folk who sang lustily without the aid of their hymnbooks. By then Dickie was articled to a firm of family solicitors with offices in Felixstowe and Melton, and seemed to have quietened down a lot. Michael hadn't seen him in years. He asked him what had happened to his Uncle Jack.

'He died a way back,' said Dickie, sounding more Suffolk in his diction than Michael remembered, perhaps because he himself had travelled a long way since that boyhood summer, sent off to music school courtesy of Herbert Jones and the scholarship his mentor had coached him to win. Jones was at the funeral too, an old man by then, which came as no surprise since Michael had kept up with him.

After the service, the three of them stood awkwardly in the Woodbridge street, Dickie sweltering in a thick tweed suit, Mr Jones complaining of the cold, and Michael with little to say to either of them beyond the usual pleasantries - about the weather and the progress of his latest composition, about the few friends and acquaintances held in common. Dickie was surprised that Michael had become a composer, having thought that engineering was more his line.

'Jack lived the life he wanted,' said Dickie in response to Michael's belated condolences, 'and that's more than can be said for most folk.'

Michael had arranged a funeral tea at Woodbridge's best hotel, nothing fancy: Scotch eggs, sausage rolls, miniature pork pies, breaded chicken thighs, mountains of egg and cress and beef paste sandwiches, potfuls of tea and a plentiful supply of soft drinks (his grandfather had remained stoutly teetotal to the end). Dickie declined to join them. He had a client to see, he said, although Michael doubted the urgency of his business.

'Well, stay in touch,' he said, shaking Dickie's hand and receiving Dickie's card in exchange for his own. *Richard Watson*, it read, *articled clerk, Nelson & Peebles*.

Herbert Jones stayed on, quizzing him about the festivals he had attended and the reception to all his works, which Jones clearly knew by heart, each in order of composition. He had once shown Michael his music collection, with its separate shelf reserved exclusively for Michael's work. Michael felt gratified but also a little disquieted that he could be shelved away so neatly, in so modest a space.

After he had put Mr Jones in his taxi, Michael shared with the Chapel folk their memories of his grandfather. A fine upstanding member of the community, they said, God-fearing to his boots. Michael acquiesced, keeping his true feelings to himself. If his grandfather had feared God a little less and loved his fellows a little more they would have been a lot happier, his grandmother most of all, who had endured the old man's martinet ways with such saintly grace that Michael could only suppose she was storing up credit for the afterlife her husband had so generously promised her.

Had Maddy been with him he would doubtless have acquitted himself better, but he was not to meet Maddy for another few years, at a festival in Heidelberg where she had gone for a summer convention of Lacanian psychoanalysts and he was the guest of honour at the première of his Martian symphony. Maddy would have known what to say to his grandfather's co-religionists, words of comfort over their loss and of praise for the man who had done Michael more harm than good, and whom he bitterly resented for his narrow-minded ways.

His final handshakes over, he walked through the town, astonished at how little he remembered, but Woodbridge lay outside his boyhood orbit and he came here only with his grandparents. Redevelopment had further confused his memories and he had to seek directions to the quayside, where baskets of gaudy primulas graced the entrance to the public conveniences, making the town appear brighter than before. After a short detour to the tide mill and the wrecks still mouldering like whale carcasses in the ooze, he hired a taxi to take him on to Bawdsey, past his grandparents' terraced cottage (he didn't stop) and down to the sea by East Lane Farm. The barn was still there where he and Dickie had roller-skated on the cracked concrete, now repaired. Larger than he remembered, the barn had new extensions to either side but was still mystifyingly empty. Seized by a whim, he asked the driver to stop by the gun emplacements behind the sea wall and return for him in an hour. Sensing the driver's reluctance, he gave him a tenner with the promise of more to come.

Built to withstand enemy assault, the gun structure smelt even more strongly of mud and piss, its subterranean passageway choked with beer cans and milk cartons stuck fast in the slime. For reasons he couldn't fathom, it turned its back to the sea, the gun slits pointing into the landscape.

He climbed back out of the shelter and walked towards Shingle Street, looking down at the granite boulders between the causeway and the mud-brown sea. This is what he would later remember: flat earth, big sky, busted trees, a tussocky turf that put a spring in his step and a smile on his face because he liked it even then.

Walking out into the marshes that day brought it all back: bike rides with Dickie and his induction into the Blues, swigging Jack's whisky when the old boy was too drunk to notice or care, daring each other to enter the gun shelter, the usual misdemeanours of young boys without an outlet for their high spirits. The worst they ever did was to untie the painters of small boats beached at low tide beside their buoys at Bawdsey Quay. When the tide flowed back in, the boats bumped their way upriver, causing a furore. One boat sank, the others were safely rounded up and the ferryman's boy took the blame until exonerated by a cast-iron alibi that placed him over in Felixstowe at the time. He still lost his job and the real culprits escaped detection, leaving Michael with a sense of empty triumph that his wickedness should escape unpunished. The one thrashing he did receive – for telling grandfather about the angel of the marshes – was for something he hadn't really done.

The Bible says it plain as day. Thou shalt not kill. Thou shalt not commit adultery. Thou shalt not steal. Thou shalt not bear false witness against thy neighbour. What did you see, boy?

I saw an angel out on the marshes. Honest to God.

And what was the angel doing?

The angel sat astride a man and pecked at his liver. You could see the blood on the angel's lips. There were lots of them, Grandad, feet like pillars of fire they had, and flaming trumpets. Whole choirs of angels, I promise you.

That's the devil talking. I'll beat it out of you if it's the last thing I ever do.

And that's what his grandfather did: thrashed him until the devil flew out of his body and he never spoke of the angel again, not even to Dickie who pestered him with questions he was forbidden to answer, causing a breach in their easy familiarity as they went their separate ways. They still rode their bikes along the Suffolk lanes, but excursions into the marshes were henceforth forbidden and from that point onwards he felt tethered by his grandfather's endless probings about where he was going and what he had seen, making it impossible to slip away.

And so it continued until he was reunited with his father in the big house from which all trace of his mother had been removed. And after his father remarried (to his housekeeper, an economical arrangement) he fell into the care of a succession of aunts and uncles and mentors such as Herbert Jones who set him on the path that would eventually lead here, to this track that dog-legs into the Pevensey Levels where he walks purposefully, listening to the wind rustling through the reeds, diesel trains rattling along the coastal track, *rattle-te-tat, rattle-te-tat*, the *ka-ka-ka* of a lone seagull and the drone of an aircraft flying so high it might be a spy plane, but is probably a commercial airliner like any other.

The voices have at last gone silent. He looks at the sky, which continues to darken but the storm is moving more slowly than he had expected.

He reaches a kind of cattle pen constructed on a bridge of railway sleepers, where two ditches converge. Here the land flattens and the sky opens out, bringing him ever closer to his childhood memories. He could shut his eyes and pretend he knows his way to the other side, but that would be dangerous.

The track he is following delivers him to the dead end of a ditch and a barbed wire fence.

Forced to retrace his steps, he stumbles across the carcass of a swan in a patch of thistles. The bird has no head, no feet, no neck, no innards, just an empty ribcage of red-streaked bones and dirty-white wings that are large enough for a pint-sized angel, or a diminutive albatross. He wants to hurry past but the bicycle is holding him back and he is frightened of sliding into a ditch. Marshes are treacherous places at the best of times.

The path proper heads off at a diagonal towards a low metal gate and a line of fence posts dropping down into water. Far away a dog barks, and a grown lamb calls to its mother.

There are other sounds too that take him back to that day he spied Fairground Jim and his girl in the marshes.

Now as then he feels a tightening in his chest and the same compulsion to walk towards those sounds issuing from behind the reeds. The only difference is that now he knows what those sounds mean. He knows what he will see when he goes through the next gate and gets a clear view of what is happening beside the reeds.

What he doesn't know is whom he will see when he gets to the other side but this is a public path. If they want privacy they should do it in the dark, like him and Maddy, cleanly and out of sight.

The bolt on the gate clangs open. They must have heard it but they don't stop. They must want to be discovered and that's why they come here, to do it under the open skies where the three paths meet.

His brain struggles to process the information it receives.

The girl is crouched over the man like a winged gryphon or a sphinx. Her back is arched and she seems to be pecking at his stomach. She has strawberry blonde hair that bristles like a brush. The man holds her around the waist and thumps her up and down. Her top half is naked but she clings to a tiny polka-dot skirt hitched high. Her lips are as red as her skirt and she is shouting the man's name. They would know him if they looked his way but the two have eyes only for each other.

He sees in an instant how he could have mistaken her for an angel. She is joyous and free as a bird. Like the man on the ground she is giving, not taking. They have no need to hide themselves away.

He would like to be the man there with her, no question about that. He would like to throw himself into the moment that has no before and after, only now. Here. With you. Yet what happens to him is equally miraculous. He feels a great lifting of his spirits as the knot of his dilemma is finally untied.

How can he have been so blind? It's not Maddy who will lead the threatened community to safety. Maddy is his wife and he loves her still, but the good spirit can only be Nancy, whose innate sense of freedom and generosity will engender a fresh beginning, after the flood – yes of course, Nancy who draws goodness out of the sullen earth and Maddy who tries to deny her, as she has denied him so much already, even on their wedding night when he wanted her so badly. Maddy would never lie with him in a field as Nancy does with Stas, not caring who might see them.

He has to get home, to fix the sights and sounds in his head. Every second's delay threatens the success of his enterprise. He hears it clearly now, but for how long? Jumping on to his bike he cycles back the way he has come, through the clanking gate, past the dead swan, on to the cattle pen straddling the ditch. The first gate opens fine but the second is tied with twine, which his useless fingers cannot untangle. Chucking Arthur's bike over the gate, he vaults the bars and takes the shortest path across the fields, pursuing the arc of Nancy's voice, which starts low and rises skywards, sloughing off the dust and dirt of the earth as it soars ever higher. If he can only follow her voice across the marshes, he will leave the darkness behind.

* * *

For Alice, the journey went without a hitch until the outskirts of Battle, where roadworks had created a bottleneck for Saturday traffic heading for the coast. The day was beginning to lose its promise, but the coast has a climate of its own. She would know what the weather held in store only when she reached the A271, where the road travels due west along a low escarpment, giving her the first clear view of the sea.

As she waited for the temporary lights to turn green, she wished she had spoken to Michael before she left. Although their weekend was pre-arranged, he might have been expecting her on Friday; and while she believed in adding spice to anticipation, she didn't want to make him cross. Glancing at herself in the mirror, she also wondered if her new haircut was a good idea. The colour suited her at least, a rich auburn that turned her eyes an alluring green.

She shifted uncomfortably in her seat. Her new underwear was beginning to cut into her buttocks. She could only hope it was the way she was sitting and not an indication that she had bought the wrong size. If the knickers really were too small, that could only mean she was putting on weight and would have to take herself in hand – not this weekend, however. The menus she had planned were on the generous side, she thought with a chuckle, in more ways than the obvious.

Ah, the traffic is moving at last. Hurry along there, the lights won't stay green forever. Well done. I knew we could just squeeze in before the lights turned well and truly red. And please don't hoot at me. In my shoes you would have done exactly the same.

18

Already a queue of cars had built up at the gates to the crossing. He pushed his bicycle to the head of the queue where a passenger in the front car was chatting to the giant of a gatekeeper. As casually as he could, Michael unhooked the gate for pedestrians, his heart pounding from his dash across the marshes. He moved through the gate.

Stop Look Listen said the sign. Best do it twice, and listen for the throb of rails down the line.

'Hey! What the hell are you playing at?' shouted the gatekeeper. 'That's fucking lunatic, that is.'

He turned just in time. The gatekeeper was bounding towards him, waving both arms. Down the line he saw a flash of yellow and green. The rumble started a fraction of a second after that. He was stuck halfway through the gate. Too late now. He felt the ground tremble beneath his feet, then the train whooshing past in a blur, the fast train to Eastbourne. He shut his eyes, appalled at what might have happened.

Without thinking to open the gates, the gatekeeper towered over him, shouting into his face. 'You fucking idiot,' he screamed. 'It's always other people who have to clear up the mess, scrape the body parts off the track. Ever thought of that? Them cars are full of kiddies. Why the hell should they be traumatised for the rest of their lives, just because you can't be arsed to fucking wait. Think you've got troubles? We've all got those, mate, but take them back to your own sodding patch. Go on, piss off. Your sort makes me sick, you fucking wanker.'

A car at the end of the line began hooting loudly. Although

he would have liked to mount his bicycle and ride away he knew his legs would simply buckle under him. He let the line of cars overtake. As they did so, passengers and drivers turned to stare.

Unsteadily, he pushed his bike down the short stretch of concrete road to the raised dyke, and beyond that the calming sea. Leaving Arthur's bike propped against the low wall he climbed up the shingle ridge and stood looking out to France. The sky to the east was darkening still; the storm would surely break soon. He was shaking all over, and his face was wet with tears of shock and shame. At least the wind had died and the sea turned eerily calm, flopping on to the shingle with the gentlest of drags.

Breathing deeply, he forced his conscious brain to shut down. Nancy's voice had disappeared, so had Maddy's, but he knew that if he could only blot out the fuzz of that shameful incident at the crossing he could coax them back into life. He had got so close. He wouldn't give up now.

The door to the storeroom was open when he got back to the beach house, as it often was; no reason to think there was anything odd there. As usual, he left Arthur's bike under the house then climbed the steps to the wooden balcony at the top. His key didn't seem to work until he realised the door was unlocked. How stupid of him. He had left by the French windows to the beach and must have forgotten to lock this door.

Even in his shut-down state he recognised something odd about the kitchen, a faint scent of flowers instead of the usual airlessness, and a breeziness that meant he must have left the door to the sea open as well. That was careless beyond belief. Anyone walking along the beach could see the house was empty and slip inside.

He stepped through the kitchen into the small lobby connecting the bedroom, bathroom, kitchen and living room. His heart flipped right over. She was sitting in one of the wicker chairs, looking out to sea; that deeply familiar head, luxuriantly styled, a rich auburn shot with golden lights. She had found him as he always knew she would. *Maddy. Oh, Maddy.*

He was running across the wooden floors towards her, light bursting in his head, and his heart. She had come back to him. He wasn't abandoned. He could carry on, produce the masterpiece that lay within his grasp, stop the dreadful sliding into despair.

She was rising to greet him, holding out her arms. Fat forearms, like an opera singer's. Maddy is willowy and slim. A chiffony dress, worn like a tent. *You're not Maddy. Who the hell are you? What are you doing here?* Lips that are moist and ruby red. Big lips. Pouty lips. A bubble of spit on her tongue. She is squeezing him with massive arms against a marshmallow chest. He can't breathe down here. It's dark and damp, shockingly intimate. No flowers can disguise the rank odour of musk. She's clawing at his shirt. *Let me go, please. Get away. I'm hurting.*

She has him in the bedroom, white and shadowy. The tent is coming off. Underneath are big breasts squashed into a tiny lace handkerchief of white, the same white triangle down below. She looks trussed up like a chicken. Belly like a whale. Now his shirt is coming off and she is unbuckling his trousers. She's pushing him backwards onto the bed, still wearing his socks, and his underpants. He is fighting for his dignity along with everything else.

Take it easy. Relax. You work too hard, that's your trouble. I've been

thinking of this all week long. Oh yes. You can do it. I know you can.
That's good. Bit more. Oh yes. That's so smart. Don't talk. Let me do
all the work. Just a little bit more. Feel with your body, not your mind.
That's it. Oh yes. You wonderful, wonderful man. Tell me truthfully,
this is what you wanted, isn't it?

Isn't it?

★ ★ ★

When the telephone rang for the third time that afternoon, Alice
reckoned she was finally in a fit state to answer. Michael was still
out cold in the bedroom, the lamb. She had made herself a light
salad, skimmed the Saturday papers, considered but rejected
the idea of calling Geraldine (one, because it wasn't a
conversation she wanted Michael to overhear, and two, because
it was undignified to crow). She had also rejected the idea of
waking Michael and taking him for a walk up the beach. The
threatened storm had mysteriously transformed itself into an
all-enveloping sea mist, unseasonably cold and damp, and while
she was accustomed to such capricious changes in the weather,
she feared for Michael's constitution, which did not look
especially strong.

Abandoned for far too long, the man clearly needed a woman's
gentle touch. She looked forward with relish to the meal she had
planned for the evening after a cocktail or two at the pub: half a
dozen oysters each; asparagus freshly flown in from Kenya, frothy
with melted Normandy butter (pace her carbon footprint); a
light salad of rocket, pistachios, basil and pine nuts; banana flambé;
and fresh figs to plug any gaps. Then a moonlit walk, if the sea
mist would only clear in time. She had wondered about some of
the sexier Futurist recipes. 'Edible Landscape' sounded fun, as

did 'Ultravirile', but the fiasco of her dinner party had persuaded her to curb her culinary ambitions. If Michael's spirits began to flag, she could slip them into the conversation, which struck her as an acceptable compromise.

When the telephone rang again, she was ready to accept the call. As she would later say to herself, she had genuinely assumed the call was intended for her. Before leaving for the coast, she had changed her answerphone message to give the Pevensey number, as she really was expecting a call from her publisher on his return from a marketing trip to New York.

'Alice Pearson,' she said without thinking, because that was how she always answered the phone.

'Oh.' The woman caller sounded confused. 'Sorry. I must have dialled the wrong number.'

'Not at all,' said Alice. 'If it's Michael Anders you're after, he's in the room next door. He's working himself into a lather, the poor man, and is now sleeping like a baby.'

'I see.' After an awkward pause the woman said: 'I wonder if you would give him a message.'

'Of course,' said Alice warmly. 'I'd be delighted to, as soon as he wakes up. You'll have to hang on while I find a pencil. There always used to be one by the phone. Michael must have taken it somewhere, I expect. You know how these men are.'

Where did he keep them? She couldn't find one in all her usual places. In the end she had to scrabble in her bag, and when she got back to the phone, the woman had rung off. Well, it can't have been that important, thought Alice, troubled nonetheless by a faint suspicion that she may have acted out of turn. These men, they really ought to put their lives in order. They can't have everything their own way, can they?

When the telephone rang again some ten minutes later, she hesitated before answering. What if she were to complicate things further? But if it was that woman calling back with her message for Michael, it was surely better to answer than not, or the woman would think her a very unreliable companion.

'Alice Pearson,' she said again, a little more circumspectly this time, but she need not have worried. It was indeed her publisher just returned from New York, calling to let her know that everybody over there was *buzzing* with excitement about her forthcoming book.

'You know what foodies they are,' he said, 'and they simply adore the book's historical perspective. The joy of food over time, what a masterstroke. Please Alice, keep feeding us snippets about how our ancestors behaved at table. Prehistoric man, for instance: did he sit around the cooking pot, chewing the fat, as it were? Oh, he ate things raw, did he? Well never mind, you get the idea. Food as social occasion, as celebration. That's what they want, and I know of no one better equipped than you to pull it off. Your last book was a triumph. Yes, I know sales were a little disappointing but your approach was as masterly as ever and don't worry. This time we'll make a killing.'

Andrew Montgomery, Alice's publisher, was not the smartest publisher on the block but his enthusiasm was catching and Alice felt a flush of well-being that her new book might really take off. That was one of the joys of her life. She might be earning a pittance compared with some of her less gifted friends, but if luck smiled on her she knew she had the talent to leapfrog them all.

She was standing at the French windows looking out to sea when Michael stumbled through from the bedroom. Distinctly etiolated, the poor man looked in need of a shower, a shave and week in the Caribbean.

'I heard the phone,' he said, 'That wasn't …'

'It was my publisher calling with news of my latest book, the one I'm writing now.' She relayed Montgomery's enthusiasm about its probable reception in America, playing down any obvious triumphalism. He didn't seem to be listening but then he wasn't properly awake. She had clearly worn him out.

'I thought I heard more than one call.'

'Well yes,' said Alice, 'I mean …' She took a deep breath. Although instinct told her to remain silent, she couldn't lie to his face, not to someone as trusting as Michael. 'A woman did call for you earlier but she didn't leave a message, I'm afraid. I went off for a pencil and when I came back she'd gone. I expect she'll ring back, if it's important enough.'

'Who was it? You must tell me. Was it Madeleine?'

'I don't know. She didn't leave a name.

'What did she sound like?'

'What can I say? Female, a sort of … ordinary voice, you know. Older than a girl but certainly not old. Just like … any woman, really. I'm trying to think. She spoke a couple of dozen words to me, no more.'

'What exactly did she say?'

'She thought she might have got the wrong number. I gave my name when I answered, you see, which she clearly wasn't expecting, so she said something like, "I'm sorry. I must have come through to the wrong number."'

'Did she speak with an American accent?'

'Her voice was possibly a bit drawly but not, you know, out-and-out American. She could just as easily have been English.

People no longer speak properly, haven't you noticed?'

'Who called last?'

'Andrew, my publisher.'

'So I'll never know ...'

'Know what?'

'It might have been Maddy. My wife. If she thinks I'm being unfaithful to her, she might never call again.'

'Well,' said Alice, trying to squeeze a smile into her voice, 'don't you think you are being a *teeny* bit unfaithful? I don't know what you think we've been doing, but ...'

Men are such a mystery, thought Alice. You never know how they will react. She heard him in the bathroom, taps running full blast, then in the bedroom where he stormed about opening drawers. The next thing she knew he was fully dressed and pounding down the outside steps.

'Michael,' she called from the back balcony, but he didn't even look up. He was wheeling a bicycle down the path and out through the garden gate where he mounted unsteadily and pedalled out of sight away from the village, leaving her feeling hurt, confused and a tiny bit angry that he should take advantage of her like this and not even bother to explain what the dickens was going on.

★ ★ ★

They were rehearsing in the downstairs music room, Nancy, Derek, George, skinny Sophie, making a terrible racket. As he rounded the corner by the coastguard cottages he heard them belting out the chorus to an old Abba number from the 1980s, *Thank You for the Music*. Tossing his bike into a thicket he strode up the path and banged on the door, which gave way unexpectedly, decanting him on to the doormat. Once he had picked himself up he barged down the hallway into the music room where Nancy and Sophie, heads close together, were singing into a microphone, accompanied by background crooning from Derek and George.

He held up his hand.

The women stopped instantly. Derek and George blundered on. It sounded like a car crash.

Above the noise, he called to Nancy: 'Did you telephone me just now? About half an hour ago? Please, it's important.'

'Why the hell should I call you?' she asked, pulling a face.

'I thought you might have seen something...'

'Seen what?'

'You know, out there.'

'No I fucking don't.'

'Then was it you, Sophie?'

'I don't have your number.'

Nancy turned to the two men. 'Did either of you call this guy, who hasn't the manners to wait till we're finished?'

George said no. Derek said nothing.

'It was definitely a woman,' said Michael.

'Didn't you recognise her voice?'

'No. I wasn't the one who took the call.'

Nancy looked amused. 'So you have a friend staying?'

'No. I mean yes. Well, she's not a friend, exactly.'

'Who is she?'

'She's my landlady. You might have seen me with her the other week, in the pub. I went off for a walk this morning and she was waiting for me when I got back. I thought she was

Maddy, my wife, and she sort of took control. There was nothing I could do.'

'Really?' Nancy's eyebrows lifted just a fraction.

'And when the phone rang, she answered it.'

'What were you doing at the time?'

'I was ... sleeping.'

'And you want to know if I was the one who called or if it was ... someone else. Like your wife, is that it?'

He nodded miserably, willing her to admit that yes, she had called him to talk about what he had seen in the marshes – or anything else, for that matter, anything at all.

'Do you know what the woman said?'

He shook his head. 'Alice couldn't quite remember.'

They were all looking at Nancy: Derek, George, Sophie. Michael felt the room turn round.

'It's okay ...' began Nancy.

His heart leapt. So it was Nancy after all. Maddy still didn't know. He could go back to the beach house, send Alice packing, get back to his work. He might even try calling one of Maddy's colleagues in America. There must be someone who could help him track her down.

Then he felt Nancy's arms around him. 'I'm sorry Michael, I would love to say it was me, but I would be lying. I didn't call, so ...'

'It must have been Maddy. Oh my God.'

He felt his world grow smaller.

Nancy cycled back with him to the beach house. Although he had assured her he would be fine on his own he was glad of her support, fearing that Alice might overpower him again, sexually or otherwise. As they passed the caravan site, he caught a glimpse of Stas waving from one of the caravans.

At Alice's they parked their bikes under the house and climbed up to the kitchen. Alice came hurrying through as soon as she heard the door open and looked none too pleased to discover he was not alone.

Michael was quite firm, however. After introducing Nancy as one of his singers, he said he was nearing the end of his piece and couldn't spare any more time that weekend. He was sorry if there had been a misunderstanding between them, and for the inconvenience of her wasted journey, but as an artist he had to put his music first, however awkward that might be for all concerned.

Alice, who had looked like thunder, softened at the word 'artist'. 'Michael dear, why didn't you say it was inconvenient? Of course I understand. You only had to telephone and we could have changed our plans. I'm just the same with deadlines myself. Don't you worry, I'll be gone in a jiffy.'

Right on cue, the telephone rang as the three of them stood in the living room with its doors open to the sea. Alice looked at Michael who looked at Nancy who indicated that he should answer the phone before somebody else did.

'Michael Anders,' he said simply but firmly as he picked up the phone.

Afterwards he would wish that he had recorded their conversation, or at least made notes to fix the eddies of their words, and silences. It was Maddy, of course, just as it was Maddy who had spoken earlier to Alice.

'It gave me quite a shock,' she said in that new voice of hers, 'discovering that you have a new woman in your life already. I was angry at first, because you were doing something behind my back, but after thinking it through I very quickly came to see that it endorses my view of our relations.'

Michael had tried in vain to protest. 'She's not a new woman. She's my landlady.'

'So she comes with the property? That's handy.'

'No it's not like that at all. Alice lives in London. She came down specially to see me.'

'Nice name,' said Maddy icily. 'Do your relations with her bring you a discount, or is she an added extra?'

'That's not fair.'

'You are hardly in a position to complain about fairness. But actually I don't care a fig about you and this Alice woman, or what you might have been up to since I went away. It's what is happening to us that interests me.'

As she talked, Michael tried his very hardest to understand what she was saying but a great big lump of hurt got in the way. And however hard he listened she wasn't making any obvious sense.

What Maddy *seemed* to be saying was that in the beginning they had been a bright and glittering couple (glittering to whom, he wondered, or did she mean glittery like the stars?) but now they had floated off in different directions like hot air balloons, drifting in the thermals. He saw Maddy in her basket somewhere over the North Atlantic, looking back towards the twinkly lights of New York while the stars in the night sky were growing dimmer. Hadn't Stas told him something about that? How the cosmos was simply fading away because there weren't enough young stars to replace the old ones collapsing all around them?

Soon the universe would be choked with the cold dark corpses of dead stars, dead loves, dead swans, piling up like debris in the marshes. No, the dead swans were floating in from his own life, not Maddy's, and he was about to put them into his work. He smiled. It was all getting so confused.

'Excuse me,' she said, 'do you find this funny?'

'Maddy my darling, where are you?'

'In America,' she snapped.

'But where in America? Are you still in Princeton?'

'Where I am has no bearing on what I am trying to say.'

'And what is that, my darling?'

'That you and I aren't doing each other any good any more.'

'Did we ever?'

'What do you mean?' She sounded surprised.

'I'm not one of those vitamin drinks you're always wanting me to try. It's not your goodness I want, but your joy.'

She said: 'Joy? I don't think you ever gave me that.'

He said: 'Maddy, my darling Maddy, why don't you come back to me so that we can talk face to face? I want to see you, hold you in my arms. If you would only tell me where you are, then I could come to you.'

'How often must I tell you that it doesn't matter where I am? I would feel the same wherever I might be.'

He thought: but it does matter, doesn't it? You are not here with me, in spirit or in reality, so you can't protect me from the Alices of this world, something at which Nancy is far more successful than you ever were, my darling Maddy. Nancy has taken Alice outside and is talking to her out on the patio, pointing at the sea, the sky, making quite sure that Alice doesn't have a spare second in which to contemplate coming back inside, because the one thing I absolutely cannot take right now is any more static on the brain while I survey the collapse of my very own lodestar. If you go Maddy, my darling one, it will be like the sun suddenly dropping out of the heavens. Can you continue to revolve around a black hole without getting sucked inside? Stas would know. I must ask him the next time we meet.

'I have to ask you Maddy, is there someone else in your life? Is that what is really going on?'

Long pause. Then Maddy's voice turned all English again. 'What is it with you men ,' she said, 'that you can't accept the idea that one day your wives and lovers might simply want to move on? I mean, why must there always be someone else? Maybe I'm just being honest for a change, refusing to pretend that things are okay between us when they are patently not. Michael? Are you there, Michael? You've gone very quiet.'

Maybe that's because I feel very quiet, he thought. The time for shouting will come but right now I have just two thoughts floating about my head. First, that it is imperative I keep Maddy talking indefinitely and thereby indefinitely postpone the full torment she has planned for me. Second, that what I really want to do is to retreat into a tiny ball and drift away into a deep black sleep where I am safe from the hurt that Maddy is inflicting, wilfully and in cold blood. All those professional hours she has spent listening to other people's pain, she must recognise the pain she is causing me. Of course I've gone quiet. That's what happens when you hurt as I am hurting now.

'Maddy...'

'Michael?'

'I love you. At least ...' He faltered.

'What?' she was drawling again, transatlantic. The snapping tone was reserved for her English voice.

'That's what I've always thought, until just now: that I really do love you.'

It was her turn to pause. 'And now?'

'Now that you're about to leave me ...'

'I haven't said that.'

'Oh but you will. I can see the trajectory of our lives together. Now that you're leaving me, I don't know any more. I don't know anything any more.'

'I'm not sure I'm hearing you properly.'

'I'm not sure I'm saying what I mean.'

Why was he talking like this? Maddy was – is – the centre of his universe. He feels a certain terror, but also an incredible lightness. He is rising into the air like the angel of the marshes, looking down at the coal black sea, rising further and further towards the heavens. Now the earth is no bigger than a small globe. He sees the allotted span of his life with Maddy, how tiny it looks, and he knows that nothing he can do or say will give him a minute longer because time itself does not exist and he is looking down at his life from the viewpoint of eternity, sub specie aeternitatis.

That's it. That's what I want for my music.

He experiences a surge of liberation. He is Leda's swan, the God that comes to her in a rush of feathers, slinky whiteness, long white neck curled like a snake. *No, think deeper. Don't take the first image that flies into your head.* He is the dove bringing Noah the olive leaf after the floodwaters have abated from the earth. *That's better.* It's the dove's second flight. The bird's first flight and the raven's have yielded nothing.

And after the flood comes silence. And then – just when you think the world all around has been utterly smashed by the waters – the still small voice of a piccolo rising like a skylark out of the marshes.

'Michael, where are you? You've gone quiet again.'

'Have I? Look Maddy, it's all too much to absorb. I'm sorry, but I can't talk any more. You must let me finish my piece. If I don't get back to it now, I might lose it altogether. Let me call you when I have more time.'

'You don't have my number, remember.'

'Give it to me and I'll call as soon as I can.'

'No,' said Maddy firmly.

'Then it's really not my fault if I can't get hold of you, is it?'

'We're talking practicalities here, not blame.'

'You might be, but we're not connecting, that's the trouble. Call me in a day or so – no, better make it two. Even working around the clock, I may not get everything finished before then. And you won't always find me here. Sometimes I'm at Nancy's.'

'I thought you said her name was Alice.'

'That's right. Nancy is a singer, some of the time. She does other things as well. I met her in the pub and now I'm working

partly round at her place.'

'So you have two landladies, I see. And do you sleep with both of them?'

'No. Well, Alice forced me into bed with her a couple of times and Nancy isn't interested in me, I'm afraid.'

'But you like her?'

'Oh yes. I like Nancy a lot.'

'No wonder you're so busy,' said Maddy and put the telephone down. Michael heard the click as he was trying to explain what Nancy meant to him: how he probably would like to sleep with her but only because he found her so sexy. He imagined everybody wanted to sleep with Nancy, every man, that is, and possibly a good few women. Maybe even Maddy herself ... Click went the phone and the line went dead. He couldn't let it bother him as he really did want to get straight to work. Nancy and Alice would have to see themselves out.

Goodbye Alice.

Goodbye Nancy. Tell Derek I'll be round soon. You, me and Sophie should get together again in a day or so, maybe sooner.

Goodbye and - thank you.

19

Alice had not intended to tell Geraldine about her abortive visit to the coast. On the drive back to London she resolved to shut herself away for a few weeks while she made inroads into the new book and then to take a holiday somewhere sexy and new, Fuerteventura, perhaps, or Martinique. Just thinking about all that hot Caribbean spice tempered with Gallic flair brought a smile to her face and a reminder that she had not eaten lunch apart from a few nibbles of the seafood salad she had brought for Michael and left behind in the Pevensey fridge along with his rations for the week. She considered adding them to his account but decided that magnanimity was the better course of action. As he had not actually placed any orders, he would have every right to object to any additional charges and the last thing she wanted to do was haggle over the bill.

Lark was pleased to see her at least, and the flowers on her back balcony were looking positively parched, even if she had watered them only that morning. But it was late afternoon by the time she arrived home, too late to start working, and when the telephone rang she answered straightaway, despite her desire to shut herself away.

'Hey, great to catch you,' said Geraldine, 'I thought you might have headed off to the coast to see that man of yours. Didn't you say you were off for the weekend?'

'I changed my mind.' said Alice. 'He wanted me to visit but I'm really behind on the book. Anyway, I've been doing a lot of thinking since I last saw you, about Michael being a married man and all that, even if he isn't exactly behaving like one.

I thought I should keep my distance until he gets himself sorted. *If* he ever gets himself sorted out, that is. Until then I intend to keep my head down and stay out of trouble.'

'That's just what I wanted to hear. But have you eaten?'

'Not yet - I'm planning to skip supper.'

'I have a better idea,' said Geraldine. 'I was hoping you might be able to help us out. We're having someone over to dinner we thought you might like to meet. He's a friend of Bill's. In fact the whole thing was Bill's idea. It's Adrian McLean, have you heard of him?'

'Not the TV chef?'

'That's the one, honey. He and Bill have been friends for years. They went to school together in Wimbledon, apparently.'

'I thought Bill went to school in Lancaster.'

'Did he? Oh well, there must have been some other Wimbledon connection. You know me, I never was very good at detail. Anyway, Adrian is coming round to supper at Bill's in the Barbican and he was bringing a girl, a woman friend, but he's just phoned to say that they've had a blazing row and she wasn't his woman anyway so he'll be coming on his own. Bill thought you and Adrian might hit it off, and even if you don't – well, you'll get supper out of us and we're rather hoping Adrian might volunteer to cook. Bill bought some reindeer steaks on impulse and we neither of us have the foggiest idea what to do with them. Say you'll come and then I can tell Bill he's done his good turn for the day so he can go back to being his grouchy old self, which suits him a damn sight better than all this clap-happy nonsense.'

'I'd love to come,' said Alice, surprised that Bill should ever want to do her a good turn. 'Just give me time to change and I'll come on over.'

'Now don't get yourself all tarted up. Adrian is the sort who dresses down and if I know you, you'll be looking great as you are.'

'All right,' said Alice, 'it's a new outfit, even if it's a little creased from all that driving.'

'I thought you said you were home all day.'

'I was most of the time, then I popped over to IKEA and got stuck on the North Circular.'

'Nobody in their right mind goes to IKEA on a Saturday. What you need is a bloody good drink, my girl.'

'I know. I'll catch the tube, is that okay?'

'Sure. You know Bill's address? Of course you do, I'm forgetting. If you come to Moorgate you can follow the yellow line almost to his door. But let me give you his phone number in case you get lost and need retrieving.'

'I've got it already, thanks.'

'Okay. See you in an hour or so.'

'See you later. And Geraldine – thank you.'

'Thank Bill, not me, it was his idea. I wasn't going to phone because I thought you were bound to have buggered off to the coast.'

Adrian had already taken over the kitchen when Alice arrived at Bill's tower block apartment. She had floated in her chiffony dress all the way to the tube and then out again at the other end, tripping along the yellow line as she breathed in the Barbican's brutal architecture. Of course she hadn't set foot in the place since that infamous night when Bill (already quite drunk) had introduced himself during a friend's fiftieth birthday party held in the Barbican conservatory. They had drunk far too much champagne and then gone back to his flat. No, better draw a veil over that one, she thought, not before remembering what he had said to her as they left the dance floor. *That was the most erotic dance I have ever experienced in my life.* Did he mean what he said, or was it just a well-worn chat-up line? She could still recall their mutual gropings behind the potted palms, and the leer on his face as she taught him a string of her best salsa steps.

Alice thought: if I had only held off for a few more nights, who knows, I might be playing the hostess at this very moment, welcoming Geraldine as my guest. The trouble with one-night stands is that you don't stay upright long enough to give yourself a decent lift-off. Still, plenty of lessons learned and I'll not fall prey to any of that spilt-milk rubbish. Bill has a truckload of faults that were bound to have tarnished his charm, after a time.

And here he was in person, having run down the stairs to let her in because the automatic buzzer was out of action, and flirting with himself in the mirror as they took the lift back up to the seventh floor. He isn't that good-looking, she thought, just big and beefy and still in possession of a full head of hair. But he seemed pleased to see her, and she warmed to that.

'A word about Adrian,' he said as they disembarked from the lift. 'He's under a terrible strain. It's rumoured that the powers at Channel 4 want to replace him with a pair of identical Korean twins who visit people's houses unannounced and cook whatever they find in the fridge. The gag is that you don't know which twin is which. I don't see why it matters, unless one of them is an accountant or something. Maybe that's the punchline. Anyway, just to warn you, Adrian is drinking rather a lot, even for him, and whatever you do, don't mention his programme. Better still, pretend you don't know him from Adam and everything will work out fine.'

Bill fumbled in his pockets for his keys, couldn't find them so buzzed the doorbell, and while they waited for Geraldine to open he gave her shoulder a comradely squeeze. Dear Bill. Maybe he made a better friend than a lover, after all.

Geraldine flung open the door holding a glass of wine in one hand and a lipstick in the other. 'Just freshening up,' she said, giving Alice a welcoming peck. 'You look great,' she said loudly. 'Come into the kitchen, there's somebody I want you to meet.'

Adrian McLean was leaning into the oven as Alice stepped into the small, meticulously planned space. First impressions can often mislead but there was something about the jaunty lilt to his hips that struck a chord, and the way he spoke to her from inside the oven. 'Don't mind me,' he said, 'Just giving it a quick scrape before I set to work. How does a little chargrilled aubergine and baked reindeer strike you for a summer's evening?'

'Oh,' said Alice, surprised by his easy informality. 'So you cook, do you? How delightful. I was frightened I would have to submit to Bill's woeful cuisine so I nearly ate first.'

A small explosive snort came from inside the oven then he stood up to greet her. He was shorter than he looked on television – only a couple of inches taller than herself – and somehow broader, but not in the least corpulent. She liked a man with a decent flank to him.

'Adrian McLean,' he said gruffly, holding out a greasy hand. 'And before you mention it, yes, *the* Adrian McLean but I don't find that very interesting, do you?'

'I'm not sure I know what you mean,' she replied, looking as blankly as she dared. 'Alice Pearson – yes, *the* Alice Pearson.'

She giggled, pleased to see the light of engagement in his eyes. 'But I don't find that very interesting either.'

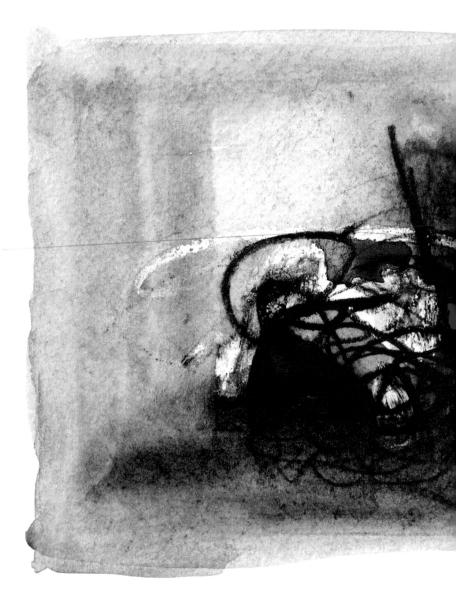

20

For Nancy, the days before Edie's funeral seeped into each other. She and Stas had reached a state of equilibrium in which they lived for the moment whenever they were together and the rest of the time threw themselves into common cause with others, Nancy into the protracted creation of Michael's music, and Stas into an idea that had sprung out of his thinking, which he hoped might raise funds for Pulkovo: a joint Anglo-Russian museum of cold war secrets that would reveal how each side had listened to the other. If the enterprise took off they could bring in the Americans, French, Germans, Mossad, Stasi, just about everybody. They all had secrets they would rather conceal, and Pulkovo was desperately short of cash.

Their nights they spent together in Stas's caravan, which Nancy had transformed into a nomad's tent from everywhere and nowhere, mixing Indian shawls and Tibetan embroideries with off-cuts from her mother's rag-trade connections, salvaged from a trunk under Edie's bed. They talked long into the night, before and after sex, which felt as natural to her as breathing. Half the time she couldn't understand what he said, especially when he talked about his work, but she loved the cadences of his speech and the offbeat questions he raised that set her thinking in unexpected ways. Colours were a recurrent theme, and the mathematics of sexual attraction.

That he would return to Russia and his wife was a given but one she conveniently ignored in their day-to-day relations. Although Stas had not yet spoken to Elena, he had made contact with her cousin Yana. Elena had been taken into hospital with suspected diphtheria and was now thankfully on the mend. Stas's evident distress overcame Yana's coolness towards him and their frequent conversations (on Michael's mobile phone) became almost cordial. Yana warned him not to get in touch with Pulkovo, whom she had called in the first days of Elena's illness. A colleague said they had received word already - he didn't say how - and clearly attributed Stas' absence from the station to a protracted vigil by his wife's bedside. Wishing to alert him to his wife's illness, she had called one of his colleagues, who said they had received word already that she was sick, and assumed Stas to be at his wife's bedside. Furious at what she took to be another instance of Stas's philandering, Yana had nonetheless refrained from revealing that wherever else the errant husband might be, it wasn't with Elena at Novorossiysk. Although unable to account coherently for his presence in England, Stas swore on his wife's honour – on her life, even - that he had not travelled outside Russia in pursuit of a woman. 'I no lie to Yana,' he told Nancy, 'but she not ask what happen after.'

Most afternoons Nancy spent rehearsing with the others at Edie's house, which the solicitor had said would soon be hers, once Edie's small estate was wound up. Michael had succeeded in disentangling their voices and now hers took the leading role. Her favourite part was where the two voices wrapped around each other so tightly that you couldn't tell which was which as they crept side-by-side deep inside the earth, burrowing, twisting, pushing like blind moles through rotting matter, then Nancy's breaking free in a sudden rush towards the light, leaving Sophie to crawl and creep upon the earth, an Edenic serpent slithering on its belly. Nancy felt exhilarated by her soaring rise towards high C, which she hit more often than not.

She also sensed that the house was adding sounds of its own to Michael's music: a deep rumble from subterranean chambers, a runaway flute from the attic, a swirling dervish dance from the thicket outside, the clunk of weights from a sash window thrown open, and a geyser bursting into flame. Edie would tell them to stop their bloody caterwauling, worse than a roomful of cats on heat it was, but Michael's best efforts would at least grant her immortality for as long as his music lasted.

Edie's funeral passed in a blur. Nancy remembered sitting in the funeral car with Derek, George, Stas, Sophie, Michael and a couple of young undertakers. Her brother Clive was to meet them at the crematorium, together with a cohort of Edie's friends and neighbours. Hoping to give Edie a good send-off, she had broadcast details of the arrangements in the *Eastbourne Herald*.

Their car arrived late on account of roadworks and she found herself fretting unnaturally. Stas held her hand throughout the journey, which took them up past the castle and on through Pevensey and Westham. He was looking unusually smart in a dark suit Derek had lent him. Michael, too, had made an effort, and came dressed in a creased but clean white shirt, black knitted tie and a bottle-green corduroy jacket that had clearly performed loyal service over the years. George and Derek wore black, as always, and Sophie her favourite oyster-grey. She herself had bought a new outfit in Edie's honour: flaming red except for black killer heels and black lace gloves. Edie would have ribbed her about it for sure.

At the crematorium their driver was involved in a minor stand-off with another funeral party, which delayed them a further few minutes. Stas kissed her openly when they finally drew up under the porch. She saw Clive waiting to one side and went over to greet him. He gave her a brotherly hug and said she looked just the same.

'How old are you now?' he asked, squinting at her like he used to when he was about to say something rude.

'Don't even think about it,' she said, 'I'm twenty-four. How about you?'

'Pretty good.'

She punched him in the chest and he put his arms around her one more time. 'I want you to meet Stas,' she said, pulling him out from the crowd. 'And before you ask, no, he's not my boyfriend.'

Stas and Clive shook hands and she felt a stand-off about to begin all over again. She went around the group, thanking everyone for coming. Jenny from the care home had brought a minibusful of Edie's friends, including a fair number of her male admirers. The one she recognised as Edie's best beau gave her a lecherous grope and a wet kiss on the lips. The community at Normans Bay was also well represented, and the shopkeepers of Pevensey Bay had turned out en masse to remember one of their own.

At her request, Derek had taken charge of the music. Edie's body advanced into the Chapel of Rest to the organ sounds of a paso doble played at double slow time. The undertakers were doing their best to smile, as she had requested. The effect was macabre rather than joyful, redeemed by the nonchalant carriage of the back four, who entered at a brisk pace bearing Edie's coffin hands-free on their shoulders. Edie was, of course, as light as a bird. Nancy tried not to cry. She thought of all that Edie had meant to her and wondered if she herself would ever mean half as much to anyone else.

After the curtains slid around Edie for the last time and her great aunt's body rumbled away to a nickelodeon tune, a cross between ragtime and Ravel's *Bolero*, Nancy and Clive led the mourners out into the memorial garden where Edie's flowers were displayed en masse under her name. The smell of lilies was overwhelming. The care home had contributed a large bouquet of mixed blooms, and several of Edie's beaux had sent their own. Derek's offering was a basketful of peonies and oriental lilies, while Stas had picked half a dozen ragged roses from the thicket in Edie's garden, tied together with string. Nothing from Michael, who annoyed her by apologising profusely. They were only flowers, for fuck's sake. No big deal.

They held the wake for Edie in a side room of the Anchor, to which everyone was invited. The landlord recounted tales of Arthur's send-off, which had ended in a notorious lock-in from which his old RAF buddies emerged only at dawn. Edie's affair was less awash in alcohol, but no less rowdy. Nancy welcomed the chance to talk to Clive who drifted in and out of her life, much like their mother who hadn't found the time to attend and, like Michael, hadn't sent any flowers. Clive was becoming more settled. He had a job as a roadie for an East Midlands band, and a girlfriend called Ellie who was soon to become his wife.

'You should have brought her,' said Nancy, 'I'd love to meet her.'

'She has a kid, little Annie, and it's a school day.'

'So I'll be an auntie.'

'A step-auntie.'

'Even better.'

Nancy told him about Edie's will, how she had left the house to Nancy and whatever remained of her savings (very little) to Clive. Nancy proposed they should pool the lot and split the proceeds down the middle. Clive said he needed the money straightaway, all of it, but would welcome his share of the house at some later date.

'No deal,' said Nancy. 'We either share it properly, or do as Edie wanted.'

'What's eating you?' said Clive. 'It'll hardly make much difference to the final amount, and you've been living off Edie these past few months.'

'Suit yourself,' said Nancy, who had no intention of revising her offer.

'Since when have you learned to stand up for yourself?' asked Clive, his annoyance clearly tinged with admiration.

'Maybe it's Stas's influence, I don't know.'

'The man who isn't your boyfriend?'

'That's right, but don't ask me what he really is.'

Clive delivered her to Stas, and they walked over to join Derek and Sophie, who never left his side but gave the impression that they weren't connected in any essential way. She had a model's trick of avoiding eye contact with whoever came her way – a perfect companion for Derek, thought Nancy. They might even be happy. She wanted to ask Michael how Edie's piece was progressing, but Stas told her that he had gone straight back to the beach house and hoped she wouldn't mind.

After a decent time at the pub, Nancy and Stas slipped away and walked up the beach in fading light towards Stas's caravan. He reminded her that his Russian colleagues were scheduled to arrive in a few days' time but she put a finger on to her lips and they talked of other things, of men and girls and happiness, and whether pigs have wings, a question Stas debated as earnestly as he did most things.

Inside the caravan they drew the hangings over the door and lit a multitude of candles, shrine-like, each in its own glass jar. Then they took off their funeral clothes and Nancy asked Stas to sing for her. He sang in Russian, of course, so she asked him to translate for her first. He was singing of the steppes, he said, the endless steppes where a coachman lies dying, and of the wedding ring he sends back to his wife. *Pro menya skazhi, shto v stepi zamyorz, a lyubov yeyo ya s soboy unyos.* Tell her I die here, in freezing steppe, and take her love away with me.

His tenor's voice, rich and true, took her by surprise. She joined in whenever she could, improvising a line of melody a couple of octaves above his, and they made such a noise that someone sent for the manager, somebody always does. They were both in full flight when the door was thrust open – neither she nor Stas had remembered to flip the latch – and a head tried to butt its way through the hanging, giving Nancy just enough time to reach for a sheet or they would have been discovered stark naked, singing their heads off.

When at last he found an opening in the drapes, the manager gave them a bellyful, his eyes on Nancy's scarlet clothes strewn about the floor, and the clinching proof of her high-heeled shoes. *Mister* Vasilyev was to get his things together and clear out; he wouldn't be welcome back either. 'This is a respectable place where guests are expected to behave properly At All Times,' he roared. 'Jesus fucking Christ, we've got families who come back year on year, little kiddies, the whole works. This isn't some fancy knocking shop where the likes of her can give you a pasting.'

Nancy hid further down the bed, having recognised the manager as one of the mourners at Edie's funeral party, but she needn't have worried. The shadows in the tent afforded disguise enough, and the man was incandescent with alcohol and rage. One spark from a candle and he would shoot through the roof.

The manager's voice grew fainter as he retreated to his office. 'I want you off site in thirty minutes, the pair of you. And don't you ever try coming back or I'll set the dogs on you. No, I'll send in the coppers. Dogs is too fucking good for you.'

Stas looked crestfallen. Nancy told him not to worry. He could come and stay at her house in the few days he had left. It was madness she hadn't thought of that before. All would be for the best in the best of possible worlds, but if the campsite owed him money, she was determined to get him a refund.

'How many days have you paid?' she asked.

'Paid? Nobody is paying me. I take holiday.'

'No, I mean how much did you pay for the caravan? They might kick you out but I'll not let them cheat you as well.'

'So deep down you have English soul?'

He ran his hand down the side of her face.

She couldn't tell if he was joking.

'Don't you worry. I learn many things here. For English, there is no free luncheon. And Nanci-er, what is knocking shop?'

She wondered if this time his question was a joke.

21

After the piece was finished, Michael felt as if his brain had blown a giant fuse and there was nothing he could do – or wanted to do – to hotwire it back into life.

He had written the final sequence at the beach house where he had spent his last few days, lacking the energy to cycle to and from Nancy's. All that was required now was to move the phone within easy reach and stretch out on the leather sofa in the sunroom. The blinds were half drawn, and the sofa well supplied with cushions.

Derek telephoned a few hours later and Michael surprised himself by holding a perfectly civil conversation. After skirting around various topics of little interest to either, Derek asked how his piece was progressing.

'I finished it this morning,' said Michael.

'In that case,' said Derek, 'may I come and see you? There's something I want to discuss.'

'What, now?'

'If that's convenient, yes. I can be with you in ten minutes.'

'I've no plans to go out.'

Derek arrived in precisely eight minutes. Michael heard him running up the wooden steps but didn't stir. The door was open. He could find his own way in.

Removing his feet from the sofa, Michael invited Derek to take the armchair opposite. Derek came straight to the point. Nancy had kept him informed about the shape and direction of Michael's new work, snatches of which he had heard when Michael was rehearsing with Nancy and Sophie round at Edie's.

He found it thrilling – a new direction for Michael and one that he was sure augured even greater things to come.

'You have a true gift,' said Derek, looking Michael straight in the eye, 'and I truly believe, from what little I have heard, that this work will catapult you into the front rank.'

Tired as he was, Michael felt the praise wash over him like a bath of warm milk.

'From Nancy, I gather your new work has come out of the landscape that surrounds us, right?'

'Correct,' said Michael. 'It began somewhere else but it's here that everything came together. Sometimes I wonder which place is which.'

'Okay, good. Then my proposition is this. The landscape has delivered itself up to your genius – I mean it, really. It's therefore only right that you should give something back, to the place and the people who helped you get to its heart.'

'You know I'm dedicating the work to Edie? Nancy asked and it seemed, well, the least I could do.'

A shadow of impatience crossed Derek's otherwise impassive face. 'A work's dedication is a private matter. I'm talking about where and how the piece will have its first performance.'

'That has to be New York. They commissioned the piece. I thought I had explained that to you already. It'll play first at the Brooklyn festival some time in November. I've got the exact date somewhere.'

'Understood. New York will host the official première of your cantata, of course. I have in mind something more informal, here in the landscape that gave it birth. A fair exchange, don't you think? You say you've finished, but there must be a few passages that are still a little raw, a voice here or there, maybe an instrument that doesn't quite work. I see you nodding – that's bound to be the case. Well, if you will leave everything to me, I propose to help you by arranging an informal performance of work in progress – nothing official, no tickets, no money changing hands, no record of what we are doing, nothing more than an impromptu performance in the marshes to let the place catch its own echo and to let you – the antennae and transmitter of those self-same echoes – gain a view of the piece as a whole. Look on it as a preliminary dress rehearsal, if you like, before a few invited friends. Honestly, you needn't worry about a thing. I shall take care of everything. All I ask is that you put in an appearance and listen to the magic you have snatched out of thin air.'

For the first time in their conversation – possibly in their entire acquaintance – a thin smile spread slowly across Derek's face.

Michael shut his eyes, limply offering himself up to the other's enthusiasm. Was this the breakthrough he had been working towards all these years? He imagined the dying notes of his cantata drifting into an electrified silence, followed by swelling applause. Derek had mentioned the g-word, but was he a good judge? There could surely be no harm in hearing his work performed for an impromptu audience of friends. Brooklyn couldn't object, if word ever got out. Every piece has its birth pangs as Derek correctly implied, the passages you would re-think if you had only heard them through the ears of a proper audience. Per Woudstra had talked of resurrection, which could apply equally to his career. Failure had become a frighteningly real prospect of late.

'Are you sure no one will get to hear about this?'

'Scout's honour,' said Derek.

'But the piece has sucked me dry. I couldn't possibly go straight into rehearsal.'

'No worries. Give yourself a break from the whole business, and when you come to hear the work played back to you, it will seem as if you are experiencing it for the very first time. That can only do it good.'

'You'll want me at rehearsals, surely? I've never walked away from something I've written. And my publishers will want to see it.'

'Hold off your publishers for the moment. If you're that burnt out, leave everything to me. I promise it'll be for the best, especially if you want to protect yourself from any possible fallout from Brooklyn. The score speaks for itself, no?'

Michael nodded.

'Then what's the problem? Unless you are not yet ready to let go, of course. Tell me honestly, is that how you're feeling, a little *maternal* towards your own work?'

Derek's eyes were terrifyingly blue.

Michael sank back into the leather sofa. The word 'maternal' carried a faint sneer. Wiped out was a better description: brain dead and drained of any ability to fight. He waved his hand in a gesture which Derek appeared to take as acquiescence because he leapt to his feet and went over to Michael's worktable.

'Is this it?' he asked, his hands hovering over the score.

'Yes,' said Michael, turning away as if to avoid any taint of collusion.

'You'll not regret this, I promise you.'

Derek scooped the score into his bag and retreated backwards out of the room.

'Regret what? What are you doing?'

'I'll be in touch in a day or so,' said Derek, his voice growing fainter as he swept through the kitchen and down the outdoor stairs.

Michael felt a momentary panic. He got to his feet and hurried to the door. Derek was by now running back across the lawn.

'You'll take good care of it, won't you?' Michael shouted.

'With my life.' Derek stopped and was looking back towards the house. 'Don't you worry about a thing. I'll arrange something as soon as I can. Give me a week, plus or minus a day or two, and in the meantime, just relax. I'll send Sophie to see that you have everything you want.'

'I'd rather have Nancy,' said Michael.

'Nancy it shall be.'

Derek was as good as his word. Nancy came to see him several times, usually with Stas in tow. They looked so young and hopeful, the pair of them. They reminded him of the Startrite kids setting off hand in hand with their satchels and shiny new shoes. Nancy, who had never heard of the Startrite kids, said that Stas would be returning to Russia soon, but more than that she wasn't prepared to say.

Still feeling acutely dislocated, he asked her how Derek's arrangements were progressing.

Nancy said that everything was in order. They rehearsed most mornings with a bunch of musicians who had materialised from nowhere and now filled every spare corner at Edie's, plus a further contingent who had pitched their tents in the campsite down the road. George had taken over the catering and proved himself a wizard at gargantuan stews, while Derek disappeared most afternoons to London and occasionally to Brighton. She also heard him on the telephone hiring stewards and portaloos and generally talking business under conditions of extreme secrecy.

'You'd think he was planning a war, not some poxy music performance. Sorry – you know what I mean.'

She told him about the venue, found for them by Stas: a disused barn close to the site of the old radar stations, which they had revisited with a Colonel Little, ex-military intelligence, whom Stas had met through the local library while researching his museum of cold war secrets.

'The library put Stas in touch with him,' said Nancy. 'They have a pamphlet he's written on the coastal battery at Normans Bay, right by Edie's house. He's cute but … kind of weird.'

'If he's army …'

'Ex-army. Must be well into his seventies by now.'

'Ex-army, okay, what do you expect?'

'He asked Stas a whole bunch of questions that don't advance us very far. Like how Stas got here in the first place. Who the fuck cares? But you'll love the barn – it's close to the lane that leads on to the radar stations. When we went back with the Colonel it really spooked me. You walk into dead space, where everything falls silent. No chattering birds. No wind in the reeds. Even the insects seemed to switch themselves off, like we were walking out of time.'

Michael asked if Derek had expressed any views on his music.

Nancy shrugged. 'You know Derek … He never gets very excited about anything.'

'He said some jolly nice things about me when I first handed the work over to him.'

'Was that before or after you agreed to his plan?'

'Before, I think. But he seemed pretty genuine.'

'That's Derek for you. He did say one thing that made me laugh, when he played us the opening track. He said the spooks are out there listening and all they pick up are effing angels, but he didn't mean that critically. He must think you're worth cultivating or he wouldn't go to all this trouble. Don't worry Michael, everything will be fine, I promise you. I like your cantata very much, so does Sophie, now that we've learnt to inhabit its space.'

She wanted to know his plans. He said he should probably return to London straight after the performance but kept putting off a call to Alice, who seemed equally keen to avoid speaking with him. So he stayed home at the beach house, eating Alice's dinners and sleeping much of the day. At night he often walked the beach, watching the moon cut a silver path across the sea. (It never shone red again.) He hated leaving the house in daylight in case Maddy should call although he knew she probably wouldn't and he wasn't terribly sure what he would say to her. But as he admitted to Nancy, Maddy's non-calling affected him deeply. To move out of this strange state of stasis he needed a signal from her and when none came he shut down even further. He was a lightning conductor without contact to the earth. If she were to call now he would probably fry.

The next time he saw Nancy was the day of his cantata's first performance. She arrived on his doorstep in the late afternoon, resplendent in lilac like a carnival queen: long lilac skirt of rustling taffeta and a shiny lilac bodice stitched together from thousands of plastic sequins. 'Fucking Derek,' she said, rolling her eyes, but from the way she kept smiling at herself in the many mirrors of

Alice's house, he could tell she was pleased. Her hair was cut short again, streaked with shades of vibrant plum that matched the deep red of her lipstick.

He had lost track of time and hadn't started to get ready. Nancy cajoled him into the bathroom then helped him dress in a clean cream shirt and crumpled suit she ironed haphazardly. She wouldn't let him wear a tie. Then she shut all the doors and bundled him out to Derek's waiting Mini, where Stas had taken the front passenger seat, on his lap a brown paper parcel stoutly tied with string. George the drummer sat in the back. At first he couldn't remember who George was, having exchanged no more than a dozen words with him.

Nancy had trouble arranging her skirts in the car, its material crackling like radio static as she bunched it around her waist, leaving her feet free to reach the pedals. 'Everyone okay?' she asked. Michael smiled at her in the mirror and she set off con brio as usual, racing past the suntrap bungalows and hurtling around Pevensey Bay's one-way system then up to the roundabout on the main Bexhill to Eastbourne road. Here she took the small road leading into the Levels, pulling off before they reached the pub at Wartling. Stewards in fluorescent vests directed them to park in a field that was fast filling up with cars.

Michael felt anaesthetised, an observer rather than a participant. He had recently finished a major piece of work and his wife had just left him. This last was an assumption rather than a fact but one whose veracity was hardly in doubt. If he could only clear away the fog in his brain he might have some idea how he felt, but his out-of-body state had to be viewed as a blessing that saved him from experiencing the full misery of his predicament. At least Alice's dinners meant that he was reasonably well nourished and able to withstand the unaccustomed crowds.

They were standing in the field. George had drifted off and Stas was rubbing his hand up and down Nancy's skirts, making them shimmer and squeak. Michael wished he could do the same. 'You are performing tonight, aren't you?' he said urgently to Nancy. If Nancy would only sing his cantata, then all would be well.

Nancy said of course she was singing, why else would she tart herself up like a fucking Martian? In fact she had wanted to abscond – Derek was being a real pain – but Sophie had persuaded her to change her mind.

'Sophie said she had never realised how well our voices go together. Apparently if you shut your eyes, you can't always tell who is singing what, which makes that changeover bit in the middle really spooky. Listen out for it, later on. When it works it scares you half to bits. I feel as if I'm talking in tongues – Sophie's tongue – and that's creepy.'

They walked slowly towards the gate, past a couple of low brick buildings and great slabs of concrete that reminded him of the barn at Bawdsey. A hulking pillbox pointed its gun slits towards the coast, the perfect backdrop for a couple of soldiers in full battle kit who leaned against the entrance, nonchalantly smoking. Their presence seemed oddly normal. Remove the dust sheets and you must expect a few walking ghosts to enter the frame.

Now they were walking towards the great barn along a concrete road, the cracks in its surface laced with ribbons of weeds. More cars were turning off into the field behind them. The metal gate to the barn was coiled with barbed wire and padlocked. Somebody had erected a makeshift wooden stile over the fence. He reached for Nancy's hand. He has been here before, of course, many years ago. Everything was leading him back here to where his music had its beginnings, in Fairground Jim's washboard skiffle and a pack of roller-skating boys and girls whooping around the barn's makeshift arena, their cheap skates rumbling over the concrete.

The crush of people pushed them on towards the stile. Nancy was pulling him forward, trying to save her skirts from the stampede. Dressed in uniform black, the audience presented a common face. Men in suits or leathers, no ties; the mostly blonde women stepping daintily over the rutted concrete in their dancing pumps or impossibly high heels. He couldn't help but stare. Most were considerably younger than his usual audience. He wondered what would they make of his music. He wondered what *he* would make of his music now that he was coming at it cold.

Their turn at the stile. Stas went first, then Michael, then Nancy, who caught her skirts on the barbed wire. Michael fiddled about in her underskirts to free her. He fought the urge to fondle her foot.

They reached the barn doors, where Derek was greeting people as they went in. He seemed to know everybody by name. Sophie stood by his side, plainly dressed in a long drab shift that accentuated her height and angularity. Her nipples jutted through the cloth like a couple of ear plugs in the wrong place. Michael wondered if she and Nancy had just happened to dress so very differently, or if this was part of Derek's plan. The women kissed each other on both cheeks then Sophie gave him her hand, which felt as limp as a dead fish. Her dress seemed wrong for the Maddy part but it was much too late to complain.

Reptilian Derek looked the same as ever, if a little high on the adrenalin of the occasion. 'Good turn-out,' he said to Michael, breaking off from his conversation with a flamboyant white-haired man in dark glasses who reminded him of Andy Warhol.

'I'm not sure I'm ready for this,' said Michael in a low voice.

'Don't you worry,' said Derek smoothly, 'everything's under control. Let me introduce you to Peter Kourkolos, he'll be conducting.'

Michael turned in consternation to the Warhol type. 'Not me,' said the man, shaking an arm in plaster as if in explanation.

The real Peter Kourkolos stepped forward, a barrel of a man squeezed into a taupe satin shirt who looked far too young to give the piece the gravitas it required.

'Please don't take this personally,' said Michael, momentarily flustered, 'but I always imagined that Derek would conduct the piece. He's seen it through its gestation and knows something about me. Had I known, I would have come to rehearsals myself.'

'No problem,' said Derek. 'This is work in progress – nobody is expecting miracles and anyway, Peter knows the work inside out already. I've seen to that. You need to go in now. When everyone is ready, I'll say a few words then you'll get up and say a few more, then you'll sit back and listen to what Peter does with your music. It'll be a revelation, I promise you.'

'What on earth shall I say?'

'Whatever you like. People will be too keyed up to remember much about anything. Walter FitzWilliam is here from *The Times*, you should probably have a word with him afterwards. We're going for dinner in Bexhill, you will join us, won't you?'

'But the première isn't until New York, we can't have the press here. We shouldn't be doing this at all. When you said you wanted to invite a few friends down to listen, I thought you meant just that.'

'Relax. There's no one here who isn't a personal friend of mine in one way or another. Walter appreciates the sensitivities. Just enjoy the occasion – you won't regret it, I promise you. But I really can't talk now. Peter, I need you backstage. Hello, yes, how're you doing? Glad you could make it. Let me introduce you to the composer, Michael Anders. Michael, I would like you to meet Gabrielle Angeli, she's with *Vogue*.'

It was horrible. The Gabrielle woman swept him inside, enveloping him with her personality in a way that reminded him of Alice, but when she saw someone she really *had* to talk to (the white-haired man who was furiously waving his plaster cast at her) she cast him adrift. Stas was corralled into the far corner, out of reach. He felt a rising panic as more and more people pressed into the barn. Its breeze-block and corrugated-iron walls were surely too flimsy to contain the crush. An unglazed window ran the length of one side, giving views of the flat horizon of the Levels broken by a line of straggling pines and willows.

The barn was filling up fast. Late arrivals crowded around the opening. Inside it was standing room only, apart from the lucky ones in the front row who crouched on fresh bales of straw.

At the end closest to the entrance was a makeshift stage next to a derelict caravan into which he had seen Nancy, George and Sophie disappear with Peter Kourkolos. On stage stood a Steinway piano, a handful of chairs and music stands, a drum kit, a couple of huge amplifiers and the usual spaghetti wired up to a control panel to one side. Where were the seats for the orchestra? He wanted to push his way to the front and send everybody packing. It wasn't right to exclude him like this. How could he ever have let this happen? Derek was trying to steal his work, his life, before he was ready to hand it over. Half of him wanted to make a scene and the other half to run away, a conflict that tied him to the spot.

A metal gate clanged shut. Murmured conversations slowly died away. From somewhere outside came the faintest hint of a choir, seraphic voices carried on the breeze, or was that coming from his head?

Derek emerged from the caravan and walked to the front of the stage. Sporadic applause from around the barn: these were Derek's friends, or the names in his book at least. The only one clapping with real enthusiasm was Stas, who had pushed to the front and was now sandwiched between the woman from *Vogue* and the man with the plaster cast.

'We are about to have the privilege of listening to a new work from one of this new century's brightest talents,' said Derek in a mellifluent voice (new to Michael) that perfectly judged the barn's acoustics. As Derek was waving in his direction, several heads turned to stare. 'I'll not embarrass him by listing his many accolades and achievements, but take it from me that Michael Anders and his music are known and loved from St Petersburg to Seattle and all the places in between.

'As Michael will be the first to admit, this work is still in the final stages of composition and that's why I have asked you down here today to this impromptu concert in the marshes, which I really must stress is provisional and not exactly official so if we have to evacuate the building for any reason, I ask you to move swiftly back to your cars. Is that understood?'

There were murmurs of assent. A woman laughed nervously.

Somebody called out, 'Do we get our our money back?' to which Derek replied, 'You came here for free, Charles, so don't try that one on me.' Scanning the crowd, Derek sent Michael an apology of a shrug. 'Some of the piece you will hear tonight has been pre-recorded. This was simply a matter of logistics. Aside from the opening section, Michael wasn't present at any of these recordings, and I ask you to imagine you are hearing and seeing a live orchestra.

'But that's enough from me. Thank you for taking the time to share this event with us. I know you won't regret the effort you have made to be present at the birth of a new work that will be celebrated for many decades to come.'

Derek was waving him towards the front. As soon as he pushed his way forwards, he felt his panic evaporate. If they didn't get the work for themselves a few random words from him were unlikely to make much difference. The chances are that they didn't give a shit about his music anyway. They were here for the occasion, each one hand-picked by Derek, and that's what they would remember.

He gave his hand to Derek, who hauled him onto the stage. The faces in the barn looked friendlier than he had imagined. Stas was positively beaming. Perhaps he shouldn't prejudge them, as he hoped they would not prejudge him.

I ask you to be gentle with the piece, that's all.

'Thank you for coming, and welcome,' he said, his voice sounding as unnatural to him as Derek's. 'I want you to find in this piece what you will. Hope, joy, pain, confusion – it's all there, and the past, and the present, and the future, even if they get a bit mixed up and come at you in the wrong order. But who knows what the right order is? Time is a funny thing. When you write music, this is what you are dealing with: sounds that happen in time and the silences in between. It's all about causality; and when you start playing around with time, you can make things happen before their cause. I find that interesting. In music it means you can make a note before the hand strikes the instrument, or before the brain has decided which note to play. As the composer, I get to choose, and if you don't like my version, remember there are plenty of other ways of putting the notes together, fiddling with time, as it were.

'But let me tell you a little about how I came to write this piece. I travelled here because my wife is away in America and I found I couldn't write at home. She has left me, by the way, and isn't coming back but that's a story for another occasion. If I had gone anywhere else, I would have written a very different piece because it was only here, as I was writing my music, that I stumbled across something that happened to me a long time ago – so long ago, in fact, that I truly believed even the memory had been erased.

'Writing this piece has taught me to think very differently: that you can re-order the past but you can't erase it. Nothing is ever truly lost. Here on earth, matter never simply disappears, it just turns into something else. The same with emotions. Hate becomes love, love becomes hate, we take a bath in the cool waters of indifference. And when things get broken we really should let the angels fix them, or at least find another use for them. Like my Russian friend here,' he waved at Stas, who became suddenly of interest to Gabrielle Angeli at his side. 'He wants to turn our wartime relics into a museum of secrets, Anglo-Russian secrets from the cold war, and good luck to him, I say.

'The episode that sparked this piece harks back to my

grandfather, a very upright man and Baptist to his boots. I thought I hated my grandfather but I don't any more. And I never wanted to kill him, not even to prove a point. Without my grandfather, I would never have invented the flaming angels, which would consequently never have found their way into the piece you are about to hear tonight, a piece dedicated to Edith Fisher and named the *Angel Cantata* in my grandfather's memory. Listen carefully and you may be able to hear the angels singing. You don't need to believe in them. I write music for angels and my wife leaves me but which comes first? Do angels cause phenomena or are they really effects? Did my grandfather give me the idea of angels all those years ago or am I now making a gift of them to him?

'It's okay Derek. I see you think I have said more than enough already, well, I have and I haven't but I'll get off this stage and let the music speak for itself as music always should. Good night, I'm going, good night, good night.'

He couldn't bear to hear the music all the way through. It was too familiar to him and also too strange, a part of his flesh and an artificial limb he could simply unstrap and leave on the operating table.

After Nancy, Sophie, George, fat Peter and a second unknown musician had slid noiselessly onto the makeshift stage, taken their bows and waited for the isolated coughing to subside, he felt quite sick with anticipation. Peter turned his back to the audience. Nancy and Sophie stood to the fore, George took the drums and the other musician (who looked more like a rock musician than a pianist) sat himself at the Steinway. When silence finally settled, Peter nodded towards Derek, who retreated noiselessly to the control panel, and the first crackle of static erupted from the amplifiers on either side of the stage: the raking radar sounds they had recorded in Brighton, and the blipping number codes enunciated in Queen's English by an unidentified woman, followed by the distant drone of approaching enemy aircraft.

He still wasn't convinced that the piece would hold its audience – not this audience, perhaps not any audience. As the radar gave way to the orchestral notes of invading armies, there were things he wanted to delete, notes and silences he wanted to add, changes that would alter the phrasing to give it pace and life. And was it right to leave his two female singers standing motionless, utterly silent, while the radar crackle swirled around them like a restless tide?

A couple of well-dressed women next to him began to fidget. Were they bored already? One of them flopped down noisily in the straw. The other continued to hop about restlessly then followed suit.

Oh Christ, thought Michael, maybe it's my fault. Maybe I should have brought the singers in earlier. But wait. Give it time. Let the sounds create their own meanings, their own silences. All you need is a little patience and goodwill.

There, what did I tell you?

A communal shiver ran through the barn.

Even the women at his feet leant forward towards the stage. Nancy had begun to sing the German part of Scholem's *Gruss vom Angelus,* her voice as rough and muddy as that very first time he had heard it slithering out of the sea fog, when he walked the beach at dusk. *Mein Flügel ist zum Schwung bereit / ich kehrte gern zurück.* There comes Sophie, her English rendition gliding over the German, *My wing is poised for flight/ I would gladly turn back*. He saw Derek at the controls visibly relax. From this moment he knew that everything would work out for the best, even if the world was so very imperfect.

In the end, Michael was driven outside not by nerves but by elation. He had done it. The piece would work as he had intended. Oh, there were still parts that needed attention: you can always improve a piece by cutting out anything extraneous to the central idea, any ornamentation that doesn't add something of itself or take you by surprise, but the central idea had wormed itself into the very core of his music. *Don't ask me to put the idea into words because then I would have written a book, not a cantata for two initially similar but ultimately contrasting female voices.*

Just listen, can't you, to the voices of the two women, and the pianist plucking at the entrails of the piano like his flaming angel. Listen to Nancy's cavernous voice, the voice that smells of mushrooms, brown sliding into black and burrowing deep into the earth. And look, there's Maddy/Sophie, silvery grey in colour when she's up in the sky but growing yellow as she turns stormy, sucking up anger and bile. Now they are sliding along together as they exchange words and phrases from Walter Benjamin: *The angel would like to linger* (this sung by Nancy), *awaken the dead* (sung by both), *and mend* (Maddy/Sophie) *what has been broken* (solo Nancy).

Quick, follow their twistings and turnings as they hand each other the next line until Nancy breaks free and they both grow stronger, Nancy leading the community to safety while Maddy, dearest Maddy, stays trapped in the earth. Watch her whip-lashed body as she thrashes this way and that amid the storm blowing in from Paradise; the storm that will breach the shingle dyke and unleash the waters that flood across the land, already drowning under the discarded junk of ages long past.

And from the music he has created he sees, breathes, smells the English landscape, imagining the blue rim of the South Downs to the west, the dyke to his back, the rising slopes of Wartling Woods to the north, and in the distance the flat lands of Shingle Street and Bawdsey in the sparkling East Anglian light, spinning their original magic.

The ferocity of the flood takes him by surprise, the boiling sea evoked in a deliberate nod to Britten's *Peter Grimes* by the strings playing a D major chord with added C♯, overlaid with flutes, clarinets and tumultuous harp. Then the flood drains into silence, a silence so prolonged that it invites the first tentative clapping, immediately cut short by Nancy's voice rising like a young skylark out of the marshes, and the unbearable sweetness of the horns' dominant seventh chord beckoning us forward to the future until at last it loses itself in the sea's eternal rhythm and fades imperceptibly to nothing.

The applause, when it comes, is thunderous. Michael leans against the rough concrete of the barn, wild-eyed, overcome by his music and the power of Nancy's voice.

Nancy can scarcely have taken a bow before he sees her running out of the barn with Stas who has now unwrapped his parcel. They disappear to the end of the field. The clapping continues and he hears his name called repeatedly, like a football chant, *Mi-chael An-ders*. Just before he steps back into the barn he is startled by a great whooshing sound and a rocket shoots into the night sky, bearing (as he will later discover) a good part of Edie's ashes. Edie goes out with a big bang, the rocket painstakingly constructed by Stas bursting into chrysanthemum colours that crackle and cascade down to earth, pinks, greens, bad-taste purples amid myriads of silver stars.

And so, thinks Michael, as he composes his face to meet his public, and as he will so clearly remember some twenty years later when he muses on the visit of the young music journalist, *I write this music to play in this barn, setting off a chain reaction that travels back in time to a little boy in short trousers who is roller-skating round and round that other barn to a scratched Lonnie Donegan record, his own long distance call from the future to the past. And because that boy chooses to respond to the music's undeniable call, a life unfolds in one direction and not in another and had I not written this piece now, the shape of my life would have been unutterably different.*

Postscript

On Tuesday 27 July 2010, a delegation of Russian astronomers and physicists took off from St Petersburg's Pulkovo-2 Airport bound for the Herstmonceaux Observatory in East Sussex, England. The purpose of their visit was at once professional and political. In particular, they wanted to alert the scientific community to a plan hatched by associates of the FSB (successor to the old KGB) to develop a large section of their own Observatory's very beautiful site into luxury tourist accommodation.

At the airport one of their number, a certain Stanislav Gregorovich Vasilyev, went missing between arrival and check in. As it happened, no one could quite recall his presence at the airport; the group had split into several factions who came together only as they took their seats in the aircraft, when Vasilyev was found to be missing. His reputation for erratic timekeeping received much ribald comment, and his friend Piotr Kharitonov wondered if the episode might finally cost him his job.

The main delegation's aeroplane developed engine trouble soon after leaving Russian airspace, forcing it to make an unscheduled stop at Helsinki in Finland. Here they were grounded for nearly twenty-four hours while spare parts were dispatched from Moscow. All were amazed to discover their missing colleague waiting for them at the Sussex Observatory when they finally arrived. As his name appeared on the roster, he had encountered no problem in gaining admittance and had enjoyed the establishment's hospitality for a full extra day.

But Stas never got his cold war museum. As Nancy suspected, Colonel Little had not been entirely straight with them. Having requested background checks through the intelligence services on his new Russian 'friend', the Colonel quickly discovered that Stas's entry into Britain was irregular. In fact there was no record of his having entered the country at all, although it was never satisfactorily established whether this was because he had travelled illegally, or whether lax border controls were at fault. Once they had ascertained the impending date of his scheduled departure, the authorities chose to turn a blind eye to Vasilyev's unauthorised stay rather than risk the ridicule that would almost certainly attend deportation proceedings of a man who had never officially arrived.

Stas went back to Russia and to Elena, as expected. He often thought of Nancy, without any sense of regret – he had taken his love for her back to his homeland, and hers for him, and their continued friendship transcended the distance between them. How he had come to Britain, by contrast, interested him scarcely at all until the following summer, when reports began to circulate of extraordinary experiments conducted deep beneath the Italian Apennines. These suggested that subatomic particles known as neutrinos might in fact travel faster than light, albeit by nanoseconds, thereby confounding one of the basic tenets of Einstein's special theory of relativity. If a neutrino can travel faster than light, why not man, in one guise or another? Although the results were later more plausibly attributed to faulty wiring in the test equipment, the experiments opened up for Stas and his colleagues a whole new universe of improbabilities, which they continue to explore with open minds, whatever the consequences.

Acknowledgements

This novel was inspired by the landscapes and musical traditions of East Anglia, starting with Yannis Kyriakides' remarkable *ConSPIracy Cantata* performed at Bentwaters Airbase, Rendlesham, Suffolk, on 8 June 2002, as part of the Aldeburgh Festival. I am also indebted to Giya Kancheli's *Imber* (conceived by Artangel, Jeremy Herbert and James Macdonald and performed at Imber village, 21-23 August 2003) and to Mark Kidel's film of the event, *Imber: England's Lost Village* (Artangel Media in association with CTVC, 2004).

For help with the music I turned to David Matthews, *Landscape into Sound* (St Albans, Claridge Press, 1992), and 'The Music of English Pastoral' in Anthony Barnett and Roger Scruton (eds), *Town and Country* (Jonathan Cape, 1998), supplemented by Christopher Palmer, *Chaos and Cosmos in Peter Grimes* in C. Palmer (ed.), *The Britten Companion* (Faber and Faber, 1984); and Alex Ross, *The Rest is Noise, Listening to the Twentieth Century* (Harper Perennial, 2009). The philosophy and practice of time travel I borrowed from Sergei Krasnikov, *Time Machine (1988– 2001)* (St. Petersburg, n.d.); and the wartime relics of southern Britain from Peter Longstaff-Tyrrell, *A Sussex Sunset, RAF Pevensey & RAF Wartling, 1938-1964* (Polegate, East Sussex, Gote House Publishing, 2001). Walter Benjamin's reflections on the angel of history are taken from the two-volume German edition of his writings, *Shriften*, ed. T.W. and G. Adorno (Suhrkamp Verlag, 1955), author's translation; and the futurist recipes adapted from Filippo Marinetti, *The Futurist Cookbook*, trans. Suzanne Brill and ed. Lesley Chamberlain (London, Trefoil Publications 1989).

Aside from obvious historical figures the characters are fictional, and no resemblance is intended to persons living or dead.

The author and publisher are grateful to Faber and Faber for permission to reproduce lines from *Viral Landscape* by Jo Shapcott.

First published in 2013 by Full Circle Editions

Parham House Barn, Brick Lane, Framlingham, Suffolk IP13 9LQ
www.fullcircle–editions.co.uk

Set in Plantin Light & Gill Sans
Printed on 120 gsm Munken Pure FSC® Mix Credit.

Book design: Jonathan Christie

Printed and bound in Suffolk by Healeys Print Group, Ipswich.

ISBN 978-0-9571528-1-6

Note on the typeface:
Plantin Light is part of the Monotype Plantin family, a modern revival
typeface that was first cut in 1913 under the direction of Frank Hinman
Pierpont. Its origins date back to the 16th century, specifically to serif
typefaces cut by Robert Granjon, and is named after Christophe Plantin
(1520 – 1589), an influential Renaissance humanist, book printer and
publisher. It is one of the typefaces that influenced the creation of Times
Roman and today features a full suite of small caps, ligatures and old style
figures.